BONVIDA'S
AWAKENING

(Bonvida #1)

A Novel

By C.D. Smith

Azariah's Compass Publishing,
Embrun, ON Canada

ISBN: 9798358170667

Interior design: Ellen Gable Hrkach
Cover Design: Chris Smith and James Hrkach
Images: Adobe Stock

Azariah's Compass Publishing
Embrun ON Canada

My book is dedicated to my deceased grandmother, "Buba," who believed in my writing and would tell everyone that I'd be an author one day.

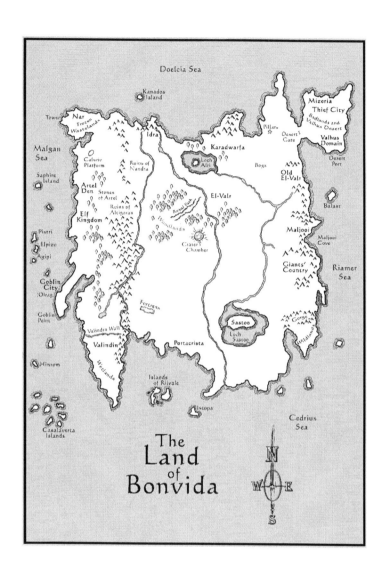

The
Land
of
Bonvida

A shining light and gloomy dark battled
before the doors.
The light overpowered and locked the dark
In a Hematite gem and tossed it into the abyss.

Inside the dome, the being of Great Light appeared,
Sofos, the ruler, the master, the creator.
His appearance changed at his every command.

To his left stood Artel,
Wolf and protector.
And perched on his right,
Advo, the transparent dove.

On a table before them lay six shiny gems,
An opal, a topaz, an emerald,
A sapphire, a ruby, and a diamond.

Outside the dome,
The fallen gem of darkness
Cried out to a banished friend.

The She Serpent, the betrayer
Obedient to the darkness,
Picked up the gem and slithered
To the crystal dome.

Tossed on the table by the She Serpent
The gem the dark color of Hematite.
The darkness locked inside had a cunning plan
To destroy Sofos and his masterful design.

The darkness broke from Hematite
And struck.
But with one mighty roar,
Sofos exiled the darkness and the serpent.
With haste, Sofos used the six gems to create a land.
He named this place Bonvida.
The darkness should have no place there.

Part I

Chapter 1

Dane, son of Desmond, stood at attention with four other warriors in a line on the plateau, all eyes on the brass door. The wind, consistently strong, whipped his hair in front of his face, blocking his eyes for a moment from the intense orange sunlight reflecting off the glossy crystal dome. While his heart hammered within him, he forced himself to remain composed. After all, he alone carried the Sword of Bonvida and wore the topaz shard on a leather cord around his neck.

Two heartbeats later, the oval doors of the dome creaked open and blue light streamed out, stretching across the plateau. Dane and the other warriors lowered themselves onto one knee. He struggled to keep his head up as he gazed upon Sofos, who appeared today as an enormous golden-brown bear. The bear? Sofos only turned into the bear if he was upset or angry. Normally Sofos would be a tall golden-brown stag with antlers that intertwined. On a rare occasion, he appeared as a beam of light, but the bear? Something was not right.

Sofos stood for a moment atop the few stairs that led to the dome and scanned those on the plateau, peering at each warrior in turn as if preparing them for some grand announcement. Then he spoke with an ominous tone. "The darkness is awakening."

Dane closed his eyes and turned his head to the side. Sofos' words shivered up his spine and to the center of his mind. He knew about the darkness. In the beginning, Sofos created six gems to build a place of peace and prosperity, but the darkness known as Hematite tempted She Serpent—Sofos' long-time ally—and together, they turned against Sofos. Hematite wanted to kill Sofos and overrule everything with darkness. Thankfully, Sofos used his power to send She Serpent and Hematite away to

1

a realm of darkness.

Resolved to do whatever Sofos asked of him to help conquer this evil, Dane opened his eyes and concentrated on the great bear before him.

Sofos descended the steps and lumbered towards his kneeling warriors, each step conveying absolute confidence. While known for his compassion and wisdom, his eyes held a devastating expression today, something only a close warrior would recognize. Sadness.

Sofos signaled to Dane, nudging his muscular shoulder with his wet snout. Dane and the other warriors arose.

"Scout the plateau," Sofos commanded, standing on hind legs in the middle of the group. "The darkness fell from within our home."

"Whom are we looking for, Sofos?"

"Luvanasis."

Dane's heart sank. *Luvanasis? Can this be true?*

Memories flooded his mind. *His father, in a long grey cloak, carried a young child. He bent down, looking at a young Dane. "Son, this here is Luvanasis. We found him in a burning village. He will stay here with us."*

Dane gripped the handle of his sword, readying himself to do whatever he must, regardless of their friendship. "What do we do once we find him?"

Sofos lowered his massive head for a moment but then swung it high, standing seven feet tall. "Chain him and his repulsive followers. Send them to the edge. I will deal with them there."

***

Dane skidded down a rocky slope, his boots kicking up dirt and his gaze fixed on a nearby grove of evergreens and deciduous trees. Plenty of hiding places for Luvanasis in there. Wherever Luvanasis hid, they would find him. Each warrior had taken a section of the plateau to search.

He had taken the path to the right of the dome and would not meet up with another warrior until he neared the far edge of the plateau.

As he passed a thin, crooked birch tree, he continued to remember the old story. *After sending the darkness away, Sofos used the gems to create everything. The opal created the warriors and Skyarl realm*—a place he could only imagine, since few had the privilege of visiting it. Most would only see Bonvida, the land thousands of feet below them. The land that he and his bloodline had to protect.

A rotten branch snapped beneath his boot, making him jump and shoot a gaze in all directions. Seeing no one, he took a deep breath of forest air and resumed his trek through the woods, watching his step and recalling a memory.

Dane ducked behind a bush and nudged the thin young man next to him. "Your ambush better work, Luvanasis."

Luvanasis glared at him. "It will work. I am filled with a marvelous will and power that you don't even know."

Dane chuckled. "Oh, Luvanasis, you know having power and control are wasteful for us."

Luvanasis grumbled under his breath, and his eyes turned fiery. "You'll see."

The bushes before them rustled, then a loud snap, followed by the squeal of a pig.

Luvanasis sprang to his feet. "See, I'm the great ambusher."

Dane huffed away the memory. Other than loving ambushes, Luvanasis was a hothead. If one thing went wrong, Luvanasis would flare with anger.

Dane shook his head and wound his way through the forest and up an incline. The thought of fighting Luvanasis bothered him, not because he feared losing but because they had grown up together. *What had caused Luvanasis*

3

to turn towards the darkness? Had he always been like this and only showed his true colors now?

Emerging from the forest, the back of the dome loomed before him. He had come full circle. He drew closer to the crystal dome, staring at his reflection. His mind kept dragging him back to the creation of everything.

After creating Skyarl, the realm only a few have seen, Sofos used the other five gems to create Bonvida. The five gems each left behind a single shard, which Sofos swept up. He knew that the darkness would try to destroy everything. Then Sofos used the blood of a warrior and the dust of Bonvida earth to create Dane's father, Desmond, and four other followers.

Dane snapped out of his reverie and turned away from the dome. He needed to continue searching. He dashed down another incline and neared a strange rock formation with trees growing out of it. Maybe he would find a cave or—

Something slammed hard against his back, throwing him forward. He flung his hands out but not in time. His face hit the jagged ground, slicing his cheek and lips, and the air whooshed from his lungs. Allowing himself a split second to recover, he made a move to roll over, but someone—some*thing*—stopped him.

Hands with rough skin and claws restrained his arms and then tugged him onto his feet. Creatures unlike anything he had seen before held his upper arms with three claws on spindly legs. More creatures—a dozen or so—gathered around. He shuddered as he turned to examine a few of these creatures.

Deep cracks surrounded their eyes which seemed to bulge from their sockets. Their mouths resembled a human's. The stench, like the odor of decomposing flesh, made him gag.

The creatures dragged him a few steps towards the

rock formation. A warrior in dark armor leaped from a shelf on the rock and stood before him, peering at him through eyes narrowed and sharp like a python's. *Luvanasis.*

"What are these things?" Dane shuddered again, disturbed by the hideousness of the creatures clutching his arms.

Luvanasis' lips curled up in a smile, although his expression remained joyless. "These are my followers . . . my Arcods." He paced around Dane. "You've been out here looking for me, haven't you, Dane?"

"Have you really betrayed us, Luvanasis?" Dane's heart clenched even to suggest it, but he could believe nothing else.

Luvanasis rolled his eyes. "Betrayal? Such a harsh word, Dane. I don't see it as a betrayal."

"You set yourself against Sofos." Tears welled in his eyes. "You are my closest friend."

"I found something that will sustain me much better than friendship."

The Arcods loosened their grip. Ready to fight the creatures off, to fight Luvanasis himself if he had to, Dane took advantage of the moment, shoving one Arcod to the ground and drawing the Sword of Bonvida.

The blade grazing the sides of the sheath made a threatening sound. Several Arcods drew back. The sound would usually cause any enemy to flee, but Luvanasis threw a threatening look to his Arcods, and they all remained in position.

Dane wasted no time. He impaled the Arcod on the ground before it could rise. The other Arcods shrieked and scurried off through the trees.

A grin stretched across Luvanasis' face as he watched the last Arcod scuttle away, leaving the two warriors alone.

Dane readied himself to strike at his friend. "Come with me, Luvanasis. Sofos has ordered me not to harm you. Though I wonder why."

Luvanasis studied Dane, his hand inching to the hilt of his sword. "I have a destiny, Dane, and that destiny is to kill you and to fulfill the commands of Hematite."

"Hematite? We do not follow Hematite." Dane gritted his teeth. Hematite, the darkness, used She Serpent and had been locked away in Calsriv, the realm of darkness. What had Luvanasis to do with Hematite? "Snap out of this, Luvanasis. You're one of us. You're a warrior!" he cried, panic rising with his voice.

Luvanasis looked Dane straight in the eye with a cold blank stare, devoid of all emotion, as if he had locked up their friendship in a box and tossed it over the edge of the plateau. Luvanasis tapped the hilt of his sword and, without another word, tugged his blade from its sheath. With a mighty shout, he struck at his friend.

Dane blocked the swing and countered, not letting the pain of betrayal take over his mind. The two warriors' blades clashed and pushed against each other.

With a kick to the leg, Luvanasis gained momentary control over Dane and readied his sword for a blow.

Despite the pain, Dane maintained his balance and jumped far enough back to avoid his sword. He reached for the shield on his back, a smooth metal protection, decorated simply with three intertwining circles. Sunlight reflected off it, blindingly bright. Dane directed the light to Luvanasis' eyes while he struggled to latch the shield to his wrist.

Luvanasis growled and, with one swipe, knocked the shield from Dane's grasp before he could secure it.

He and Luvanasis danced around the shield, both of their guards raised. Luvanasis feigned a swipe at Dane's right, which Dane prepared to block, but then Luvanasis grabbed the shield and tossed it aside like a frisbee.

Giving up on the shield, Dane wiped sweat from his brow, shinnied the rock formation, and leaped off one side, swinging his sword. He knocked the blade from his enemy's hand. Landing hard on the ground, he and Luvanasis dashed towards the blade, like two dogs going after the last treat. Dane secured Luvanasis' blade with his boot and directed the tip of his sword to Luvanasis' neck.

Luvanasis raised his hands in surrender. "Easy now."

Thankful he won the duel, Dane grabbed the shackles from his belt. He glared at Luvanasis, hoping to communicate the hurt filling up within him. Then he wiped his nose, and putting his grief aside, he cuffed Luvanasis' wrists.

Luvanasis grumbled under his breath and gave a taunting wink.

Dane squeezed Luvanasis by the arm, giving vent to the anger still in him as they marched back to the dome and to Sofos.

Chapter 2

Without a word, Dane escorted his old friend through the forested area. Luvanasis did not struggle, complain, or try to fight since Dane had caught him. *Strange.* Once up the incline, one side of the Sacred Dome came into view. Luvanasis scoffed and spat towards the crystal. Dane squeezed Luvanasis' arm and marched him around to the front of the dome.

Warriors rushed from the lush forest to meet them. Dane pulled Luvanasis to a halt. He did not want to interrupt Sofos, who stood engaged in conversation with two warriors. A moment later, Sofos waved him over. Dane shoved Luvanasis in the direction of the two warriors, who then grasped the prisoner from either side. Luvanasis stood front and center, a few feet away from Sofos.

"Your Arcods are captured, Luvanasis, and waiting for you." Sofos turned his gaze to the two warriors. "Take him to the edge of the plateau. We will join you in a moment."

Luvanasis twisted his shoulders, trying to loosen the two warriors' restraints, while giving them a taunting glare. "Whatever you have planned for me, Sofos, I assure you I will have my revenge. As will Hematite. And, Dane"—he turned his black snake-eyes to Dane—"when I do, I'm coming for your bloodline."

Sofos gave a nod, and the two warriors and Luvanasis turned around. After a brief pause, they marched off, heading for the edge of the plateau. The forest rose up on one side and rounded boulders with a few scattered trees on the other.

Watching the warriors take Luvanasis away, Dane shook his head. Still reeling from the discovery that his best friend had turned against him, he turned to Sofos with frustration. "I don't understand. Why would he turn on us? He was loyal. He was my friend."

Sofos remained silent as more warriors returned. "Dane, do you remember the name Shiesta?"

"Shiesta?" He tried searching his memory for the name. His father had told him stories . . . "Aye. She was one of my father's close allies until—" A fresh stab of pain in his heart made him wince. "She betrayed him."

Sofos nodded and continued to speak in a calm voice. "Shiesta accepted the lies of Hematite, and she vowed obedience for herself and her descendants. From then on, her heirs have been known as Dark Descendants. Hematite, in turn, created the Sword of Darkness, which they alone can wield."

His father's memories flooded his mind. He flipped through them until he found the one . . . When his father had locked Calsriv and put the She Serpent into slumber, Shiesta had died. "What does Shiesta have to do with this?"

"Luvanasis is her child," Sofos replied.

In disbelief, Dane stepped backward, bumping into one of the four warriors. "How is that possible? My father found Luvanasis as a child in a burning Bonvidian village. My father and his followers saved him."

"Interesting how life works, isn't it?" Sofos remarked, shifting his position, his golden fur glimmering in the sunlight.

"Now, what do we do?"

"We do what must be done."

Sofos eased himself to the center of the five warriors and directed Dane to stand at his right side. He tilted his head up, indicating that they would all walk forward together.

Pushing against a strong breeze, the smell of spring air filled Dane's nostrils while dread filled his heart. With Dane's next step, the rocky ground gouged his boots, and his stomach turned at the thought of what they were about to do, but he kept pace with Sofos and the other warriors. Everything would work out as it should.

He concentrated on the edge of the plateau. When Sofos had spoken of it, he'd made it sound menacing, but Dane had been to the edge. He always enjoyed standing there and looking down, a strong breeze blowing through his hair and the land of Bonvida thousands of feet below him. Why did Sofos send Luvanasis to the edge? What was he planning?

After a fifteen-minute hike—that seemed like hours—the forest on his right gave way to level, barren land. A crowd of Arcods had gathered in the distance, in plain view of their path, close to the edge and likely close to Luvanasis.

As they continued forward, the odor of decomposing flesh took over, obliterating the pleasant spring smell. He held back a gag. The Arcods gurgled and growled, the ugly sound making him want to cover his ears.

Luvanasis, in his dark armor, stood front and center, chained to metal hooks that poked from the ground. The Arcods, also chained, stood behind him. Their claws scraped the ground. Some shoved each other; others tried to jump and attack like a pack of hyenas. One made direct eye contact with Dane, its eyes bulging. Dane tried not to look, but utter terror fascinated his attention.

Sofos plodded forward on all fours, moving towards the man in dark armor. "Luvanasis," he said, his voice shaking the plateau. "You have broken my trust. You have awoken and accepted the darkness. For that, I banish you to the Calsriv Realm, the realm of darkness, the realm that the She Serpent and Hematite created, and there you will stay."

Luvanasis tugged at the chains around his wrists. "I will find a way to destroy you and all that you hold dear: the land of Bonvida and all who dwell in it." He yanked the chains, the metal clanging, and gave a vengeful smile. "I will release the darkness in Calsriv, and with the Sword of Darkness, I will awaken the She Serpent. After destroying Bonvida, we will return here and kill you!"

Enraged, Sofos lifted himself onto his hind legs and growled, "How dare you speak to me that way." He dropped to the ground, landing on all fours, and proceeded to approach Luvanasis.

Dane gripped the hilt of his sword and took a protective stance at Sofos' side. After all, it was his duty to protect Sofos.

Luvanasis fidgeted with his chains, and then he rushed forward as if challenging a fight, but the chains snapped tight, holding him back. He held his position, glaring at the bear.

Undaunted, Sofos leaned so close that his wet nose touched the thin, pointy one of his enemy.

Luvanasis stepped backward, twisting his wrists and tugging at the chains.

Sofos laughed, watching Luvanasis withdraw, but then his expression fell. Suddenly, Luvanasis' chains loosened their restraint. He must have been pulling at the hooks in the ground, hoping they would loosen.

Sofos shut his eyes.

Before anyone else had a chance to move, a dark blue funnel appeared at the edge of the plateau, creating a spinning portal. It expanded and grew three times taller than Sofos. The whooshing sound and the way the portal spun made it resemble a tornado, although it remained in one place and caused no damage—other than dreadful fear. The warriors had known about the existence of portals, but most had not seen one until now. Sofos could create them at will to transport beings from one place to another. He must have planned to use this one to send

11

Luvanasis and the Arcods to Calsriv.

One by one, the funnel snatched up the Arcods, sucking them into the portal against their will, their long arms thrashing and claws snapping. After the last Arcod disappeared, the funnel glided across the ground, stopping over the end of Luvanasis' chains. The chains dragged Luvanasis towards the portal.

Panic in his every move, the man pulled himself towards the bear and screamed. He tugged harder and harder until one of his wrists from the shackles was free and grabbed at Sofos. "You will come with me." Luvanasis grabbed Sofos around the neck.

Sofos tried to pull away but could not free himself from the grasp.

Coming to Sofos' aid, Dane loosened his grip on his sword and shoved the huge bear aside. He tackled Luvanasis to the ground. Dane and his opponent grappled for the loose chain. But it was too late.

His feet lifted from the ground, and he floated alongside Luvanasis. Luvanasis stopped struggling and laughed. Dane made an effort to free himself from the pull of the blue funnel, tried to return to his friends and Sofos, but Luvanasis grabbed him around his waist. The portal acted like a magnet on his body, tugging him, dragging him closer and closer. He reached a hand out in desperation.

Dane's breath caught in his throat as a warrior ran towards his outstretched hand. But Sofos stopped her with his large paw.

Why would Sofos stop her? Everything drifted further away, and his surroundings became a darker shade of blue, twisting, with a dizzying effect. The portal sucked him in. He had no escape.

Before the portal closed, Sofos spoke to the other warriors. "Dane will be all right. He is a descendant of Desmond. He wields The Sword of Bonvida and the power that it will one day carry. His bloodline is destined to bring peace." The sounds of those closest to him became faint.

"What about the five shards?" one of the warriors asked, his voice muffled.

Had he failed his destiny? As the portal closed, he heard Sofos' calm response.

"The five shards that created Bonvida must be recovered and placed in the grooves of the sword's handle. Only then can his bloodline destroy the darkness. This event has just been the beginning . . . Dane must keep faith in himself, his bloodline's destiny, and in all of us here."

As the voices trailed off, everything and everyone that Dane had known vanished—except for his enemy.

Chapter 3

Dane opened his eyes and gasped for air. His heart raced out of control. He lay in a pit of thick mud, with grey smog above him. Where was he? He flailed his arms, searching for solid ground, wanting back on his feet.

Something flew high above the haze, drawing his attention. The creature's shadow grew closer and closer. A thirty-foot, long-necked bird flew toward him. It made a disturbing screeching sound as it circled him.

Dane shuddered. Any second now, that bird would dive down and feast on him. He survived the fall into Calsriv and had no intention of dying now. If only he could find the linking platform that Hematite used to try to get into Bonvida all those years ago. Maybe from there, he could cry out to Sofos for help, hopefully, before Luvanasis found him. Or that bird.

He rolled onto one side and struggled to pull himself up from the thick mud pit. An angry guttural voice cried out in the distance. The Arcods? Were they close by? Could they see or smell him? He remembered separating from Luvanasis as the portal opened in Calsriv, but who knew how far he was from his enemy?

With every move he made, the mud sucked him further down until he sank to his hips. Sick with panic but determined to get himself out, he kept trying. The bird let out an ear-piercing screech and swooped closer to him.

Defensive instincts kicking in, he remembered his sword. He wrapped his fingers around the hilt and tried to draw the sword out, but a layer of thick mud made his hand slip. And still, with every move, he sank deeper. And the sounds of the Arcods grew louder.

The bird swooped in closer yet—

Fighting against the mud, Dane tried twisting around to keep his eye on the creature.

It zoomed in from behind him and opened its mouth wide. Its tongue shot out and spread like a claw. Before Dane could react, it grabbed him from behind and lifted him from the pit.

Dane almost lost his breath from the shock. Even though he feared what the bird might do to him, he felt relief that he had made it out of the mud pit. As he moved through the air at great speed, zooming away from the mud pit and the Arcods, chunks of mud fell from him.

The bird slowed and circled closer to the ground. Dane drew his sword and, with one strong swipe, sliced off the bird's tongue. Dane free-fell for a moment, then slammed hard onto the ground. Pain shooting through him, he let out a yelp, which echoed throughout the realm.

Drops of blood rained down from the bird, sprinkling his face. He struggled to his feet, but the tongue, slimy and rough, still bound his waist.

The bird circled in the smog until it collapsed on the ground behind him, squalling a deafening sound. Then it burst into thousands of tiny versions of itself, and they each flew off into the unknown of Calsriv.

Breathless, Dane crawled out of the dead tongue's grasp. Easing himself up, he sheathed his sword. His ribs and back burned like fire and hurt, even more, when he touched them. He would likely develop a huge bruise from his left hip to his armpit.

He stood hunched from the pain and looked all around, gazing at the realm in dismay. He heard stories of this dreadful place, but none of them compared to the reality before him.

Rather than blue sky, darkness and gloom hung over the whole realm of Calsriv. Beneath thick smog, muddy and rocky ground stretched out on all sides. In the distance loomed a volcano, its fire glowing a vicious orange and red. Pockmarks covered the landscape, as if bombs had fallen, destroying any hope of beauty, leaving nothing but sadness.

This pathetic realm had come about when Sofos banished She Serpent and Hematite. Having nowhere else to go, Hematite had used its powers to create Calsriv and other forms of darkness. Hematite had created a platform, too, linking Calsriv to Bonvida. Shiesta had used that platform to release She Serpent from Calsriv, and then the two of them set out to take over Bonvida. Dane's father, Desmond, put an end to that threat, inducing the serpent into a slumber. Then Sofos closed and locked the platform, ensuring that Hematite and its darkness would never again escape . . . unless someone with a similar darkness were to free them from Bonvida and break open that platform again. Would Luvanasis attempt it? Did he carry his bloodline like his mother, Shiesta?

Dane glanced over his shoulder. Where was Luvanasis now?

***

Luvanasis skidded across the Calsriv ground like a meteorite hitting Earth. He pulled himself up, spat dirt from his dry mouth, and gazed upon Calsriv. His Arcods scuttled towards him from different directions, dragging their spindly arms. As he rubbed the side of his head, he glimpsed a Calsriv bird circling prey—most likely Dane. He pointed to the bird. "You Arcods, head out and bring Dane to me. I want to kill him."

While the Arcods scuttled away, Luvanasis rested on a boulder and gazed at the volcano looming before him. Somewhere hidden within the volcano, Hematite awaited his arrival. He must have Hematite's advice, and he longed to hold the Sword of Darkness like his mother had done all those years ago.

After some time, the Arcods returned empty-handed. Disappointed, Luvanasis shook his head and marched up the trail that led to the top of the volcano. The Arcods sighed as they dragged their long arms and followed him up the steep incline. With each step, the temperature grew hotter and hotter.

The trail leveled out, and the bowl-shaped crater at the center of the volcano came into view. Molten magma glowed from the cracks at the bottom of the crater. Warmth filled his lungs, and ash dusted over him like snowflakes. *Good.* He made it to the top of the volcano, but hundreds of crevices lined the inner walls. Where could Hematite be, and how would he get down to him?

"I know you're down there," he shouted, his voice bouncing off the walls of the volcano. Suddenly his ears perked.

Something whooshed through the air above. A dark scaly dragon with ten horns around its head emerged from the foggy sky and hovered nearby.

Luvanasis drew back, pressing his hands against his chest, as if to keep his heart in place. He gazed into the creature's empty eyes. He had never seen a dragon before. The only dragons he knew of belonged to Hematite and were locked in Calsriv. His mind rattled, trying to remember the Bonvidian history of this dragon. "Kanado, you are fearsome. Take me to your maker, Hematite."

The dragon placed its tail on the lip of the volcano and indicated for Luvanasis to step onto it.

Luvanasis turned to his Arcods. "Stay here out of trouble until I return."

The Arcods grumbled and growled as they sat on the rocky ground.

Luvanasis stepped onto the tail and climbed to the center of Kanado, observing its broad wings. "You once showed Bonvida much pain until Desmond, and two of his followers brought you back down here. I promise you, dragon, one day you will show your flames again."

17

The dragon swooped down towards the bottom of the crater and the cracks of molten magma. Hot suffocating air rushed past them. The creature headed towards the largest of the crevices and landed gracefully just inside it. The cave went back some distance, shadows playing under torchlight.

Luvanasis strode deeper into the dark cavern, an orange glow ahead. Stalactites of various sizes dangled above him. He maneuvered past a pocket of magma and then glowing orange stones. He stepped through an arch, which made a sort of doorway to an open area with ledges on one wall. The ledges seemed to hold bedding or storage.

A misshaped throne made of rocks stood in the center. The seated figure on the throne trembled. It moved like liquid, like slime trying—unsuccessfully—to form into something or even someone. On closer inspection, Luvanasis realized that the figure was Hematite. Should he sit and speak or remain still and silent?

At that moment, a haunting voice surrounded him and filled the whole cavern. Hematite slid out of the throne and slithered to Luvanasis like water moving through pipes. "Luvanasis, you have made it. But I sense something, someone else here too. This is only the beginning of a long journey."

***

Having caught his breath, Dane labored across the jagged lands, creating a path for himself, fully alert to everything. Moments ago, the bright, beautiful sunlight shined on him, and now he was here. No sun in sight. Nothing but smog and gloom.

A few paces more and a repeating drumbeat came from all around him, along with cries of agony. He rested one hand on the hilt of his sword in case anything should jump out at him.

Dane reached a stream of murky water that came from a rocky hill and curved away from him. A dried tree trunk arched over the river further down, where it made a small lake. The murky water hid the bottom of the stream, but he did not care. He managed to lower himself to his knees and then drank savagely. Then he waded into the cool waist-high water, easing the pain in his ribs, and washed the mud off himself. As he splashed his face one last time, something pinched his leg.

A black leech as long and thick as a squirrel had attached itself to his thigh. He pulled out the small knife that he had strapped around his ankle and eased it under the leech.

"That'll only make matters worse," came a woman's voice from behind him.

Dane froze, knife poised under the slimy creature. Taking her advice, he withdrew his blade, straightened, and turned around.

A young woman with deep purple hair, braided and draped over one shoulder, stood on the riverbank, gazing down at him through green eyes. Judging by her beauty, she did not come from this realm. "My name is Lavender. I'm a survivor of Nandra. Who are you?"

He wiped water from his face and climbed, dripping, to the riverbank. "I am Dane, a Warrior of Sofos, protector of the Sword of Bonvida."

With a playful smile on her lips, she touched the purple braid draped over her shoulder and asked, "What brings you to this cursed realm, Dane, Warrior of Sofos?"

Dane paused, gathering his thoughts. "I did not come here of my choosing."

Her eyes twinkled, and she tilted her head.

He could not look away from her eyes, green like untouched grass.

Averting her gaze, she spoke again. "We saw the portal

open."

He raised an eyebrow. "We?" Nobody came to Calsriv by choice, and Sofos banished no one here without reason.

"Villagers of Nandra and I watched two men and creatures fall. Creatures that we've seen roam this realm. All of them dark except one."

"Yes, the warrior Luvanasis and his Arcods." He gritted his teeth as the struggle replayed in his mind. If only he had broken Luvanasis' grip on him . . .

She said, "I came to find the one. I came to find you."

"How do you know that I'm not dark?" A smile stole its way onto his face, but he forced it away.

She hesitated for a moment. "I saw you before."

Her manner, her words . . . yes, he could trust her. "I was dragged here by Luvanasis just as he was banished with his army. He was once my friend—"

"Why was he banished?"

"He was planning great chaos." Dane stepped closer to her, the pain from the leech hurt with each stride. "You said you saw me before. Can I ask when?"

"When the warriors came to warn the Bonvidians of Nandra about their wrongdoings, you were one of them. Three days later, those who did not flee or die were cast here by Sofos." Lavender paused and lowered her head with grief in her eyes.

Dane placed his hand on her shoulder. He, too, remembered the day Sofos cast out Nandra.

She clasped his hand and squeezed. "We're not all bad, though, at least I'm not. I was young when it happened." Without waiting for a reply, Lavender bent down and peered at the leech. "Forgive me. We should get that sucker off your leg. May I?"

He smirked, wanting to make a flirtatious comment, but he could come up with no words.

The exiled Bonvidian woman dug into a small pouch and pulled out a tiny glass jar with a cork. She tugged the cork until it popped off and then poured the liquid onto the leech.

He bit his lip as a burning sensation spread through his leg.

In the next moment, the leech dropped off his thigh. It flip-flopped on the ground and then splashed into the stream.

"Thank you," he exhaled, sending a sharp pain through his bruised ribs.

Lavender tucked the jar into her pouch. "Come with me. My village is in the forest. I can take you there." She pointed west towards the treeline. "And you need to heal." She glanced down at his ribs, as if knowing all along of the pain he had been trying to hide.

He examined her for a moment. *Can I trust her?* His heart said he could, but the warrior in him urged caution. *Well, in any case, at least I can search for the platform along the way.*

"Follow me." Lavender moved a strand of hair from her face and smiled.

Giving in to his heart, Dane smiled back and followed her through the rough terrain of Calsriv.

After walking for some time, Dane peered overhead, hoping no birds or dragons would find them. "There's no sky."

Lavender glanced up at the smog. "It's always like that. It gets darker at night. We have no stars, no moons, no sun," she said with a sad tone. "I miss them, the sun and blue skies, the crescent moon, and the star-filled skies. The smell of the grass, those times when the dust of snow would blow over Bonvida from the Frozen Wastelands." Tears glistened on her cheeks.

Dane felt bad for her. She should not be here. She should be out of Calsriv and back in Bonvida. "You're not of this realm, Lavender. I can see your goodness. You deserve to be back in Bonvida."

Hours later, they neared a forest of bony, bare trees. All dead. They stepped over branches and bricks, rubble from the city of Nandra. A shattered home here, the remains of a marketplace there, the citadel bell turned on its side . . . it was a haunting scene, like ruin after a hurricane.

Lavender soon pointed to a few wooden huts. "Welcome to Nandra."

Dane stared out at the growing crowd of Bonvidians from the fallen city of Nandra. Men, women, and children in raggedy clothes and with dirty faces. They moved slowly, as if they'd never seen a stranger before. Some hid after getting a glimpse of Dane. Others clutched tools as if ready for a fight. Dane's heart sank with sorrow over what they'd been through. How had they survived so long in such a place?

"Sofos came to us in a vision when we arrived," Lavender said. "He told us that he would protect us from . . . from whatever is out there, from what created this place. We have been rationing everything all these years. Scavenging for supplies. He said one day someone would come to us. I believe that to be you." She fell silent. "In any case, let's find you a place to rest, and we can eat."

Chapter 4

Dane's stay in Nandra turned into weeks, which then turned into months. With each passing day, Dane worried more about Luvanasis. Was he still alive? Was he causing destruction somewhere else in Calsriv? Or was he searching for Dane? If he reached the village of the Nandrians, would he cause trouble here? Not wanting to bring trouble to these people and hoping to return to Bonvida, Dane did find the linking platform beyond the forest where he was living.

As time passed, Dane settled himself quite well amongst the Nandrian Bonvidians. He spent his days helping villagers gather food and rebuild their wooden huts. Some villagers avoided him, but he earned the trust of most of the others. His friendship with Lavender grew into love, and before long, Dane and Lavender married. His gut told him there was more to come for him and Lavender than a quiet life in Nandra.

One evening, Lavender came up to Dane as he sat gazing out the open door of their hut. She rubbed his shoulders and pressed a kiss on his neck. His tense muscles rolled with each press of her hands. "You seem worried about something. Is everything okay?"

After taking a deep breath, he turned and gazed upon her beautiful face. "I'm just tired." He moved a stray lock of her hair aside. He did not want to tell her about the depths of his concern or about the nightmares haunting him.

She pressed her forehead to his. "Don't lie to me . . . it's Luvanasis, isn't it?"

"I'm going to rest my eyes." He gave her a kiss and settled himself in the bed in the corner of their hut. Then he lay gazing at the ceiling, reluctant to drift off to sleep, even as sleep beckoned.

A topaz gem shot towards an abyss, and land formed. Next, a sapphire exploded above the land, causing water to appear and form into rivers and lakes. A ruby landed after that, and mountains and stones rose up.

Then an emerald exploded, bringing about all types of plant life. And finally, the diamond hit a corner, creating a desert and clay shapes.

Sofos swiped five fragments of the gems with his paw. He created a sword and placed the shards into a groove in the sword's handle.

A dark shadow hovered over Lavender, who cradled a crying infant. The shadow became more vivid and turned into Luvanasis. The baby screamed.

The five shards flashed around the baby as a cloud of dark flames invaded the land of Bonvida.

Suddenly, Dane sprung up. Drenched in sweat and his heart beating faster than ever, he flung back the covers.

Lavender rushed to his bedside and hugged him. "I heard you tossing in your sleep. Is everything okay?"

He eased her arms from around him and held her hands. Gazing deeply into her eyes, he whispered, "We are to birth a son, and he will destroy Luvanasis."

She trembled and drew back. "How will he destroy him?"

He got out of bed and went to the shelf where he kept the Sword of Bonvida. Drawing the sword from its sheath, he admired it, the thick blade, bronze on the edges and silver inside. Gold strips encircled a silver hilt with a diamond shape and a fish carved into it. At the base of the hilt, in the center, five irregularly shaped cavities lay empty, waiting for their stones.

"Crafted by Sofos, this sword was made to defeat Hematite and—with aid—to destroy the other darkness of Hematite that comes to harm Bonvida, darkness such as Luvanasis," Dane said.

Lavender gasped, worry on her brow. "What if he finds out that we're to have a son?"

Speaking cautiously, Dane glanced at the sword. "He will try to kill him, so we must keep it secret between us and those of this village, but since this place is home to darkness, he will eventually find out." Dane slid the sword back into its sheath and returned it to the shelf.

Lavender sat on the bed, tears streaming down her face. Dane came over to comfort her.

She stopped weeping, gave him a courageous smile, and then embraced him.

Dane's heart melted, and he could not resist kissing her. While her beauty surpassed any woman he knew, he admired her courage and inner beauty more.

That night Lavender and Dane conceived a child. Dane stroked Lavender's hair as she slept in peace, but then sounds of terror echoed in the distance. Not wanting to wake her, he planted a kiss on her cheek and eased out of bed. Dane dressed, grabbed his sword, and made his way out of the hut. He crept out of the village and through the dead forest until he reached the linking platform.

Standing on the cool stone, he gazed up at the dark night smog. Tears streamed down his face as he gave way to feelings of abandonment. "I am to have a son. He can not live like this. Luvanasis' darkness is getting stronger. Sofos, if you can hear me, send me a warrior a few days after the birth of my son."

***

Nine months later, Lavender birthed a son. They named him Atticus. The Bonvidians of Nandra celebrated the birth of Atticus in the traditional manner. A few villagers played drums while others danced and clapped their hands around a fire pit, everyone rejoicing in the celebration.

Sitting on a log bench under a canopy, Dane enjoyed

watching the villagers dance, eat, and laugh. Amid the celebration, he knew that word of his son's birth would soon spread to Luvanasis. His family could not remain long with these Bonvidians. However, on this day, he would forget his fears and rejoice.

A hand squeezed his shoulder. He sucked in a breath with a jolt and then turned.

Airmo, a heavyset villager covered in war paint, stood behind him holding a rusted sword.

"Airmo, you startled me." Dane laughed, relieved.

"Dane, I bring news." Airmo sat beside him and watched the dancers as he spoke. "Scouts spotted Luvanasis in the distance. He is making his way here fast. He will arrive within half an hour, so time is precious." Airmo lowered his eyebrows as if trying to keep a strong face.

"I best get going then. The moment Luvanasis arrives, do whatever necessary to keep him at bay." Dane jumped up and rushed through the celebrating villagers, nodding to one here and one there. He passed several huts and darted inside his, finding Lavender holding their newborn son, Atticus. He gazed at his son in awe and kissed his tiny forehead. "Lavender, we must leave now," Dane whispered, trying to keep the fear from his voice.

Lavender promptly rose and wrapped the baby in a blanket and held him close to her breast.

Dane removed his sword belt and strapped it around Lavender's waist. "We must take this with us."

Concern furrowing her brows, Lavender cradled baby Atticus close to her chest and gazed at him. "Our son has no idea what destiny and greatness lie before him," Lavender whispered.

Swallowing back emotion, Dane focused on their urgent situation. The idea of his son carrying the Sword of Bonvida and one day facing Luvanasis popped into mind. He shook the thought away.

"Dane, are you sure this will work? What if the portal doesn't come? Or Luvanasis—"

He caressed her face. "Have faith in Sofos, and faith in our son. I spoke with Sofos internally. Everything will work out according to plan. He will send a fellow warrior through to be sure nothing goes wrong."

"Where will the portal be?" Lavender's eyes welled with tears as she gazed at their son.

"At the platform, beyond the village." Dane wiped Lavender's tears. He did not want to live without Atticus either. If only there were another way.

Lavender grabbed a blanket and nestled Atticus close to her bosom, and the three of them exited their hut. Dane spotted Airmo rushing towards him with a torch. In silence, he handed Dane the torch.

Dane and Lavender, with the babe in her arms, left the village of Nandra. They fled through the dead forest with a torch as their only source of light. Hopping over stumps and logs, their clothes catching and tearing on branches, they finally reached a clearing. Here they paused to take a breath.

His heart pounding hard, Dane peered around. If only he had a better light with him in this darkness. Shadows of the night made it difficult to see the path that lay before him.

Lavender scrunched up her eyebrows as she peered at him through worried eyes. "Everything will be okay."

Moments later, screams came from the village. Lavender turned towards home, though they could no longer see it through the trees, and she froze.

Dane swallowed a lump in his throat. "We must keep going. The portal is near."

He and Lavender pressed on, weaving their way through thickets of trees with bare branches tangled together and past clusters of tumbleweeds. As they leaped over a fallen tree trunk, they found themselves in another clearing. This was it! A large stone platform rose up in the midst of rocky ground.

Dane and Lavender rushed to it and stepped onto the platform.

"How does this work?" Lavender stood in the middle of it, scanning the intricate arrangement of stones beneath their feet. "Where is the portal?"

A gust of wind rattled through the trees. On impulse, Dane checked behind him to make sure nothing was coming. "He should be here soon." He raised his eyes. "Sofos! Sofos, we're here. Send a portal."

After speaking, he gazed at his son one last time, kissed Lavender's forehead, and stepped off the platform.

Lavender tilted her head. "Dane, what are you doing? When it comes, we have to go through."

He bit his lip. "Lavender, the portal will come fast. There will only be room for you, Atticus, and the warrior who will guide you through to safety in Bonvida. Which means I cannot come. You and Atticus must go."

Lavender's jaw dropped.

Like a flash of lightning, a light blue portal the size of a doorway appeared. It looked nothing like the spinning portal that had sucked Luvanasis and the Arcods away. This one stood still and flickered like a weak light, it looked like it might close at any moment. Silence assured him that it would not suck anyone into it like the last one did him.

A warrior in a long brown cloak stepped out. A necklace with a flame emblem in the center dangled from his neck. "Quickly. The portal will close soon," the warrior said softly as he gazed upon baby Atticus.

Lavender turned to Dane, tears in her eyes.

His heart aching more with each passing second, Dane pulled the topaz shard from his pocket and stuffed it into

Lavender's hand. "My father gave me this, and it must pass to Atticus. He must always have it on him."

She nodded and strapped the leather cord which held the topaz around her neck.

"It is one of the five keys to destroying the enemy," he told her, though he had told her many times before. "It's one of the five shards of Bonvida." His heart burst with the thought of never seeing his wife and son again. "I love you," he cried and kissed her one last time. "Go!"

His gaze still fixed on his wife and child, Dane backed into the shadows of the forest.

The warrior, Lavender, and baby Atticus stepped into the light blue portal. Cradling Atticus in one arm, Lavender touched the light blue portal, but her hand went right through it as if it were made of water. In the next moment, a woosh filled the air. The portal closed and vanished.

Dane stood alone yet again in Calsriv. His legs wobbled. He wanted to collapse to the ground. Tears streamed down his face as he realized that he might never see his family again. Suddenly the hairs on the back of his neck raised. He pulled himself together, cautiously turning around.

Before him, two arm's length away, Luvanasis stood cracking his neck from side to side. He wiped his narrow sword on a nearby tree trunk. "Where are they?"

Dane's blood boiled. He had not seen him since the plateau. "Not even a hello? Or a how've you been?" Using caution, he leaned to one side and reached for the knife at his ankle—his only remaining weapon, a small hand knife not suitable for the fight he felt brewing. "They're in a safe place, Luvanasis. You failed yet again."

Luvanasis clenched his jaw. His eyes showed no sign of mercy. He took one stride closer to Dane. "I am no failure. I and my Arcods have slaughtered villagers in our search for you. You are in my domain, Dane. You might as well give up."

Rage growing inside, Dane made a fist. Did he really have to kill those villagers? Trying to appear calm, he twirled the knife between his fingers. "I won't back down. You can taunt me all you want, but it will only make me stronger." He charged at Luvanasis, his knife poised for an attack.

Stepping aside, Luvanasis drew his sword and swung.

Dodging the strike, Dane swerved and jumped onto Luvanasis' back, wrapping his arms around Luvanasis' sweaty neck and bringing his knife to his skin.

Luvanasis growled and staggered backward while sheathing his sword. He kept a firm hold of Dane's knife hand while also trying to free himself from Dane's grip around his neck. After grappling with Dane for a moment, he flung himself backward, and they both landed hard on the ground.

The air whooshed from Dane's lungs, and pain shot through him, but he did not let go of Luvanasis' neck or his knife.

Luvanasis clawed at Dane's arms and wrists.

With his back pressing against the hard-packed ground, Dane wrestled, trying to stab Luvanasis in the neck but never getting his blade close enough to do the job. In the blink of an eye, his wrist popped out of place, and he lost his grip on his foe. He held his dislocated wrist close to his chest and dragged himself away from Luvanasis. The adrenaline kept him going, overriding the burning pain of his hand.

Luvanasis jumped to his feet, unsheathed his sword, and lunged at Dane.

Dane leaped to safety, just missing the blade. "You're out of practice, Luvanasis," he taunted.

Enraged, Luvanasis swung his sword furiously.

Dane dove behind a small rotting tree. The swoosh of the sword grazed his hair and smacked the tree, causing it to fall over. He jumped up, stabbed Luvanasis in the knee with his knife, and skidded across the ground, dirt getting in his eyes. With his palm, he swiped the dirt from his face.

Luvanasis simply stood there, seeming unaffected by the knife. Did he even jab him?

Dane glanced at his knife-wielding hand. He felt the blood drain from his face. The blade of his knife had shattered. But how? Was it Luvanasis' armor? He tossed the handle into the shadows.

The sound of Luvanasis' chuckles echoed around him. "You don't get it, do you, Dane? Only one weapon can destroy me now, and you sent it away." Luvanasis approached Dane as he spoke. "But not to worry, one day, one of my descendants will unlock the platform to this realm. And I will arrive in Bonvida. On that day, I and all the darkness will be released, and we will conquer Bonvida."

The words slithered into Dane's ears. He could run, but what good would it do? Luvanasis would find him in this realm of darkness.

Luvanasis stood behind him now. "And when I do, I will find your child."

The chill of Luvanasis' cold breath tingled the back of Dane's neck, and he shuddered.

Then Luvanasis rested a hand on his shoulder. "I will kill him before he has the chance to kill me."

Dane breathed deeply. His friend-turned-enemy raised his long sword. How he hoped one of those birds would swoop down right now and eat Luvanasis. But no, this was his fate, a sacrifice so that his wife and son could escape. His mind flashed with images of Lavender and baby Atticus.

He focused on the incoming blade. The sharp steel grazed straight from his shoulder down to his left hip. All breath left him in a gasping scream. His chest opened up. He lost control of his body and collapsed to the ground.

Luvanasis stepped over and peered down at him. He pressed his sword into Dane a second time.

Dane gasped once more, raising his head.

Luvanasis knelt and held Dane's head. "Shh, sweet Dane, it will all be over in a moment . . . I will be sure to tell your son how brave you were." He dropped Dane's head on the ground.

Everything around Dane blurred as he watched Luvanasis stroll into the darkness of the forest. Blood filled his mouth, and he coughed, managing to mutter one last word.

"Atticus." His surroundings faded . . . until he passed.

Chapter 5

Overwhelmed, Lavender pressed baby Atticus to her chest as she gazed through the pale blue portal to a darker blue night sky and shadowy surroundings.

The warrior exited the portal first and motioned for Lavender to follow. Still marveling at the strange form of the portal, she closed her eyes as she stepped through the translucent perimeter and into a grassy field. The portal disappeared even before she could glance back at it.

A deep breath of the fresh Bonvidian air left her momentarily hypnotized by the beautiful aroma of nature around her. Large stones lay scattered across the area. A peaceful crescent moon and stars lit up the midnight blue sky above them. The moon in Bonvida remained a crescent all year long, except for once a year when it became full. On that day, all the kingdoms held a council meeting known as Winter's Moon.

Lavender sighed. She hadn't seen such beauty in such a long time. The land around her brought the image of Dane to her mind, but she wiped it away. She had to bury him in the depths of her heart so that she could remain strong and carry out his wishes.

The warrior stuffed a map into his pocket, approached her, and put a hand on her shoulder. "We must continue with our mission for the child's safety." He paused, a hint of compassion flickering in his eyes. "There is a farmhouse not too far from this pasture. You must leave your child at the door."

Lavender's heart ached, and she shook her head in disbelief. Was she strong enough to go through with this?

"They are expecting Atticus and will care for him as long as is needed. I will take you into hiding."

"Why can't I stay with my child?"

The warrior stopped in his tracks. "He must grow up amoungst the people, learn their ways and go unnoticed until an appointed time. I'm sorry, Lavender, but it's a must."

Lavender nodded. She had to accept and let her son live his best life.

The warrior led Lavender through the field in silence, with only the sound of crickets chirping their night songs. In the distance, a kingdom sat on a hilltop, flickering lights from lanterns glowing through the tower windows. "That is El-Valr," he said.

She stared at El-Valr's domain. Everyone loved El-Valr, a kingdom bustling with activity. It had the greatest army, with soldiers always ready to protect their land. They wore their El-Valr crests proudly, an image of Sofos as a Stag in the center of a green square surrounded by light turquoise.

The Royal El-Valr Family was kind and loving to all, but they had not always received the same kindness from the islands or from Mizeria, the kingdom in the Bonvida Badlands. She Serpent had taken her anger out on the original El-Valr, leaving it in ruins, so they re-situated themselves on this hill.

Just then, Atticus' small hand wiggled from the blanket and reached out towards the kingdom. With her heart constricted at the thought of giving her only son away, she took his little arm and swaddled it back into his blanket.

The blue of the night sky had deepened on their trek. Before long, a little farmhouse came into view, light glowing from two windows. Lavender sighed with relief. An unfinished stone wall surrounded the cozy wattle and daub home. As they approached, they passed a small, gated garden with neat rows of cabbage, herbs, and onions. A barn, not much bigger than the little house, stood further back, the open doors revealing stacks of hay, which the family likely sold to nearby villagers and traders in Portacrista.

Leaving the warrior at the edge of the garden, she paced alone towards the door of the farmhouse, tears welling in her eyes and her heart shattering. With each step, she sensed Dane's presence. Atticus' eyes fluttered open, his attention fixing on her. She tucked the blankets around his little body, then kissed him and set him on the porch at a safe distance from the door.

Kneeling beside him, she reached for the leather cord that hung from her neck and pulled it over her head. The moonlight glinted on the topaz shard that dangled from it. Dane had entrusted this to her, and she must now ensure that it stayed with Atticus. Tears streaming down her face, she stuffed it into a fold of his blanket.

"I love you, my boy," she whispered, emotion strangling her every word. "We will meet again. Until that day, I won't be far." She kissed Atticus again and wiped her eyes.

Resolved now, Lavender stood up, took a deep breath, and knocked on the door. Not wanting to break down with sorrow, she ran to the side of the little house and peered around the corner.

The farmhouse door opened, and a Bonvidian couple appeared in the doorway, their gazes snapping to the little bundled baby on the porch. Wasting no time, the woman bent down and picked him up, her expression one of great joy. "He has come," she said, carrying the baby inside. The man shut the door behind them.

***

The warrior and Lavender continued through the fields, moving in the direction of El-Valr, passing boulders and clusters of trees. The warrior scanned the area on both sides as they trudged along.

As they entered a misty area, he slowed his pace and nodded. "Your son is extraordinary, Lavender. He carries your husband's bloodline. He is a true descendant." They continued to take small steps, inching deeper into the

35

mist.

"Where I take you now, no one can see or enter except those of the chosen descendants. Lavender, since you gave birth to Atticus, you have the privilege to enter this area."

He handed her a knife that hung from his belt. "There is a stream nearby, where you will find an endless supply of water. The soil is rich with plenty of vegetation and small creatures to hunt."

Clutching the cold knife handle, Lavender peered into their mysterious surroundings. She took a long deep breath and then strode forward alone into the mist.

Part II – Eighteen Years Later

Chapter 6

With his spirit flying high this morning, Atticus pulled on his best tunic and fastened his belt around his waist. He checked all the pouches that hung from his belt—oh, his journal. He snatched the journal from his unmade bed and tucked it into the largest pouch, then he sat on the end of his bed and grabbed a boot.

The view from the window in his cramped bedroom caught his attention. Rays from the rising sun shot across the land in every direction, touching the twelve kingdoms and beyond. Strips of light red and blue kissed in the middle of the sky, with puffy white clouds scattered around.

A great yawn took over Atticus as he stepped to the water pitcher on the rickety table by the door. He splashed cool water on his face, refreshing himself. He had barely slept a wink last night. He hadn't been able to stop thinking about his plans for today, his eighteenth birthday. And then, sometime after midnight, the ground had shaken. Unless he'd imagined it.

Moving closer to the bedroom window, he leaned on the sill and watched a flock of geese gliding through the sky and honking away at each other. He breathed in the chilly but fresh spring air, taking in whiffs of hay from the barn next to their small thatched-roof home. A breeze rushed over him, stirring up sentimental feelings. He reached for his topaz necklace—the only thing his birth parents had left to him—and pressed it close to his heart.

Seven years ago, this very day, his adoptive parents told him the truth, that he had been given away only a few days after his birth. Never meeting his birth parents still bothered him from time to time, especially on his birthday.

The sound of four paws pattered along the wooden

floors outside his room, then the door squeaked open. He brushed his thoughts into a safe little box in his mind as a furry head nudged under his hand.

Atticus grinned, looking down at his sleek black dog. "How yah?" he said, scratching the top of her head. "Oh, Carrie girl, today is finally my eighteenth birthday, which means I'm going to do something special today. I haven't told Mum or Dad yet." He bit his lip, his stomach turning.

The dog plopped down, lifted a rear leg, and scratched behind one ear.

Atticus pulled his leather journal and a feathered pen from the pouch on his belt and climbed onto the window ledge to get a broader view of the land. Carrie whimpered, begging for another head scratch, and rested her head between his tummy and curled up legs. He opened his journal and flipped to a blank page. His journal helped him release the emotions that he kept bottled up inside him.

"Psst, Atticus, over here!" came a young female voice.

He turned and peered out his window.

His sister, Daria, stood poking her head out her window, her tousled brown hair dangling past one shoulder. She smiled, her dimples popping out and a playful expression in her hazel eyes.

"Morning to you, Dar." He chuckled, closed his journal, and tossed it onto his bedding.

While a fairly sensible and strong-willed girl, she had a playful, adventurous streak too. Daria, in a long white tunic and blue shawl, proceeded to climb out her window and shuffle towards his window along a wooden beam on the side of the house.

He jumped back into his room and helped her in. "You could have walked around."

"Where's the fun in that? Happy birthday, brother." His sister, one year older and a half-inch taller than he was, flung her arms around him and hugged him. "Any big

39

birthday adventures planned?"

"Aye, you know how I've been planning on applying to be a knight for El-Valr ... Well, today is the day!"

Daria beamed with excitement and gave him a gentle punch on his shoulder. "I am so happy for you. I hope you get in! I mean, I know you will!"

While Daria's enthusiasm warmed him, a hint of anxiety still niggled him. "Do you think they will be fine with me applying?"

"Who, our parents? Of course they will, Atticus. They want the very best for us. I know your birthday can sometimes feel sour, but they love you, Atticus."

Atticus slumped onto his bed, thankful for her support. "You know me better than anyone else does. You always have my back, Daria ... I don't want to let them or you down."

"You'll never let us down, especially me, Atticus. I know if you get accepted, you'll be off on marvelous adventures with the princes and the knights"—she flung her hands in the air, a dreamy look in her eyes—"protecting the land and all its inhabitants. You'll be living your dream. And I also know that if I ever run into trouble or need you, that you'll come back."

His mind filled with images of him alongside the other El-Valr knights, fighting creatures and keeping order across the land. He liked the idea of holding a sword. A sword made a warrior strong. "Of course, I will. You're my sister."

"Now c'mon." Daria tugged the sleeve of his tunic. "Let's get downstairs and see what is for breakfast."

He stood up and followed her out of the room and down the crooked stairs into a small kitchen. Not expecting anything, he spotted a single thick pastry covered in white powder on a plate.

Atticus grinned like a child, his mouth watering. "A

berry jam pastry? How did you get a hold of this?" He immediately sat down and bit into the soft breading, deep purple jam spilling onto the tablecloth. His memory rolled back to the first time he'd ever tried a berry jam pastry . . . so scrumptious and mouth-watering. The Elves never skimped on the fillings like other bakers in the land did with their cream-filled pastries.

Daria stuffed logs into the stove and grabbed a jar of dough, all the while watching him enjoy his birthday treat. "I went to the El-Valr market the other day, bumped into an Elf vendor selling their specially made pastries. Mum and I knew how much you love them."

"Thank you!" he said with his mouth full and berry jam dripping down his face.

"Happy birthday, Atticus!" their mother said as she and their father stepped into the kitchen. They both kissed the top of his head.

"Now, I know it's your special day," Dad said, "but we still have our chores. We've got hay to pile up and a house to refurbish, so after breakfast, we get to work."

"Daria, later today, I need you to collect some wood," Mum said.

Atticus wiped berry jam from his chin and pushed out his chair, all eyes fixed on him. He hesitated but then forced himself to speak. "Mum, Dad, I have to tell you something."

His parents exchanged glances.

"I'm going to apply to be an El-Valr knight, and I want to do it today, after my work is done, of course."

His parents smiled, beaming with excitement. They hugged him.

The morning passed quickly. As Atticus hurled a stack of hay onto the pile in the barn, his stomach growled, and he longed for a drink of water.

"Oh, Carrie girl, we have how many left?" He stepped

out of the barn and counted ten more stacks. Wiping his sweaty brow, he peered out into the distance, to the hill upon which sat the Kingdom of El-Valr. A pearl staircase protected by a gate led up the hilltop into the domain and—

What's this?

A small army of mounted knights rode towards the gate. So few? Were those the princes returning? Where were they coming from?

Carrie tilted her head and panted.

"Aye! Good idea, Carrie girl." Atticus glanced at the sun. He had enough time for a brief excursion. "Let's follow them." They followed from afar, running through the green pastures, passing by groves of trees, and leaping off large boulders.

As he focused on the royal horses, the toe of his boot slammed into something, and he toppled forward. Landing facedown on a clump of grass, he glimpsed a large root poking up from the ground. Groaning and hoping none of the princes noticed his embarrassing fall, he picked himself up and dusted his clothes. Not wanting to lose sight of the princes and their knights, he took off after them again.

Out of the corner of his eye, he caught Carrie running with determination towards a patch of trees in the pasture. The patch of trees—he stopped pursuing the princes for a moment and had to take a second glance—they did not look familiar. Why had he never noticed them before?

Carrie neared the edge of the trees, not slowing one bit.

"Carrie, wait! Where are you going?" Atticus gave a last glance back in the direction of the princes and knights, then he turned towards his dog and the strange patch of trees. He jogged to catch up.

As he stepped beyond the treeline, Carrie bounced up

to him and barked as if wanting him to follow. A strange mist rolled from between tree trunks on every side.

They continued through the mist, embracing the peacefulness of this place. He passed two trees arched over bushes and purple-flowered vines. After continuing a bit further, he paused at a clearing. An old stone well stood before him. Carrie romped around the well, barking playfully.

The different flowers that surrounded the well, orange, yellow, and magenta ones, captivated him with their beauty. A soothing voice echoed from inside the well. Intrigued, he shuffled forward and peeked over the edge.

A vine with pale purple flowers grew along the insides of the well, down beyond where the sunlight reached. Why had he never found this place until now? Atticus' mind battled, part of him wanting to leave the well and another part wanting to climb inside and explore like a knight of El-Valr would do. Maybe he should return home and tell Daria. She would love to explore with him.

The desire to climb into the well grew from a seed to a plant with deep roots and strong leaves. "I'll be right back, Carrie."

Head cocked to one side, Carrie wagged her tail.

Atticus climbed over the edge and grasped onto the vines. Then hand over hand, boots against the inside of the well for support, he climbed downward, excitement growing inside. After a few minutes and still not reaching the bottom, he peered into the darkness beneath him. How deep was this well?

He meant to continue his steady descent, but his hands, sweaty now, slid a distance down the vine, and he lost his footing at the same time. Heart leaping into his throat, he tried grasping the vine with both hands, but he lost his grip and hurtled downward.

Just as he landed hard on the bottom of the well, he saw a pair of hands reaching out to him, but then his head cracked against stone, and everything went black.

Chapter 7

Daria maneuvered a wooden cart of firewood down a bumpy trail in the woods between home and El-Valr. Lifting her gaze to the treetops and the crystal blue sky, she spotted a cloud in the shape of a whale. Continuing her way down the trail, the sound of familiar barking came from a distance to her left.

She stopped pushing the cart and wiped sweat from her brow as she turned in the direction of the barking. A strange mist gathered between tree trunks a stone's throw away. Curiosity beckoned her to investigate. She gripped the smooth wooden cart handles and raced towards the mist, hoping that no logs rolled out in the process. She reached the edge of the woods, where the mist curled around roots and tree trunks.

The mist swirled with her every step, keeping her aware of her surroundings. The barking and whimpering of the dog grew stronger. A few steps in, the mist parted, revealing a well surrounded by the most beautiful arrangement of flowers. Curious, she continued to pace forward.

Carrie rushed from around the well, came to her side, and tugged at her sleeve ... trying to tell her something

Daria, following the dog's orders, stepped closer to the well, and peeked inside. She could see nothing more than a long dark hole. "What is it, girl?"

Carrie jumped up, placing her front paws on the well's edge.

Daria was filled with worry. "Carrie, where is Atticus?" She shook her head. Daria tried not to look down the well again, but something nagged at her. Could he have fallen into it?

She grasped the cold stone sides firmly and leaned over it, hoping to spot movement in the darkness or even to hear his voice. "Atticus!"

Her voice bounced off the walls of the well. She waited but got no reply.

Suddenly, a rumbling sound came from deep in the heart of the well. Without warning, rain burst forth from the sky above. The ground quaked the way it had last night. Panicking, she shouted again, "Atticus! If you're down there, we have to go!"

While her voice still echoed in the darkness below, stones broke loose, and the well caved in. Daria jumped back. Her jaw dropped, and her heart stopped beating. She sprang forward again and grabbed a stone before it settled on the heap. Maybe she could unbury the well. As she tossed that first stone aside, a sheet of rain overpowered her, forcing her away from the well.

She put her arm over her eyes. "I'll be back for you, Atticus." She sprinted out of the mist with Carrie trailing behind her. The whole land had darkened, and rain pounded the earth.

Daria jogged through the plains, her eyes set on home. Maybe their parents could help find him. With every breath, she shouted Atticus' name, hoping that he hadn't fallen into the well. Carrie followed close on her heels, barking repeatedly. But still no sign of him.

The rain calmed enough for her to see her surroundings better. As the path curved around, the bells in El-Valr chimed. She approached an overlook with a view of the kingdom, and then she froze.

A battle was being fought in the plains before the El-Valr castle, strange-looking creatures battling mounted soldiers. Some of the creatures marched in different directions. What was happening? The bells meant trouble, warning everyone who heard them to go into hiding. Soon the echo of bells filled the Bonvida sky. The other kingdoms were responding to El-Valr. The land was under attack but by what? Or who?

Fear overcoming her, she patted her belt to find her small hatchet, then she pulled it out in case she came across any of those horrid creatures. Thankfully, they were far enough away that they posed no immediate danger, but they might head her way.

Further down the path, two figures ran towards her. Her parents? They must have rushed from the house in search of her and Atticus when the ground shook and the rain started.

"Do you know what's happening?" Daria asked as they came close. She had never seen her parents in such a fearful state.

Her mother grabbed her by the shoulders. "Daria, where is your brother?"

Panic overtook her, rendering her speechless for a moment until having to force out words. "I don't know. I think he fell into the well down the path."

Her parents exchanged glances, their expressions strangely peaceful.

"Daria, he will be fine. We do not have time to explain right now because we are on the brink of dark times." Her father's eyes welled with tears. "You need to run, hide until it is safe." He gazed in the direction of the ugly creatures.

She wiped rain and tears from her face. "What aren't you telling me?" she said, her voice rising with panic.

Her father held her close. "We love you. You must go."

"Where will I run to?" Daria asked.

"For now, just find shelter anywhere but here." Her mother pointed in the opposite direction of the battle between the soldiers and creatures.

"Please, you must hurry and go." Her father gave her a hug and kissed her head.

Daria's mother squeezed her. "You are a brave young

woman, Daria."

"We have to save Atticus. What if he's hurt?" Daria cried out.

"Don't worry about Atticus." Her father's eyes seemed oddly peaceful.

Confused about their attitude and frightened, she ran off with Carrie at her heels, trusting in her parents' judgement.

Two hours later, Daria stopped to catch her breath between a grove of trees and open farm fields. Her teeth chattered and goosebumps popped out on her legs and arms. Thankfully, the rain had stopped, turning into a cold mist. She gathered her damp hair in one hand and tied it into a messy ponytail, wishing she had done it earlier, but she had been too focused on running.

"Oh, Carrie." She turned and went quiet, not seeing the dog. Where did Carrie go? When did she lose her?

She squatted down and pressed her face into her palms. The idea of losing Atticus, her parents, and now the dog struck her hard. Standing up again, she tried to force herself to think of the best place to hide. A kingdom would be the safest place.

She continued jogging down the trail and soon saw others traveling on a crossroad that led towards Idra, a peaceful kingdom between two mountains. Villagers carried bundles in their arms or on their backs. The slope of the land revealed a village ahead, no more than ten minutes away, she guessed. A log fence surrounded the village, men shouted outside the gate.

Drawing closer to the village, the commotion she had seen from a distance became clear. Bonvidian men, armed with swords and various iron tools, fought against those same hideous creatures she saw earlier. Daria froze at the sight of those ugly creatures swinging their long arms, their eyes bulging from their faces. What were they?

One creature ran with a flaming torch and then set the village wall ablaze. The smell of burning wood filled the air. In the next instant, a horrible stench overpowered the burning odor. Her neck warmed, and something breathed heavily behind her, making her skin crawl.

Gripping her hatchet, she whipped around to face it.

The creature yanked her to the ground with a clawed hand. It stood above her, pinning her down by her neck.

Rather than struggle to free herself, she swung her hatchet at its arm. The stench consumed her, and drool dripped onto her face. She squeezed her eyes and mouth shut and swung again. She just could not die this way . . . death by a stinky creature outside some little village in Bonvida.

Something hissed through the air and landed nearby with a loud smack.

The creature loosened its grip and tumbled to its side.

She opened her eyes and shoved the lower part of the dead creature off her. Then she climbed to her feet and backed away from the thing, its dead body less threatening but still hideous. She glanced about to see who had saved her life.

Two stocky Dwarves with fiery orange hair stood on a nearby boulder, each holding specially crafted bows.

With gratitude, she walked up to them, brushed a strand of hair from her eyes, and offered a formal bow. "Thanks for that. My name's Daria."

The two Dwarves jumped off the boulder and came up to her, standing no more than three-and-a-half-feet tall, one with dreadlocks and the other with curly, puff hair. When they smiled, dimples popped out on their innocent-looking faces. "Ello, Daria, me name's Tidy," said the one with dreadlocks. "This here is me brotha', Spit." Tidy spoke with an Irish accent similar to one from Letterkenny, Ireland.

The two Dwarves clasped her hands and tugged her along. "Come with us quick. We best hurry off."

Daria caught her breath and stared over her shoulder at the chaos. The village still burned, villagers scattered, and those creatures could pop out from anywhere. She could think of no other choice. Besides, these two Dwarves seemed trustworthy.

Daria only needed to jog to keep up with them as they ran to a grove of thin pine trees.

Spit pointed to a white-spotted horse with a brown mane. It stood tied to a tree. "Oie! There it is, our horse!"

Spit lowered onto all fours next to the horse. Tidy climbed onto his back and struggled to pull himself up and into the saddle.

Then Spit stood up. "Well, c'mon, Daria, help me up. We don't got all day now, do we?" he said with a cheerful grin.

With a chuckle, Daria bent down and cuffed her hands. Spit's heavy boots pressed onto her palms as he tugged at his brother and seated himself in the center. Next, she placed one foot in the stirrup and hoisted herself up and over.

Tidy tapped the horse's side and gained control of the reins. The horse neighed and proceeded to gallop. "You shoulda seen us earlier when we first found this beauty of a stallion."

Daria held onto the sides of the graceful creature. She had only ridden a horse a few times in her life, but she'd always wanted one for her own. Glancing over her shoulder, she watched the nightmare fade away into the distance. "Tell me somethin.' I thought Dwarves usually wielded axes, but you two carry bows and arrows."

The twin Dwarves chuckled in unison. "Aye, Daria, that is quite true, but us two, we wanted to be different from all the other Dwarves in these lands, make a special name for ourselves. Have you ever tried archery?"

49

"I've always wanted to learn."

Spit cranked his neck back, trying to look at her. "Well, how about we teach yah? We could use someone like you. I feel we are in for quite a battle."

Daria smiled as the horse trotted alongside a large dark blue lake. Trees curved over parts of the lake and long strands of grass poked up along the rocky banks. In the center of the lake was an island with an ancient temple that overlooked the waters. Daria had visited Loch Alri with Atticus and her parents to fish, and during festivals. Loch Alri was a popular location to gather. The lake connected two rivers. One ran west through the Dwarven Forest and met the lake's far side. The other swerved south and split into branches in the Woodlands.

The horse paced through the Dwarven Forest, heading in the direction of cliffs beyond the trees. The Dwarves lived there. After traveling peacefully for some time, Daria glimpsed odd stones littering the ground ahead. No, not stones. Bodies. The bodies of fallen Dwarves and those hideous creatures lay scattered about them. "What are those things?" she asked after some time.

Spit made a low growling sound and then shrugged. "Murderers."

"We 'ave no clue, actually. Some ugly beasts sent to ravage the land. Hopefully, our great Dwarf King Courtneilous will know." Under his breath, Tidy added, "He'll know what to do about them."

As the horse trotted through the Dwarven Forest, birds chirped in the trees, and chipmunks played tag.

Excitement filled her as a clearing and the cliffs came into sight. She had never been to the Dwarf Kingdom before. She'd always thought that Dwarves guarded the forest outside the kingdom, hiding in trees and bushes or even under boulders.

The aroma of the forest—tree bark mixed with smoke

from campfires carried from a distance—brought peace to her.

Finally, the forest cleared, and large cliffs rose before her eyes. A long white steel gate stood in the open field, and behind it was a fire-lit tunnel. In the clearing outside the gate, units of Dwarves in all different shapes and sizes assembled. Some carried axes, others clubs with metal spikes.

The twins waved to the other Dwarves.

"Wouldn't want to get poked in the eye with that." Tidy chuckled as he pulled the reins back, and the horse halted.

Daria and the two Dwarves climbed off the horse and strode to the kingdom entrance. Daria tried not to feel awkward as everyone watched her waiting for the gates to open.

The twins looked up at her. "Well, Daria, welcome to Karadwarfa," Tidy said. "Our home is your home. How 'bout we go get us some answers on what in tarnation is goin' on in Bonvida." Tidy cracked his knuckles, and Spit wiped his face.

As she followed her two new friends, she turned back one last time. Whatever was happening in Bonvida, at least she was safe with the Dwarves.

Chapter 8

An army of thirty soldiers stood at a rocky shoreline. A wave from the deep blue Bonvida sea rolled inland, nuzzled their ankles, and slid back, leaving behind foam bubbles. The smell of salt water blended with the smell of the Evergreen Forest just behind them.

Each soldier removed his armor and waded into the calm Bonvidian sea. Within seconds of their toes touching the salty water, their bodies clenched—no chance of backing down from the El-Valr ceremony now.

Prince Victor, the youngest of the three El-Valr princes, peered to his left upon the oldest, Prince Damien, born five years before him. Damien strode into the water with his head held high and shoulders back. He always walked like he owned the room, carrying a glare that some would read as menacing.

As he continued to wade into the icy water, Prince Victor tried to stand as straight as he could to match the height of his two brothers. He almost reached the height of Raldon, the second son. The three brothers did not share any resemblance. Maybe it was due to their father having married a second queen after his first one had vanished.

When the water reached his waist, Damien raised an arm towards the sky. "Today, you soldiers will become more than just fighters for this land."

A breeze blew, sending chills right to their bones. Victor shivered, and his brothers both held onto his sides. He rolled his neck from side to side in preparation.

"Accept the vulnerability and become more than just a man," Damien exclaimed.

Victor's brothers dunked him under the seawater. Seconds passed. Then minutes. His lungs screamed for air, and he snapped open his eyes—the saltwater stinging. He fought his instincts, which told him to break free from his brothers' restraint.

Just when Victor could take it no longer, Damien and Raldon pulled him up. "You're worthy of fighting for the land," Raldon said, slapping his back.

Victor gasped for air and pushed his silver hair from his eyes. The taste of saltwater lingered in his mouth. Oh, he could not wait to get back onto the dry land and get the taste out of his mouth.

Victor accompanied his brothers to dunk the nearest soldier and then the next and next, until all of them had their turn.

After the dunking ended, Victor, his brothers, and the other soldiers trudged to the shore and to their belongings. As he stepped onto the shore, pebbles gouged his bare feet.

The three brothers dressed and put their armor back on. They led the army up the shore and through the forest. The trees of the Evergreen Forest smelt of early spring. Wild pear trees and apple trees budded while the oak and birch trees bloomed. The usual chatter and activity of the woodland creatures silenced.

Victor strode alongside Damien.

"You did well once again, little brother." Damien chuckled.

Arriving at their belongings, Victor drew from his backpack a piece of bread and cheese, put them together, and took a bite. "Well, it is my fourth time," he replied with his mouth full.

Damien brushed his dark brown hair from his forehead. "Oh, Victor, didn't mother tell you not to talk with your mouth full, especially since you're a prince?"

Victor swallowed his food. "Aye, I believe she did, but who have I here to impress, Damien, you?" He chuckled as he sat down on a log.

Evening fell upon Victor and the El-Valr soldiers as they pitched their tents. The sunlight dimmed, shades of orange now visible through the treetops. The air grew chilly, and night animals began awakening from their sleep. Victor helped Barlos, the lead commander of the El-Valr army, take out materials to make a campfire.

After getting the fire going, Victor sneaked away from the campsite and back to the sea. He loved how the crescent moon reflected off the sea and how the stars filled the night sky.

Victor fiddled around in one of his pouches and pulled out a tiny seashell with a marking on it. He threw the seashell into the sea and then paced back and forth.

A few moments later, a Bonvidian female—a Bru— appeared amidst the waves, swimming to shore. She waded out of the water, her scaly skin and fishlike face glistening in the moonlight.

Victor found it strange that the Bru breed of Bonvidians lived in the depths of the sea and were the only sea creatures that could breathe on land.

This particular Bru, out of the luck of the draw, would one day be his wife. His father hoped that this arranged marriage would ally them with the Bru colony. Over the last few months, Victor had grown close to her. While he had wished to marry someone that he chose, someone that would warm his heart, he did not want to disappoint his father—or even the rest of the kingdom. He wanted to do whatever was best.

"Victor!" She gasped with excitement and ran to him.

Lena grabbed Victor's hand, and they walked towards Damien and the other soldiers. A scattering of tents surrounded a blazing campfire. Victor stood to the side, observing his brother Damien. This had always been Damien's favorite part: branding the soldiers with the seal of El-Valr. As Damien dipped a steel pole with a symbol of the stag face of Sofos into the fire, Victor rubbed his own wrist and the coin-sized mark of the stag.

The cry of a soldier filled the dark forest and caused Victor to turn away.

After the branding ended, Barlos lumbered over and stood on a log, his large belly bulging from his shirt. "Tomorrow, we head home to El-Valr, and when we do, we go back stronger. Tomorrow we will also be accepting new candidates to join our army. You have all moved up in ranks. Congratulations," Barlos shouted.

New recruits . . . how Victor loved watching the process for applying to be a soldier.

Sleep beckoned, and he yawned, turning to Lena. "I need my rest. Will you be joining us on our way back to El-Valr?"

Lena took off a pair of gauntlets with blades on the wrists. "If I am permitted."

The next day arrived as they packed their belongings.

While Victor folded up a tent, he looked over at Raldon, who arranged items in a bag. "Did you feel that small tremor last night?"

Raldon raised his eyebrows. "You must have been dreaming deep, brother. I didn't feel a tremor."

Damien squeezed Victor's shoulder, interrupting them. "Brothers, we must leave soon."

Raldon tied the bag to a saddle. "Aye, we are almost ready. Which way do we want to go?"

Damien stepped aside. "I know the way home. Don't you worry, brother,"

Once everyone packed their belongings, the brothers led the soldiers through the flourishing green forest with the Grey Stone Mountains in easy sight.

After zigzagging through the woods, a jagged and narrow mountain pathway stood before them.

Victor observed the treacherous path, not liking what he saw. They would have to proceed single file to go down it. "Should we go around it? It looks too tight."

"If we do, it'll add another day to our journey," Raldon replied.

Victor glared at Damien. "I thought you knew the way, Damien."

Damien shrugged and glared back at him. "Guess we took a wrong turn."

Victor sighed. Damien hated being proven wrong, but they had taken another route to get to the forest. Why weren't they taking that same route back?

"We will travel in single file," Damien announced.

Frustrated, Victor opened his eyes wide and huffed. "Go through? Damien, that's not a smart idea. We should turn around and follow the trail we used to get here."

Damien ignored Victor and peered down the jagged path. "Single file," he snapped.

Victor shook his head in disagreement. Why would Damien wish to take such a dangerous trail?

Victor and his two brothers led their soldiers down the jagged path. One side of the cliff rose higher than the other. They maneuvered around shrubs and boulders that brushed against the horses' bodies and the riders' legs. A steep cliff rose on one side.

To ease the tension, Victor whistled a Bonvidian folk song, and his brothers and Barlos joined in.

A few minutes later, Raldon, who rode before Victor, stopped whistling and jerked a glance upward as if noticing movement above them along the stones. Then he glanced over his shoulder at Victor and gestured upwards with his chin.

Victor peered up and he, too, glimpsed something. A strange creature—likely one of many—readied a bow and arrow, peering down at them.

Attackers? Victor reached for the smooth tusk horn that hung across his back, and he blew to signal danger. They could only go the speed of the lead knight. One wrong step would cause a collision of horses and soldiers.

An arrow sailed down, striking a soldier and knocking him off his horse. Victor and the soldiers nearest him positioned their shields above their heads. Gruff shouts came from behind, then another signal horn blew. Flight mode kicked in as the line hustled forward. Arrows came from every direction. More of these creatures must have arrived.

Victor glanced back at his soldiers. Some had fallen, while others barely held on. They drew nearer the exit of the jagged path and, hopefully, the end of this massacre. If only he could get his hands on whatever those dangling-arm things were.

He sighed with relief as he exited the path and lowered his shield. His brothers, Barlos, Lena, and the other soldiers had made it through. He counted the heads of the other soldiers, making note of at least fifteen. He peered down the jagged path, only to shut his eyes at the sight of bodies.

He glared at Damien. If they hadn't taken this wretched path, the other soldiers would be alive.

Before he could speak his mind, Damien cleared his throat. "Whatever those creatures were, we'd best make haste. We need to warn Father."

Victor, his brothers, Barlos, Lena, and the remaining soldiers raced through lavish green fields and over hills filled with flowers and small animals. They passed a barn and continued through the pastures.

Out of the corner of Victor's eye, he glimpsed a Bonvidian no less than two years younger than he, following them on foot. The lad tripped over a root but recovered quite well. Victor lost sight of him as the follower went into an unfamiliar misty area.

The El-Valr horses headed up large handcrafted stairs and through an open city of stone and marble houses and buildings. Bonvidians walked and chatted, some even singing, while others bargained in the open markets. Before reaching the castle, they passed a blacksmith hammering hot steel.

The horses trotted up a set of stairs to large wooden stables. At the stable, Victor and the others dismounted and turned the reins over to servants. Victor, his brothers, Barlos, and Lena stood before large maroon maple castle doors which opened majestically.

Walking into the castle, Victor admired the architecture. A large staircase welcomed them. Statues, stained glass windows, and paintings lined the long hallway, along with rows of alabaster and closed doors.

Their father, King Arldin, stood admiring a painting of a three-headed creature. He wore a long red robe and a golden crown atop his wavy brown hair. "My sons," he said with his arms outspread, ready to embrace.

Raldon hurried to the King. "Father, we came across strange creatures . . . They attacked us."

His father's jaw dropped. "What?"

Lena stepped forward. "Whatever they were, I believe they are not of this realm. I believe they're of Calsriv." She took another step closer to King Arldin. "My father told me stories when I was little. They are part of the prophecies of Desmond, locked in Calsriv until one day when the darkness of Hematite re-enters Bonvida. They can only be defeated once the heir of Desmond arises."

King Arldin glanced at Barlos. "Ring the bells. Alert the other kingdoms. As of now, Bonvida is under siege. Gather everyone within the kingdom at once!"

In obedience, Barlos darted back down the halls.

King Arldin rubbed his grey beard. "Sons, we must lead

the coming battle. It may feel hopeless, and this darkness may overwhelm us." He paced back and forth, staring at Victor and his two brothers. "It may bring us to our lowest points." He stared at Raldon and then stopped before Damien. "But no matter what, my sons, no matter what, do not give in to despair or defeat. Do not let the fear or the loss dishearten you."

He gazed up at a stained-glass window of Desmond. "Because there is hope. A hope in someone who is to come and save us from this wrath. It may not be today or tomorrow or even in a year." He turned around and looked at Victor. "When this chosen descendant of Desmond does arrive, you can be sure that the light will shine again. And when it does, the land will be saved, and this darkness vanquished."

Before King Arldin could say another word, the castle shook, the painting of the three-headed creature fell off the wall, and debris dusted their heads.

Another tremor like last night.

Victor clenched a fist. "Father, we will do whatever it takes. This place will one day be ours, and we need to be strong enough to protect it."

Raldon nodded. "What about you and Mother? You're the king and queen. You should come with us."

King Arldin lowered his head. "No, my place is among my kingdom. I will stay here, and I will protect it the best that I can. I fear that El-Valr will be the first kingdom to fall. You all better hurry." King Arldin hugged each of his sons.

Victor strode from the castle shoulder to shoulder with Damien, Raldon, and Lena, shoving open the maple doors and heading into the pouring rain and driving wind. This was his land, his kingdom, and no one was going to take it from him.

Standing on the highest step, Victor scanned the city

streets. Soldiers gathered civilians and escorted them to a bunker. Victor eyed his older brothers. "Viva Bonvida." He wrapped his hand around the hilt of his sword and drew it out. He marched with the others down the steps and through the emptying marketplace.

He spotted a single creature devouring cakes from a stand.

The creature shrieked as it turned its bulging eyes to Victor and his brothers. Then it growled and waved its claws in a threatening manner.

Readying himself for an attack, Victor tightened his grip on his gold-handled sword with jewels glittering the edges.

The creature charged at them, its long arms flailing. Almost upon them, its mouth opened wide, revealing sharp teeth and drool.

Wasting no motions, Victor swung his sword and sliced off its head. He and his brothers chuckled. If they faced nothing more threatening than this, then they would have an easy fight until the chosen one arrived.

The brothers and their soldiers moved on, picking up their pace. Screams and growls and the clanging of metal filled the air. As they reached the top of the steps on the hill, they stared as soldiers and creatures battled together.

The chaos flowed down the pearl steps and into the plains.

The three brothers turned to one another, unsure of what was to come. Victor gave them each a grim smile. No matter what, until the chosen one should arise, he had to keep hope and faith pulsing through his veins. He and his brothers and the other soldiers charged down the pearl steps of El-Valr into battle as the citadel bells rang their warning songs across the land.

Chapter 9

Atticus awoke to find himself lying atop a quilt of feathers and wool on a stone slab. As he sat up, pain rushed to the back of his head. He tried rubbing the pain away, squinting at odd purple flames in a small firepit.

A gentle but tired-looking older woman stirred a kettle that hung over the fire, her long grey hair shimmering in the firelight. A single purple lock of hair hung in front of her eyes.

"Where am I?"

The women spun around. "Ah, you're awake," she said. She paced towards him with a steaming bowl and handed it to him. "I am happy to see you up. Drink this. It will help you."

A metallic odor came from the hot red broth, making his stomach turn. "What is it?"

She glanced to the side. "It's . . . well, it's Apori blood mixed with vegetables and the waters of the Loch Alri."

He gagged and made a face, unable to hide his disgust. "Apori blood, no thank you." The very thought made him want to vomit. Apori meat, sure. He enjoyed the taste of that, but the blood? Yuk! That was a whole other taste altogether.

Her eyes glittered. "I insist, Atticus. It will make you feel better."

He shook his head and turned away. Then he turned back to the woman. "Hey, how do you know my name?"

The woman smiled and sat by his side. "Drink," she repeated, ignoring his question. She placed the bowl into his hands and up to his mouth like a mother trying to feed a young child.

Atticus held his breath to avoid the smell and then guzzled the substance down, some of it going down the wrong pipe. He coughed and hacked and took deep breaths. "That is disgusting," he said, wiping his mouth.

"Well, what do you expect when you drink Apori blood?" She chuckled.

This must be some kind of cruel joke.

She took the bowl from him and set it on a side table. Then she seemed to study him for a moment as she stroked his hair. "You look just like your father."

Atticus' ears perked. "What?"

She laughed. "I said you look like your father."

Could this be . . .? Why would *she* be down in this well? "Mother?" Atticus gazed upon this older woman, and tears blurred his vision.

She wiped her eyes, her voice tangling with emotion. "You have no idea how long I've been waiting for this, my boy. Oh, my Atticus."

They fell into each other's arms and held on tight.

She kissed his cheek. "First of all, my name is Lavender. I didn't want to leave you, but I had to. I thought of you every day."

He shoved the blankets off and climbed out of the bed. He followed her to a wooden table and sat across from her. Lanterns hung on damp stone walls, providing ample lighting for the little room. Large water barrels stood in one corner, shelves of dried food beside them.

Atticus wiped his tears. After all this time, on his eighteenth birthday, he finally met his birth mother.

She held his hands, hers cold and bony, his still soft and young.

"My parents told me," Atticus said, "that I would meet you one day and that my father had died saving us. The family you left me with, they cared for me and treated me with great love and respect. I have a sister. Her name is Daria." He took a breath and spat out the taste of the Apori blood.

Lavender smiled, her shoulders relaxing. "Atticus, I

must tell you where you come from and about the destiny that awaits once you leave this well."

Atticus tilted his head. Where was he from? His destiny? What was she talking about?

Lavender tapped her fingers as if organizing her thoughts. "You may have learned as a child or during The Festival of Gems that the opal created the skies, the warriors, the moon and sun and stars . . . and Skyarl. The other five gems created the rest of Bonvida and left behind shards. Now, Sofos knew his enemy Hematite created chaos and would stop at nothing to escape and destroy Bonvida. This threat of Hematite gave Sofos authority to create a new type of Bonvidian, mixed from the dust of the earth and the blood of warriors." She fiddled with one lock of purple hair that dangled by her ear.

Atticus listened intently. He had heard much of what she told him now, but somehow it seemed more important coming from her.

"Desmond and his four followers would be the defenders of Bonvida. Unfortunately, one was tempted, grasped by darkness. Sofos had given Desmond a sword and placed in the sword the five shards of Bonvida. Desmond and any of his future descendants were destined to defeat Hematite, She Serpent, and the other darkness with that sword. Desmond's other followers were also given weapons to assist in the destruction of Hematite and its darkness." She took a breath.

Atticus leaned in closer. He knew pieces of the story of Desmond. The way she spoke about these historical stories ignited his desire for adventure. The excitement of being a knight of El-Valr deepened. It was time. He needed to leave the well, and then he could apply. Maybe his mother could live with his adoptive parents. *Wait a second* . . . What did the legend of Desmond have to do with him being stuck in the well?

Lavender cleared her throat. "You are the only one who can destroy Luvanasis. He has found his way out of the dark realm of Calsriv and into this beautiful land of Bonvida, bringing with him the darkness. Son, you are the chosen one, the son of Dane, grandson of Desmond . . . You, Atticus, can wield the Sword of Bonvida and destroy the darkness."

Atticus drew back, not understanding what she just said. Did she just call him the chosen one? Maybe he was dreaming? That must have been it. He had fallen asleep on the hay and— *No, that cannot be it . . . This must be true.* "Mother, how can this be? All I've ever wanted was to become a knight for the kingdom of El-Valr, and now you tell me I am to carry the fate of this land on my shoulders?"

Lavender took him by his hand. "You carry special blood in you."

Atticus pulled his hand from hers and rested his gaze on his arms. He imagined seeing his blood slide and throb through his veins. So many emotions hammered his mind. *What if he failed? Was he worthy of this? Why only now? How could he alone attempt such a quest?*

She got up and went to a shelf. Then she stood for a moment gazing at the sheathed sword on the shelf as if lost in some memory. "Your father, Dane, gave this to me." Lavender picked it up and returned to Atticus. "This is the legendary Sword of Bonvida, the one Sofos created, the one Desmond used to protect this land."

He studied the sheath and the golden hilt. He had only seen paintings of the sword. They did not compare to the real thing.

Lavender placed it in his hands. "Behold the Sword of Bonvida," she proclaimed.

Atticus pulled the sword from the sheath and held it aloft. The handle shot waves of warmth through his hand and into his body. Holding this sword seemed too good to be true. He admired the craftsmanship, running a finger along the edges of five deep grooves. The grooves, each different in shape, formed an oval.

Lavender stepped closer to him. "Those will hold the shards of the land. With this sword, you will destroy Luvanasis. And with aid from the other descendants, you will destroy Hematite and its darkness, but only once all five shards are in place." Her gaze shifted to the topaz necklace he wore. "That is one of them, the topaz shard, the shard which formed the lands."

Atticus grasped the topaz. "This tiny, jagged topaz? One of the shards?"

Lavender walked behind him and untied the necklace.

Atticus placed the Sword of Bonvida next to the sheath on the table. Then he opened his hand, and she draped the leather cord over his palm.

He took a deep breath and closed his hand around the topaz. This little piece of topaz had always reminded him of his birth parents. Now it meant so much more.

He blocked out the sounds of the crackling fire and tuned out their breathing as their hearts beat in rhythm. Then he uncurled his fingers and detached the topaz from the thin leather cord. How could this be true? He carried the fate of this land, Bonvida, in his hands. Trembling, Atticus placed the topaz shard into one of the five grooves. It clipped into the groove like the first piece of a puzzle.

Chapter 10

The sun reached its apex in the grey sky over the rough Bonvidian Sea as Zane rowed his wooden boat closer to shore. After securing the oars inside the boat, he swung his legs over the side and splashed into the cool, waist-high water. He grabbed a rope attached to the bow and dragged the boat to the rocky shore. Then he dropped to his knees and kissed the ground.

Finally, after days of constant rowing and nights of resting with worrying of his boat flipping over, he had found a safe shore. The day he fled home entered his mind . . .

Zane closed a book and stared at the title: A Tale of Desmond, Volume I. *Done with it, he pushed back his chair and paced around the circular library. Tarnished titanium bookshelves lined the walls from floor to ceiling. A large stained-glass window curved around the room. Sunlight streamed in through it, illuminating colorful images of Bonvidians holding scrolls. Reaching a tall, wooden ladder, Zane climbed up and slid the book into place on a high shelf.*

No sooner had he started down when the ground trembled—and everything else in the room shook. Fearing he would fall, Zane gripped the sides of the ladder, but it shifted away from the bookshelf. In the next instant, books slid from their places around him, and the ladder toppled backwards.

Zane crashed to the floor. A sharp pain shot up his spine, but he held back a cry. Everything continued shaking, books falling. Regaining his breath, he shoved the ladder aside, dodged falling books, and ran for cover under the desk. A moment later, the ground stilled, and everything quieted.

Before he climbed out from under the desk, the citadel bell rang and screams followed. What was going on? Were they under attack?

He crawled out from under the desk and sprinted to the window.

Zane pushed the memory away and took a breath. Raising his head, he scanned his surroundings. Two mountain ranges loomed before him, one on either side, and between them, a forested path. The odd curve of the mountain range on his right made it seem like a giant had rearranged them. Well, he was close to Giant Country. He'd once learned about the Giants and how they'd moved the towering cliffs, stacking one on top of another to create an enormous fortress and attached castle. They'd even built a regular-sized kingdom within theirs so they could receive Bonvidian visitors.

The mountains to his left were of regular height. But beyond those treacherous cliffs lay the Wildlands. Those living in The Wildlands did not want to be part of Bonvida. They loathed the land for some odd reason. Sure, the twelve kingdoms within Bonvida had their own disagreements at times, but The Wildlands hated the entire land. They hated it so much that they'd tore down the bridge that had once connected the two parts of the land.

Zane got up and lugged the boat to where the tide would not draw it back. Gazing at the mountains again, he shook his head and laughed at this accomplishment. He had rowed from the kingdom of Maljooi along the coast by himself. Unlike those of the kingdom of Sastoo, he was not athletic. He had some muscle tone but nothing he would gloat about. He was a young scholar who had escaped a fierce battle and survived. Unbidden, thoughts of that day returned to him.

Zane crept out from under the desk and ran to the window.

Out in the street only feet away from the library, horrid, big-eyed creatures with long arms tore through the gates.

67

Some used their arms to leap over walls. These creatures looked familiar.

Zane turned away as he tried to place them. Then he remembered. He'd read about them in the stories of Desmond. These were Arcods, Hematite's creatures. Wait . . . that would mean . . .

His heart dropped to the floor. It was happening. The darkness had been released.

He squinted out the window again. The ugly creatures were attacking everyone they came across, grabbing civilians and corralling them into groups, killing those who tried to defend themselves. In the midst of the chaos, his parents and uncle were grouped with other civilians.

Sick to his stomach, he turned away. He could not bear to see more. He whipped to the desk, grabbed his bag, and raced out of the room. He stepped into a stone hall filled with paintings and statues of knights in armor. With one hand on the doorknob, he stopped. Then he turned back and snatched the sword from the closest statue. He had never used one in his life, but how hard could it be?

At that moment, a growling echoed in the halls, and his blood ran cold. The creatures had found their way inside this building. He hid around a corner.

Heavy footfalls grew closer, as did a horrendous smell.

Holding his breath and hoping to avoid being seen, he peeked around the corner.

A lone Arcod lumbered closer and closer. A few more steps and it might see him.

Mustering courage he did not know he possessed, Zane leaped out and thrust the sword into the creature's chest. Its huge eyes turned to him in shock, then it gurgled until it lost its breath.

He yanked the sword back, and it fell from his shaking hands. He collapsed to his knees. He had just killed . . . he'd just killed something.

More footfalls drew his attention. Arcods pounded up the library steps.

He had to go, but his legs stuck to the ground. Come on, come on, legs! Let's go! *He sprang up and snatched the sword from the floor, his hands tingling. The reality that he had just killed something overpowered his mind. But he could not think of that now. He had to go.*

Snapping from the unpleasant memory, Zane rubbed his fingers with his thumb, a technique that always seemed to calm him, especially when he did not have his books. Back to work, he leaned into the boat and grabbed a pack, a cloak, a belt with two daggers, and a thin sword in a navy sheath with a large "M" engraved in the center. The "M" stood for Maljooi, his home. Maljooi, the city of scholars. He kissed the "M." Those raised in Maljooi normally grew up to become professors, politicians, advisers, or historians. He desired to become a historian, the most famous historian that Bonvida would ever know.

Lastly, he reached for a glass jar. The jar held only a handful of assorted nuts. His stomach growled at the sight of them. He had fled so fast that he'd only managed to grab two large canisters and this jar of nuts, which he had to ration.

Ready now, he faced the towering mountains and the forested path. The fact he had managed to leave home and escape those creatures through one of the secret tunnels encouraged him. He marched across the shore and to the path ahead of him. Food and shelter were his top two priorities . . . and staying safe. Hopefully, none of those Calsriv creatures had reached these woods.

Reaching the top of the hill, he stopped and listened. The pine forest seemed to glare at the mountainous hills and deep inclines bundled with trees. As unsettling as the current situation was, the tranquility and alone time brushed all the anxiety away. A bird swooped from one tree to another, its flapping and chirping startling him. He would have to get used to this, especially with those Arcods around. The history books spoke of those creatures and how they followed the ruling of Hematite.

A bug landed on his face. He smacked it away and then trudged down the path through the forest, pushing away hanging branches and stomping over low bushes. His stomach rumbled louder with each step, but then he noticed a plant with berries growing along the side of a narrow path. He rushed to it, leaping over a fallen log and scaring a small animal in the process. Then he stood there for some time, eating handfuls of sweet blueberries. The juice of the blueberries quenched his thirst and filled his belly. He would never have thought such a common food could become so important to him.

After satisfying his hunger, he peered down the narrow path. He moved his lips to the side. What an odd path. Curiosity getting the best of him, he proceeded to see where it led. Time passed as the path winded up inclines and down. It curved around a large cliff and ran down a steep hill with no other paths in sight. Someone had to have made this path. But who? And why? Who would want to live out here in the deep pine forests between the mountains? He paced himself as he climbed a hill, careful to avoid tripping on roots.

Once reaching the top, he stopped for a rest. Grey clouds hung above him in the evening sky. The path led to a clearing at the foot of the hill. On the far side of the clearing stood an arched tree opening. Ever more curious, he hurried down the path, keeping the clearing and arched trees in sight. Reaching the bottom of the hill, he sprinted across the clearing. There before him, hidden in all this forest, was a village.

He raised an eyebrow at the strange entrance sign with a backwards "R" in the center. Then he passed under the arched trees. A small village lay before him with dozens of huts scattered about landscaped lawns, gardens, and tidy walkways. Barrels of water and empty food carts stood along the main road.

He fiddled with his fingers as he stepped forward. Something wasn't right. Something was different . . . This place seemed untouched by destruction. Perhaps the Arcods had not made it this far yet. But the huts looked so new and not raggedy.

He crept through the ominous village, finding no signs of life, not even a burning fire or the aroma of a homecooked meal. It was as if the villagers had vanished.

He poked his head into a hut large enough to fit five Bonvidians easily. A dark fire pit stood in the center. He bent down to check it out, finding no ash. He arose and continued investigating, approaching one of four buffalo fur beds. It, too, appeared as untouched as the rest of the village.

He shrugged. He hadn't had a good night's sleep in two weeks. If the owner of the house returned, he would simply explain his situation. He tossed his pack to the side, kicked off his boots, and stretched out on the bed for a rest.

Zane fell asleep at once, but he slept fitfully.

Bile crept up his throat. He could not do this. He had to do this. Move! *Zane grabbed the sheath from the statue that he taken the sword from and strapped it around his waist. The stairs were too risky, but remained his only way out of the building. Where would he go, though? The tunnels! He could take the tunnels.*

The footfalls grew louder; the Arcods were getting closer.

He gripped the sword tighter and darted to the stairs. As a shadow fell on the wall, he leaped behind a statue on his left and stood frozen.

The creatures thudded past him, their stench filling his

nostrils. One of the creatures grunted as the unit marched into the library.

This was his chance for a clean escape! He sheathed his sword and, two steps at a time, made his way down the steps. Then he sprinted to the back of the building and shoved the door open with his shoulder.

He stood in an alley, all clear for now. Should he go find his parents and uncle? Or would they understand if he left? Was he a coward for leaving?

He tiptoed through the alley and stopped where it met the street. A cart filled with jars of nuts blocked his way. He was about to step around it, but he would need food for the journey, so he grabbed a jar and shoved it into his bag. One of the nearby alleys led to an escape tunnel through a grate in the ground. He sprinted forward, hoping he would not cross any of those creatures.

He counted to himself and turned down the next alley. Two bodies lay on the ground. He froze, holding his hand over his mouth to stop from vomiting. He stepped over them, trying to focus on the grate. Was he really going to do this? The image of his family entered his mind once again.

Wiping a tear from his eye, he knelt and tugged at the heavy metal grate until it opened. Then he leaped inside and scraped the grate back over the hole.

A thin string ran along the side of the dimly lit tunnel. Using the string as a guide, he paced forward until he finally came to a sunny opening. He stepped out, closing his eyes from the sunlight. Once his eyes adjusted, he sealed the cove with a few large rocks.

A rowboat filled with survival necessities floated next to the dock. He climbed into it, untied it, and stared back at the sealed entrance. "I'll be back to save you, I promise. I'll come back." He grabbed the paddle and began to row out to the open sea.

Someone shook his shoulder.

"I'll be back," he muttered, his dream drifting to the recesses of his mind. Feeling rested but not ready to rise, he cracked his eyes open. Early morning sunlight streamed in through the open entrance—

Someone stood over him!

Zane sprung up, looking upon a Bonvidian woman. "Sorry, is this your home?" He tidied his tunic.

A much older woman with brown curly hair stepped back. "Not quite. Who are you?"

He grabbed his boots and shoved his feet into them. "I am Zane. And yourself?"

She smiled. "Quin."

He grabbed his pack and headed for the open entrance. "Nice to meet you, Quin."

She followed him out into the village. "Wait!"

The bright sunlight hit Zane's eyes, making him squint. Even though the sun shined, large clouds were moving in. "What is it?" Zane said, unable to control his annoyance.

Quin went silent.

He took a flask from his pack, opened the top of a water barrel, and dipped the flask in. "I don't want to frighten you, Quin, but I think you should go find someplace safe to stay." Zane lifted the flask out and took a sip before closing the lid. He scanned the village while making his way to the arched entrance with the sign that he had spotted the day before.

Quin continued to follow him. "Zane, wait!"

He sighed with his back still to her. "Yes?"

"This is a safe place," she said.

Zane raised an eyebrow and turned to face her. "What do you mean? Darkness has struck this land. There is no safe place."

She twirled her curls. "I know, Zane, but don't you see that this village is undamaged? It is so hidden that those creatures cannot find it. Zane, I know you want to go off

73

alone, but can you do me a favor?"

Not comfortable making eye contact, he glanced to the side. "What sort of favor?"

She glanced at him. "Bonvidians are scared. Kingdoms are fighting. And Bonvidians need a safe place, a refuge. If you meet anyone, send them here."

Zane bit his lip. "How will they know where to go?"

Quin yanked a piece of papyrus from her back pocket and drew a symbol on it. She handed it to him. "Take this. Tell them to head between the mountains of Giants' Country and The Wildlands and look for this symbol." She scurried around him to the arched entrance of the village and pointed to the same symbol, a backwards "R." "This is our symbol for refuge. Whoever comes here will be safe."

A sense of purpose filled Zane.

She turned and gazed into his eyes. "Sometimes I know things, even though I don't know how. When I first saw you, I knew this: you are going to find the Bonvidian who is destined to save this place."

His heart skipped a beat. Did Quin actually say that? Desmond's heir, the holder of the Sword of Bonvida? He was going to find this Bonvidian?

She leaned against the tree with its branches braided to form the arch of the village entrance. "How about some food? You must be hungry. You'll need food for your journey as well." She stepped aside.

Zane grinned.

After eating a hearty meal with Quin and packing food for the trip, Zane walked off alone. He followed the path for hours, just as she said, until he finally reached the plains. A mist floated over olive-green grass. Heavy clouds continued to block the sun. The distant sounds of battles danced in the wind.

Continuing across the plains, he made sure no Arcods were tracking him. He soon came to large boulders that formed a circle in the middle of the plains. It seemed like a great place for a rest. He pulled the papyrus out that Quin had given him, placed it on a rock, and scratched the symbol onto the rock with a dagger.

Zane folded the papyrus up again. A chill blew in the air. Oh, how he wished he had brought a blanket or something for shelter. He thought about making a fire, but if Arcods spotted the light or smelled the smoke, he would be in trouble.

Quin's words ran through his mind. He was going to meet the chosen one, the heir of Desmond. The prophetic tales were coming true. One day the fallen Hematite would try to regain power, causing chaos across the land. Then the heir of Desmond would awake and save the land from the first layer of darkness. But who was the heir? And exactly where would this take place? Bonvida expanded so far in every direction. So many kingdoms, farms, villages . . . This chosen descendant could be anywhere and anyone. And it was up to Zane to find the chosen one.

He knocked his head on the stone in frustration. How he still wished he had brought a book, especially now. What if he messed up a part of history or forgot something?

Wait! If the darkness had been released, that would mean . . . the Dark Descendant was out in the land too. Zane pondered the Calsriv platform. It was located just beyond the Evergreen Forest. Should he go there?

No, now wasn't the time to worry about any of that. He could only focus on one quest at a time. How could he find the chosen one? If he were the chosen one, he would go to The Chamber of Descendants located in the crater. Zane nodded. Yes, he would go that way in the morning. For now, though, he had to conserve energy.

By the first light of the next morning, Zane set out,

heading for The Chamber of Descendants. After several days of travel and brief rest for snatches of sleep, he glimpsed a clear barrier in the distance. He'd found it!

"Skyarl, the crater of the cliff," he whispered to himself. At one time, the dome sat in the center of the land. But in the beginning, when Hematite had released its darkness, Sofos had raised the dome and land around it into the sky. He contemplated the idea of Desmond, his followers, the Sword of Bonvida, and the other special weapons that would help defeat the darkness of Hematite.

If he were to find this chosen one, this would be the first place to look.

In the center stood the Chamber. Zane remembered reading that Desmond and his followers had built the Chamber for themselves and their descendants.

Zane climbed onto a rocky lip, skidded down the slope of the crater, and crossed rough ground and pockets of dirt.

Finally, he reached the barrier, a clear dome that covered the Chamber and part of the ground around it.

As a Bonvidian, he knew the legend that only those of ancient blood could pass through the barrier. He also knew that those not of descendant blood, who tried to pass through, would burn. Temptation poked at him. What if he was a descendant of one of Desmond's followers? What if he was the chosen one able to hold the Sword of Bonvida? But if he risked touching the barrier and he was not a descendant, he would burn. Maybe he could shove his hand in and out quickly.

He put his hand closer to the barrier, his heart racing with adrenaline. He pushed panicky questions away and shoved his hand through, squeezing his eyes, expecting to scream out in pain.

Nothing? No burn, no pain . . . He glanced down, flabbergasted. His jaw dropped in surprise.

He wiggled his fingers through the barrier. "I'm one of them . . . I'm one of the descendants!"

His mind swirled with excitement, and wonder stirred within him. "Me, a simple scholar from Maljooi?" Joyful laughter overtook him. He fixed his hair and tightened his belt. Nobody must know about this. Now he had a significant quest. "I have to find the chosen one, the holder of the Sword of Bonvida. I will aid him, and together we will find others like us. Together we will face Hematite and the rest of the darkness."

Chapter 11

Daria yawned and rubbed her eyes as she sat up in bed. Every morning she wished that the last nine months had been a terrible dream. Though she did enjoy the Dwarves' company and everything she had learned. But the thought of home, her own bed, and of Atticus still rattled her.

Once she threw back the wool cover and planted her feet on the cold floor, her stomach growled. With the food shortage in Karadwarfa, she had skipped dinner last night. Hopefully, she and the twins would bring something home today. She grabbed a robe and wrapped it around herself, then she dipped her hands into a bowl of water by her bedside and wet her face. She was still thankful about being safe in Karadwarfa. She, Spit, and Tidy had learned from the king that the creatures were called Arcods and came from Calsriv, a realm she vaguely recalled learning about. Then the king told them the tale of a chosen one, of someone descended from ancient blood, who was destined to save the land. Deep down, she wanted to believe the old tales, but right now, there was no chosen one. No sign of hope.

After dressing for the day, she met Spit and Tidy at the edge of the forest.

Spit adjusted his belt. "Daria, you ready to hunt?"

She carried a deep maroon bow with steel tips and a string made from Elves' hair. She'd found the bow a few days after arriving in Karadwarfa, when she and the twins had gone to search for Carrie. Unfortunately, the dog had likely not survived.

She raised her bow towards the cloudy sky. "Aye, I am."

She and the Dwarves strolled through the forest, their eyes set on Loch Alri. The day smelled of trees, and the forest sounds calmed as they passed through. In order to survive, hunting became the biggest source of food. The days of going into the kingdom markets or meeting traders ended with the day of Bonvida's takeover.

The smell of the Loch became stronger. Something moved in a distant bush.

Daria raised her fist, signalling for the two to stop. Since no horrendous smell accompanied the creature, she knew it wasn't an Arcod.

Understanding her signal, the Dwarves froze. "You catch your eye on something?" Spit asked.

She nodded. Dwarves weren't the best of whisperers, but these two had been learning. Daria drew an arrow from the quiver that hung on her back and placed it in the bow. Then she shifted her feet into position, raised the bow, and tried to stand steady but relaxed—the way the twins had taught her.

The bushes moved, a deer emerging. Again using the technique the Dwarves had taught her, she breathed in from her nose and exhaled from her mouth. And released. The arrow flew through the air and pierced the deer in the neck, dropping it instantly.

Lowering the bow, she raced over and looked down at her prize. A medium-sized deer with a grey-brown coat lay dead in the grass, killed instantly by her clean shot. "I haven't eaten a deer in months, maybe even a year."

The twins went to either side of the animal and lifted it up. "We feast in Karadwarfa tonight!" Spit exclaimed. "We'll carry this back. Meet you by the water?"

Daria strapped the bow around her. "Aye."

The two Dwarves lumbered back towards their home.

After watching them go, Daria followed the smell of the fresh lake water. She glanced up through the treetops to the clouds above. They were beginning to clear away to reveal a crystal blue sky. Stepping through the edge of the forest, she smiled.

Loch Alri stretched out to the horizon. The graceful branches of willow trees dangled over the water. Long blades of grass poked up between large mossy boulders scattered around the shore.

She untied her ponytail and brushed her fingers through her hair. She had spent so many days with the Dwarves, hardly finding time to wander alone in the wilderness. A pile of boulders sat in a shaded area along the water. She skipped to them, climbed up, and looked for a boulder not covered in wet moss. Finding a good one, she sat in a comfortable position and closed her eyes.

Birds chirped, and a gentle breeze made a soothing sound as it traveled over the lake. She took a deep breath to relax, but then images appeared in her mind, shattering her peaceful mood. *Searching for Atticus . . . the misty woods . . . the well caving in!*

Daria opened her eyes to rid herself of the troubled feelings that had come with the images. Strange how she and the Dwarves had been unable to find the well. She had tried so many times but found nothing.

With her focus lost, Daria picked up a stone at her feet and threw it into the lake. The stone splashed, sending ripples across the calm water. Her eyes welled, and she sniffled. She'd never even gone back to her house. She hadn't seen her parents in so long. She feared they were dead. How could they have survived those evil creatures?

Clenching her jaw, she picked up another stone and threw it into the water.

"Daria." A whispered voice came from behind her.

She scanned the treeline on her left and behind her but could only see the dark woods. Maybe the Dwarves were playing a trick on her. "Spit, Tidy, you got me."

Still staring at the tree line, she waited for the fire-headed twins to waddle out. But she saw no sign of them. "Spit? Tidy?" Her heart beat faster. She unstrapped her bow and drew out an arrow, took position, and waited.

"Daria," the voice whispered again.

Adrenaline shot through her veins. "Who's out there? How do you know my name?"

Maybe she was going crazy. She closed her eyes. A flash of Atticus in a cave of sorts glimmered in her mind. She tried to shake off the image, but it continued to tug her heart strings. Was that Atticus' voice?

Maybe, just maybe, Atticus had survived his fall and found his way out. She had to go back.

Out of the tree line, the twins emerged, waving their arms. "Daria, you going to shoot that arrow?" Tidy asked.

Relieved to see them, she lowered the bow and slid the arrow back into the quiver. "Nah, I, um, thought I heard something. Must've been the wind."

They came closer to her. "Nah, Daria, I don't believe that. What's goin' on?" Spit asked.

She tried to hold her emotions together. "I—I think my brother is still alive," she said, choking from emotion. "I have to go. If there's even a chance, then I must be at the barn for him to return."

The two Dwarves' eyebrows lowered. Tidy held onto her hands. "Daria, family is important, especially in these times. If you believe in your heart this to be true, then go." He cleared his throat.

Spit patted her lower back. "Just don't forget about us."

She crouched down to their level. "I will never forget you two. We'll see each other one day soon, I believe." She kissed both of their foreheads. Without another word, she dashed off through the Dwarven Forest.

Emotions overcame her as she set out for her old home. She blocked out the sights of destruction and waste that covered the plains. She walked and ran and walked again, on and on, stopping only when her body insisted on a break.

Finally, she reached her home. Shock overtook her. It looked nothing like before. The thatched roof had caved in, though the house walls still stood. The creatures had torn the garden apart. And the barn had a giant hole in one side.

She paced forward, childhood memories flooding her mind. A silk scarf stuck under rubble caught her eye. She bent down and tugged the scarf until it came free. She pressed the scarf to her nose, breathing in the faint smell of her mother.

In the distance, a small group of creatures ambled along. Hopefully, they hadn't spotted her. Not taking any chances, she jogged around the house and into the barn. Daylight came in through the gaping hole in the side, but the rest of the structure seemed sound. She could hide behind the scraps from the destroyed wall, or—better yet...

She climbed up to the rafters. The creatures did not seem that intelligent. She would spot them first from up here. She wrapped the scarf around her face to block the Arcod smell and leaned against a beam. Once the threat of Arcods passed, she would have to find the mist again. And once she did, she would have to finish unburying the well. "Oh, Atticus, I hope you're all right."

Chapter 12

With sword in hand, Atticus stared at a dummy made from clothes and a broomstick. He advanced, deflecting an imaginary strike by his homemade opponent. He pranced back, pretending to deflect another strike, then he crouched and jabbed the sword into the gut of the dummy. Standing back up, he pivoted and lunged, stabbing the dummy where its heart would be.

Stopping for a breath, he turned to his frail mother. She sat on a stool, watching him. He walked up to her and kissed the side of her cheek. "I'd say I've improved."

Lavender grinned. "Come and sit a moment."

He slid the sword into its sheath and placed it on the table. Something seemed off with his mother, her eyebrows furrowed, and her voice was softer than normal.

She rested her hands on the stone table. "Let's go over everything one last time."

"Okay." He took a deep breath and rubbed his eyes. He had spent the past nine months in sword training and learning about his father and all that had happened in Calsriv. But more importantly, he'd finally had time with his real mother.

He questioned where the other shards were, but his mother had no idea of their locations.

She sat up straight. "What do you seek?"

As he closed his eyes, he whispered, "Daria." He opened one eye and stared at Lavender. "Sorry, I miss her." He smacked the table with a fist.

Lavender pursed her lips. "What do you seek?" she repeated.

He closed his open eye and took a deep breath. "Daria," he whispered for a second time.

Lavender touched his hand. "Atticus, it's okay to miss

your sister. Focus on the quest, on your purpose."

He glanced at the walls around him. He had grown accustomed to this confined living space. "I seek the remaining four shards that Sofos used to create Bonvida. With those shards in my sword, I can defeat Luvanasis."

Lavender smiled. "Very good. Atticus, time is calling you to go back. You're ready."

He was filled with excitement and worry. "I've been down here for nine long months, training myself for this very day. What about you?"

Lavender lowered her head. "I can't come with you. Our time together has been short, but—oh—I'd been waiting for it for so long."

His heart raced. Not coming? What reason could she have for staying?

He arose from his seat and swallowed his emotions. Then he picked up the sheath and strapped it around himself. "So, how do I get out of this cave?" He took a step towards an opening behind a curtain.

She bit her lip. "The well caved in a long time ago, and I never told you."

He glanced at Lavender as he tightened the strap, securing the sheath. "Then how do I leave?"

Lavender glanced up and spoke to the air above as a tear rolled down her cheek. "Sofos, he is ready. Please send a portal so that he can return to his home and begin his journey."

A gust of wind filled the room, and a bright white portal appeared. Atticus stepped back a few feet as the portal warmed his insides.

She kissed his cheek. "Keep the faith, and believe in yourself even at the darkest of times."

He waited for a moment. Was this it? He got to leave, but she stayed behind. Why? He'd only had such a short time with his mother. The desire to stay beckoned. His gut tightened, but he knew he had to leave. He had a land to save. "I'll come back for you. I promise."

She turned her head away for a moment. "Go. Be who you were born to be."

Atticus blew her a kiss and stepped through the portal. It closed behind him.

The portal spun, creating a hall of swirls. He soon realized he should walk forward, but the spinning made him dizzy. He spotted something at the far end of the portal. What was it? Where was it? He took another step, followed by ten more. The portal swept away.

Atticus collapsed onto a bundle of straw. Rolling and then jumping to his feet, he tightened the strap of his sword and scanned his surroundings. He stood in a barn with piles of hay scattered across the ground. A giant hole in one wall loomed before him, jagged pieces of board at his feet. This was his barn. He'd made it back home.

Something whisked through the air, heading towards him! He leaped back just as an arrow landed in the straw inches from his boots. On impulse, he reached for the hilt of his sword, darting a glance in the direction the arrow had come. "Who goes there?"

A figure crouched in the rafters—a young woman with a scarf shrouding her face, a bow in her hand, and a quiver of arrows hanging on her back.

The woman leaped down and unraveled the scarf.

He let go of his sword. "Daria!"

Chapter 13

Atticus stared at Daria. He was relieved to see her, but she seemed so different—and not just because she brandished a bow.

"Oh, Atticus, it's you!" Daria grinned from ear to ear, her dimples appearing, then she embraced him. "Forgive me. I thought you were an intruder." She released him and stepped to the side, wiping her eyes. "I knew you weren't dead."

Confused, Atticus scratched his head. "Why did you think I was dead?" He considered the destroyed wall of the barn. What had happened to it? This was all so surreal.

Daria grabbed his shoulders. "Atticus, it's been nine months since you vanished. A lot has happened. Our parents . . ." She clamped her lips together, and her eyes welled with tears. Then she pulled him into a hug again and whispered in his ear, "They're dead, Atticus, and Carrie too. Those horrid creatures . . . they killed them."

Atticus stepped out of her grasp and bit his tongue to stop himself from bursting into tears. He kicked a nearby haystack, then released a long breath. "I wasn't even here to save them . . ."

Daria's jaw clenched. She wiped tears from her eyes. "El-Valr was attacked and left in smoky ruins. Those creatures have killed and torn apart families and villages and kingdoms. They've captured countless Bonvidians." She gripped her bow firmer in her hand. "The princes of El-Valr and their army have fled. They are building a rebellion to fight this darkness. The princes have a meeting ground in the Badlands and another with the Elves." She strapped the bow around her shoulder. "It's only a few days hike to the desert gates of the Badlands...if you want to go."

Atticus stood for a moment, but no words came. All his

mother had said must have been true. His mind was boggled. Why had he been left out of the fight until now? Fighting alongside the princes had been his dream. But what about his own quest?

Maybe the El-Valr prince in The Badlands could help. Shaking free of his thoughts, he took slow strides to the barn door. He had to see this destruction for himself.

As he stepped through the barn door, his heart sank. Their home stood in shambles as if a storm had torn through it. The creatures had trampled the garden too. He shifted his gaze to further points, to where El-Valr stood on the hill. One of their four tall towers remained, while the rest of the structure appeared only as malformed shapes.

Shaking his head, he looked at the cloudy sky, which made everything worse. So much devastation, so much pain crossed this land, his home. He brushed his hand along the sheath of his sword. Saving Bonvida was impossible. He could not do it. Too much had happened. He was supposed to save this . . . to rebuild this? His mother had said nothing about creatures, only Luvanasis.

Daria placed her hand on his shoulder and gazed upon the horizon with him.

He breathed in and out deeply and made a fist.

Daria squeezed his shoulder.

He turned to his sister. He had to tell her that he was destined to save the land. But maybe he should not tell her and should simply go alone? No, he could not do that. He sighed.

Atticus tucked his messy hair behind his ear. "Daria, I must tell you something. I must tell you what happened when I . . . I fell into a well. Inside the well, I awoke and discovered my birth mother." He cleared his throat. "She told me that I was born of ancient blood, blood so ancient that I am related to Desmond. She told me that I am supposed to save Bonvida." He pulled the sheath from around his shoulder and attached it to his belt. "Now that I see all of this, Daria, I don't believe I am capable of saving Bonvida."

Her face glowed, and her eyes glittered. "You're the chosen one?" Her grin from reuniting with him did not compare to the grin on her face now. "Why, this is amazing!"

He raised an eyebrow and smirked. "Daria, why are you excited? Don't you see this before us? You said that these creatures have torn this land apart. How am I, the chosen one, capable of saving this land? Where do I even start?" He lowered his gaze, trying his hardest to hold back his emotions. He exhaled and fell to his knees. "This is too much. I told my mother I was ready . . . but now that I see this, I realize I'm not ready. Daria, I cannot do this." He punched the ground as tears streamed down his face.

Daria knelt beside him. "Atticus, I believe that you can. You've got to believe that you can. You're overwhelmed by what you see. Don't let the enemy do this to you. Stand up, believe in yourself, and hold onto faith."

He lifted his chin, glancing at Daria. "Thank you."

She arose and helped him stand. "Now, brotha', why don't we go save our land?"

He could not help but chuckle. "Brotha'? What are you, a Dwarf speaking slang?"

She bit her lip. "Well . . . I didn't spend the last nine months in a barn. I have stories for you."

Atticus wiped his eyes and pointed to their house. "Think we can gather any supplies?"

She shrugged her shoulders. "We can go see."

The two took long strides to their house. Atticus pushed open the door, which creaked on its loose hinges.

"I'll gather what supplies I can find for our journey," she stated.

Memories flooded his mind as he looked around the house.

"Here, son. This is yours."

Sunlight created a light purple starburst in the topaz shard that Mum dangled before him on a leather cord. She smiled, but sadness lurked in her eyes as she lifted the cord over his head.

Father gave a sad smile and nodded. He opened his mouth for a moment before speaking as if unsure how to say something. "We need to tell you about your birth mother."

Atticus sat down at the small wooden table where they used to eat family meals. The table wobbled as he touched it. A partly folded map of Bonvida sat amongst other clutter. He unstrapped the maroon leather case that hung from his belt and opened it, revealing a small golden compass. He unfolded the map to examine it and placed the compass on one corner. Then he located their house and moved his finger along the map towards the Badlands. Atticus folded the map, tucked it into his back pocket, and put the compass back in its case.

He stood up to help Daria, who was now scrounging through the cupboards.

"We have enough food for now," she said. "Let's grab our flasks so we can get water at the river. We should be going."

Once outside, they strode towards the open plains.

The day drew towards noon as Atticus and Daria neared El-Valr hill. The foot of the hill had become a waste field of armor and dead bodies. Not daring to go near, they picked up their pace.

The partly cloudy day grew into an overcast evening. The sound of rushing water perked their ears and reminded them of their thirst.

The two picked up speed and soon arrived at a river of

clear water. Atticus opened his flask and dipped it into the water alongside his sister. "Looks like a good place to rest."

They lifted their flasks out of the water and took a few sips. Daria pointed at a few fish gathering in the water. "Aye, you hungry? We can try to catch a fish."

Atticus wiped the water dripping from his chin. "Fish sounds delicious. All I ate for the last nine months was Apori meat and dried oats and fruits. But I'd like to know more about you. What have you been up to since we last saw each other?"

His sister ripped a thread and hook off her satchel and tied the string around one end of the hook. She dug in the dirt nearby until she found a worm, which squirmed between her fingers. She turned to Atticus and latched the worm onto the hook. "Moments after you fell into the well, Bonvida was struck. I had to run. I met up with the Dwarves, and they sheltered me. Two of them, Spit and Tidy, one of a kind, they are. They taught me archery. And I picked up a few survival skills too." She dipped the handmade fishing rod into the river.

After catching two fish and making a campfire, Atticus and Daria sat across from each other and watched their fish cooking.

The savory aroma of fish grilling over an open fire stirred Atticus' imagination. He pictured eating the fish with roasted potatoes, fresh garden vegetables, and a special sauce. Maybe even a dessert of—

Something in a nearby tree caught his attention. A dark raven watched them from the branches. A more studied look revealed feathers of different shades of blue and four long tail feathers with red tips.

A moment later, the raven squawked—as if it did not like being noticed—and it leaped off the branch, taking flight towards the ruins of El-Valr.

Atticus returned his attention to the fish cooking on the fire. He watched the flames lapping around the sides of the cooking stone. He now only had one thought on his mind. To end the darkness.

Chapter 14

Luvanasis glared at the desolate city of El-Valr through a smashed stained-glass window. Nearly nine months ago, he'd stormed the market and castle with his Arcods. The collapsing of towers replayed in his mind's eye. He'd fought off the king and queen and kept them as prisoners, along with others, below the castle in the dungeons. He hoped to use them as leverage. Maybe he could even—

Something flew towards the abandoned market streets. A cold breeze blew over him, making the castle even colder.

The raven had returned from its current scout. What had the bird spotted today?

He raised his arm so that it could land on his gauntlet. Its talons curled and held firm to his upper arm.

He stroked the raven's red-tipped feathered head as he turned around and paced down a hall of stained-glass windows, paintings, and statues. Large columns still stood in this main hall of the castle. He did not want to destroy everything. He needed somewhere to live and to rule from. Why not El-Valr, the kingdom on the hill?

Arriving at the far end of the main hall, he peered through broken doors at the throne room. Five thrones sat at the head of the room, one each for the king, the queen, and their three children. Their three sons had fought quite a fight against his Arcods. But he'd overpowered them. The brothers and their army had split, taking off in all different directions. The El-Valr sons and the other kingdoms had had enough trouble in their fight when he'd first arrived.

Behind him, someone cleared their throat. He turned and stared at a tall, thin woman. "Raia."

She pressed her thin lips together and whistled. The raven hopped off Luvanasis and onto Raia's shoulder. She kissed the bird on its narrow beak. "Our bird spotted two travelers." Her deep black hair swooped to one side of her face. "One carries a sword . . . not a sword of ordinary make though. I sense there is something powerful about it."

Luvanasis eyed one of the stained-glass windows of Sofos, the one showing him handing the Sword of Bonvida to Desmond. He pointed to it. "Did it look like that?"

The raven cawed.

Raia glanced around the room, as if trying not to look at him. "Yes." She backed up. "There are two travelers, a young woman and a young man. The young man's name is ... Atticus."

Luvanasis smacked his fist against a pillar. "Dane's child! Dane's son has finally come out of hiding. Did they say anything about where they were going?"

Raia opened a pouch of bird seed, grabbed a handful of seeds, and held them close to the bird. "They go to the Badlands. A prince of El-Valr is apparently there."

Luvanasis clenched his jaw. "That's where one's been... Clever prince, clever prince. Raia, write a message and have your raven bring it to an Arcod unit near The Badlands." He stepped closer to Raia and rubbed under the raven's beak. "Have them enter the city of Mizeria. Kill whoever gets in the way, except for the sword holder. I want him alive."

Raia tilted her head to the side. "If we take him alive, won't he try to kill you?"

Luvanasis glared into her captivating eyes. "Kill me? He can not kill me. The shards are scattered across the land."

Raia smiled as the raven finished the seeds. "I will write your orders down."

Luvanasis glanced back to the colorful image of Sofos. "Good. When you finish that, Raia, I have something I need you to do."

She leaned in closer.

Luvanasis whispered in her ear, "Bring me my descendant. The one who freed me."

Raia took a step back. "As you command."

He pointed down the hall. "Now get out of my sight. We're wasting time." His frustration echoed throughout the empty hall.

He watched Raia stride down the corridor. Then he shook his head and shoved the throne room doors open.

His mind bit at him. Atticus, the son of Dane... His greatest fear had awakened. Atticus, the only one able to kill him, the only one able to ruin the plans of Hematite. He tucked his fingers into his palm, making a fist. Taking long strides towards the thrones, his mind continued to ponder. He'd found no sign and heard no word about where Desmond had put She Serpent to slumber.

Frustration building, Luvanasis looked around the bare room. He tore down the flags and decorations that draped the ceiling. His mind went back to She Serpent, his contingency plan. His descendant could use the Sword of Darkness to wake her.

Atticus *would* fall at his feet just like Dane had. Once Atticus was dead, he and his descendant together would find She Serpent. He shook off his thoughts as he seated himself on the king's throne. Then he picked up a golden crown that rested on a velvet pillow and placed it on his head. He may as well declare himself a king. Leaning back in the king's chair, power surged through him as he pictured his foe in his mind. "Atticus."

Chapter 15

Atticus awoke with the rising of the sun and the sounds of the rushing river near where he had fallen asleep. He yawned and stretched. Sleeping on the ground wasn't as comfortable as the feather and wool blankets he had been using for the last nine months.

He glimpsed around, taking in the colorful sky. He enjoyed the growing brightness of dawn as it wiped away the morning mist. Further ahead, probably a thirty-minute hike, a cobblestone bridge stretched over a river. Oh well. It would be better than trudging through the river. *Wait a second!* Where was Daria?

He rubbed his eyes, but Daria was nowhere in sight. Heart sinking, he reached for his belt and sword and climbed to his feet. She could not have been taken. He would have woken up at the slightest sound of trouble.

He listened intently but only heard the river and a frog or two croaking their morning conversation. He paced around their small camp, finding her bag, quiver, and bow gone too. Maybe she set out early to hunt.

Through the morning mist, someone approached . . . Daria, holding her bow in one hand and a prize in the other. "Mornin', Atticus!"

He squinted at her catch. Apori, big ones too. They did not usually grow larger than a squirrel. "Mornin', Daria."

She put the dead Aporis on a stone, grabbed the hunting knife hanging from her belt, and cut into one of them. "I didn't want to wander off too far. These little things were the only juicy option, other than the jar of berries and nuts I gathered."

Atticus turned his head away. He gagged as he remembered having to drink Apori blood mixed with other ingredients.

The mist had cleared away by the time Atticus took his

final bite of meat. He pointed to the cobblestone bridge in the distance. "We'll cross that bridge, then continue from there. I think that'll lead us to The Badlands."

Daria wiped her mouth. "You think?"

Atticus shrugged and pulled the map out of his back pocket. He traced a line with his finger. "We're here. We have to walk all this way, then cross the bog and fields, while hoping to avoid getting caught by anything. If we can make it to the pillars by tomorrow, we will be making great time."

Daria tied her hair back. "Well, let's not waste any more daylight then."

Atticus folded the map and shoved it into his back pocket. He stood up alongside Daria.

After packing their few belongings, they trekked to the foot of the bridge. He could not help but notice a fallen El-Valr soldier. His heart ached. That could have been him if he hadn't found the well. The kingdom of El-Valr would have wasted no time giving him a weapon and armor and sending him off. Now here he was being sent off anyway, not by El-Valr but by Sofos, on a quest to save the land. He and Daria both agreed to keep a close hand on their weapons. A chilly wind blew with each step as they crossed the bridge.

Atticus mentally prepared for the rough bog that lay ahead of them. By this point, the sun glared bright in the sky. It must have been mid-morning by now. It struck him as odd that they passed no animals along the way. Normally animals and travelers would have filled these fields. But now nothing, except the occasional dead body. Were they the only two living things left? Nah, that would be crazy.

Atticus pointed at a cart turned over on its side. "Let's take a break." The cart was made from pine and filled with crushed barrels. He spun one of the wheels. "Think we can salvage anything from this?"

Daria twisted her lips. "Only if it's food or weapons. Those would be the best."

Atticus tossed torn pieces of wood. A sudden pain went through his finger. He shut his eyes. *Please don't be a splinter.* Opening one eye, he gazed at a thin splinter no longer than his pinky finger poking from the side of his finger. "Daria!"

She poked her head around the side of the cart. "Ouch! Here let me help you."

Atticus stared at the sky as Daria clasped his hand and pulled. A five-second sting fired through his hand. He bit his lip to hold back a shout.

Daria waved the little piece. "Do you want to keep this as a memory? The tiny piece of wood that almost destroyed the chosen Atticus."

He shook his head and chuckled.

He and Daria walked around the cart and climbed on top. Burnt-down villages and more scattered carts lay off to the east. He pulled out the map. "We have to go towards those grey clouds there."

Something moved by one of the burnt-down villages. "Daria, do you see that over there?"

She squinted and immediately leaped off the cart. "We have to go!"

He raised an eyebrow. He had never seen Daria so nervous. He jumped off the cart and peered at whatever moved about in the village. "Daria, what is that? Why are you so scared?"

She tugged his arm. "That, Atticus, is an Arcod. See how it walks, wobbling like a drunk man. Those are the enemy's pathetic army. Usually they don't travel alone, meaning there's a unit by that village. They are probably waiting to ambush any passing travelers."

"Do you think they see us?"

Daria rubbed the side of her nose. "Aye, they most definitely have."

Atticus and Daria picked up their pace, their eyes on the bog. Every so often, Atticus looked over his shoulder to make sure no Arcods followed them.

As they drew closer to the bog, the weather dampened and mixed with a chilly breeze. A mist fell from the clouds above. Atticus squinted at the sky. At least the sun was still up somewhere behind these heavy clouds.

The bog stretched out before them, with steep hills and boulders scattered around. One wrong step and a person could sink. "Take it slow, just like we were taught when we were young," Atticus stated.

With each step, their boots sank deep into squishy mud. They held onto each other as they trudged along. With Atticus' next step, his foot slid down, and he almost lost his balance. Daria held tighter and steadied him. "I'm not losing you again."

Finding it too hard to walk, Atticus stopped for a moment and cleaned mud off his boots.

From behind them, a grumbling filled the air, followed by a growl.

Atticus spun around.

Below the incline that he and Daria had climbed stood a unit of at least seven Arcods. "Daria, we have company."

She grabbed her bow. "Get behind me. Quick!"

He cautiously walked around her, hoping not to fall.

She reached for an arrow, exhaled, aimed, and fired the shot.

She did it! One Arcod down.

The two had waited, but the remaining six Arcods charged at them. Perhaps the bog would slow them down. Wait! The bog seemed to have helped rather than hindered their speed, as if they were used to walking on such delicate grounds.

Atticus took a few steps back and wrapped his hand around the hilt of his sword. He withdrew it from its snug home.

Daria grabbed a second arrow and aimed, but the targets were moving too fast through the bog. "They're gaining on us!"

Atticus returned to his sister's side. As the Arcods got closer, a disgusting stench filled the air. If he could only plug his nose and fight.

One Arcod outraced the others. It leaped into the air.

Atticus swung his sword and impaled the Arcod. The body flopped and rolled, knocking over another Arcod. The weight of the two Arcods caused them to sink into the bog.

An Arcod jumped onto a boulder close by. Daria held her breath and released an arrow.

Atticus kept watch on the remaining three Arcods. He raised his sword high and shouted, scaring them away.

He looked to his sister as he sheathed his sword. Their first battle together. If coming battles were anything like this one, they would be a piece of cake.

They finally made it out of the bog and back onto the open plains. Atticus squinted at the sun ahead of them and glanced back at the cloudy bog behind. He kicked mud off his boots and opened his flask to sip water.

Daria sipped water too. "We don't have a lot of food. Do you think we can skip lunch and continue on?"

Atticus closed his flask. "Aye, I can hold off for a few more hours."

As the day carried on, they traveled up and down hills and over boulders and crossed through empty villages and green fields. In a particularly large field, he spotted a lonely Rieloc chomping at grass.

Rielocs were known to be vicious creatures, especially if anything came within close range of their comfort perimeter. He remembered hearing that they weighed about four hundred pounds. A trader once said that their skin was craggy, and if a person ever got slammed by one, they would likely be killed.

On the other side of the field stood a figure, possibly another traveler or a slim Arcod. Either that figure or he and Daria would likely be bait to this Rieloc.

Atticus nudged his sister and pointed. The Rieloc pawed the ground. "Uh-oh. I think he must've seen us. It's getting ready to charge."

She put her hand in front of his chest. "If we don't move, it won't charge. Let's give it a moment."

The two stood as still as statues.

The Rieloc stopped pawing the ground and turned around.

"Okay, let's go!" Atticus said. Then he and Daria continued across the field. Atticus pointed to a large rock formation in the field. They hurried to it and decided to take a quick rest. Atticus set his boot on a boulder to fix a strap. "You hungry?"

Daria rummaged through her bag. "I am. Here, we have a small jar of berries and nuts that I picked when hunting this morning by the bridge."

Atticus licked his lips. "I'll take a bit."

Daria opened the jar. A gentle breeze carried the scent of fresh berries and nuts into the air. She picked out a few, handed them to him, and took a few for herself. She closed the jar and returned it to her bag.

Atticus stretched his back and twisted to one side. The figure he noticed earlier seemed closer. Who was it? Was he following them?

Before he could ponder another thought, he glimpsed something charging towards him and Daria. "Uh . . . Daria. . . we have trouble."

Daria looked up and strapped the bag over her

shoulder. "Rieloc . . . Go!"

The two sprinted off. "I guess it followed us or smelled the food from the jar," Atticus said. His heart pumped with each stride.

As they picked up speed, Atticus peered back to see the Rieloc on their heels. He pointed to a patch of thorn bushes bundled at the foot of a steep hill ahead. "The bushes! Keep your head down before jumping," Atticus shouted.

He and Daria drew closer to the thorn bushes and dove in. Tiny thorns pierced their hands and ripped their clothes.

Trying to avoid catching themselves on thorns, they crawled to the back of the bush. A second later, the Rieloc crashed through the thorns, but it continued to charge forward. The two waited and watched as the Rieloc looked around in all directions. Not seeing them, it made a huff and wandered away.

Keeping low to avoid thorns, Atticus crawled through the bush with Daria behind him. He poked his head out, making sure it was clear. He gave her a thumbs up and stepped out of the bush. He and Daria pulled the thorns out of their clothes and hair.

They came to the foot of the hill as night fell upon them once again. Eyeing the steep hill, they both agreed to rest. They made a fire and unpacked some of the food that they'd taken from their house. As the fire crackled, Atticus leaned back and let his weary body rest.

Daria glanced at him, a smile on her face. "Do you remember the song our parents used to sing to us when we were scared at night?"

He held his hands closer to the fire to warm himself from the chill of the night. He yawned. "Parts of it."

Do you see that star up in the sky?
It's the home of the light,

The light that takes out all ye fears,
The light that conquers the dark.
No matter what comes to your heart,
Sofos will always guide you home,
And keep your light from burning out.
Now hold my hand till the sun rises again,
Never worry 'cause I'll be here, right by your side.
Rest your eyes now, back to sleep,
Shh, rest your eyes now, back to sleep.
"Goodnight, brother." Daria yawned.

As he gazed up at the stars, his eyelids got heavier. "Good night, sister."

Atticus and his sister awoke to a sprinkle of rain and the sounds of birds chirping in the thorn bushes. After eating, the two trekked up the hill, slippery from the rain.

When they reached the top, Atticus pulled out the map and compass. They could barely see their next destination. Straight ahead, beyond the pillars and Skyarl platform, was the Desert Gates which the Master of Mizeria built after a feud with El-Valr. To their left was part of the Dwarven Forest, and to their right, a mountain range of the Greystone Mountains. They even pinpointed where the Old El-Valr used to stand in the mountains.

The two hopped down the hill. At the bottom lay the head of a dead Arcod, its bulging eyes still open. Atticus held his nose, finding the smell of a dead one ten times worse than a live one. "They really are pathetic."

Daria chuckled. "They are. But you're the best swordsman I know. They will fall at your feet."

Atticus grinned. "I'm the only swordsman you know."

The clouds drifted away, taking with them the gloominess of the day. He hoped his tiredness would pass. He liked to blame his attitude on poor weather, most days at least.

On the horizon, five pillars stood. They should reach them in a few hours, if they kept to their current pace.

As the day passed, the ground changed from green grass to sandstone, and finally they reached the five pillars.

Atticus' focus shifted to the pillars, which towered higher than the eye could see. Each column had distinctive engravings. From what he had learned as a child, the engravings on each of the pillars told a story. The columns circled a massive octagon-shaped platform, and on the platform was the face of Sofos. The platform was similar to the one that his mother described to him. But this one connected to Skyarl.

Atticus was filled with excitement.

He and Daria dropped to the ground at the same time. He opened his flask and chugged water. Then he kicked off his boots to rub his aching feet. "I don't think I've ever walked so much in my life." He stretched his legs, wiggled his toes, and rolled his ankles.

Relaxed, Atticus stood up and strolled to the closest pillar, the one on his right. He touched some of the engravings. A calm breeze passed over him, carrying the smell of sandstone and dust from the Badlands. "With all the destruction that this enemy brought, how did these pillars go untouched?"

"Because they're indestructible," a voice replied. A Bonvidian man stepped out from behind one of the pillars. He bore the same shape and height as the traveler Atticus had spotted yesterday. The Bonvidian made a sweeping gesture. "This platform here goes to the Skyarl Realm dome, the realm where Sofos dwells. These pillars tell of Bonvidian history."

The man walked closer to Atticus and Daria. "Each one is different. The one you're looking at tells of the time of Desmond and his followers. It speaks of their bloodlines, which will end the darkness. The darkness which I believe is upon us."

The Bonvidian man stopped talking.

Atticus sized up the stranger. A bit taller than Atticus, his lanky build, groomed hair, and refined movements made him seem out of place in the wilderness. And then that nervous habit, rubbing his fingers together as he spoke . . .

Atticus reached for his weapon.

The Bonvidian man raised his hands. "I mean no harm. I've been tracking you ever since I saw you encounter the Rieloc. I do thank you. You saved me a good run."

Atticus glanced at Daria, seeing suspicion in her eyes. "Who are you?" Atticus said. "Why are you following us?"

The traveler glanced here and there and continued to rub his fingers together. Then he straightened and leveled his gaze on Atticus. "I am Zane of Maljooi, the city of scholars. These last nine months, I've been wandering these lands, hoping to find the chosen one, the one who will save us."

He pointed to the sheath around Atticus' belt. "That . . . that sword. I caught its reflection in the sun briefly before you two took off like prey. I had to be sure. Now I am certain. You are the descendant of Desmond." He lowered himself to one knee. "I am honored to be in your presence."

Atticus straightened. He wanted to relax his guard but kept his hand on the hilt of his sword. Just in case this stranger wasn't who he claimed to be.

Chapter 16

Atticus stared at Zane, the scholar from Maljooi, analyzing the situation. Before him knelt a Bonvidian.

So much had happened across the land. What if this man was a liar? Or a thief? Although, if he were a thief, he would not have been so caught up in conversation. Besides, from what he remembered being told about thieves, they just attacked and went their way. Maybe, just maybe, this scholar from Maljooi was genuine.

Atticus considered the situation as he admired the dry terrain and strangely shaped clay rock formations. Just beyond the desert gate, hot sands awaited them. He'd better bring lots of water.

Zane arose and pointed behind him at the desert gates. "I assume you're on your way to the desert to get the diamond shard. It is past the Badlands, hidden in Valhu's Domain and protected by the most beautiful warrior." Still smiling, Zane stared at the sheath.

Having never seen a female warrior in real life, he imagined a woman dressed in fine armor. Valhu's Domain sounded like an ancient place too. Atticus squinted at the fellow, still not sure how to take him. This odd Bonvidian . . . he seemed so joyful, so excited, like someone who had been waiting all his life to meet the chosen one. And so educated. How could he remember so much information?

Zane cleared his throat. "The emerald is protected by Artel the Great Wolf somewhere in the vast depths of the Evergreen Forest." He paced back and forth, waving his hand as he spoke. "The ruby is somewhere in the mountains guarded by Advo the Dove. And the sapphire is hidden away somewhere at sea protected by Kilo, the mythical sea beast." He held his finger to his chin. "The topaz . . . the records concerning the topaz state that it is in the dome. Probably with your parents, right? They must've given you it already." His eyes dropped to the sheath again. "Can I see it?"

Atticus stared at Zane for a moment. This stranger, a few years older than he, knew where to go. Atticus did not even know where to find the shards. He pulled the sword out enough to show Zane the grooves.

Zane leaned in close like an inspector. "Even more magnificent than I imagined. This is absolutely beautiful. The enemy must want you dead."

Dead? Atticus had not thought about that, about the enemy . . . Luvanasis. Did he know that Atticus was out in the land? Could he see him?

Realizing he had not introduced himself, Atticus reached out his hand. "My name is Atticus. This is my sister, Daria."

Zane shook his hand enthusiastically. "Sister? The prophecies said nothing about a sister."

Atticus slid the sword into the sheath. "My father was pulled into Calsriv by Luvanasis, and there he met my mother. After I was born, my father sent her and me to Bonvida, where I was given for adoption." Atticus paused before adding, "Then he died."

Zane stepped back, looking unsure of what to say next. "Do you want to hear the poem? It's about you, Atticus, you and the other descendants."

Atticus glanced to Daria, who shrugged her shoulders. "That would be nice."

Zane gazed at one of the pillars and cleared his throat.

Oh, shining light, you overcast the dark, sent it off without destroying it.

Oh, shining light, you created this place, just for me and all those here.

Five simple fragments called the shards left behind to fulfill a destiny.

The darkness came, and you banished away to Calsriv,

but soon this darkness would re-enter.

So, you sent out for thee.

One whose blood would lead the way, conquer each dark light.

With the sword of land, the shards each in place.

One whose blood brightens darkness and barriers us with light.

Another plays the poem proudly from the harp of the might.

Alas, there is the one crowned with a noble heart, with these, oh light, you use to face the dark.

Time soon came when they did just that and cast it all away.

You, oh light, for you say their blood will continue for a time uncertain.

The dark will return, and once it does, the descendants will arise, starting with the true chosen one, who will wield the mighty sword of Bonvida,

But first, he must reclaim the shards of topaz, emerald, diamond, ruby, and sapphire.

Hidden across the lands they are, for it has fallen to you,

Do not worry, you chosen ones of this light.

You are descendants of the mighty, and you will vanquish the dark light.

After finishing the poem, Zane stared at Atticus. "I wish to journey with you on this quest, to fight alongside you, and teach you whatever is necessary to help end this darkness. I will not disappoint you. I promise you now that I will go with you as far as the land reaches so that the darkness will end . . . even if it kills me."

Atticus smiled. "I accept your guidance, Zane." He gazed at the pillars and waved Daria closer. "Let's set out." He turned towards the desert gate.

Daria tapped Atticus on the shoulder. "Brother, your

boots." She pointed to the ground.

His cheeks warmed. With all this excitement, he had forgotten that he had removed his boots. It could have been worse. "Thank you, Daria."

After tugging on his boots, Atticus, Daria, and their new friend, Zane, walked beyond the pillars. As they journeyed across clay-rich soil, they passed cactuses, desert bushes, and tumbleweeds. Rugged claystone mesas jutted from the ground and soon became high walls all around them.

As mid-afternoon approached, they drew near the brass desert gates. Poorly built pillars held the gates, and mesas stood on either side. A wooden ladder leaned against one pillar, something a scout could use to scale the wall.

Atticus approached the gates and grabbed onto one of the bars. More Badlands lay before them. Next, they would enter Valhu's Desert. Somewhere in the desert, the diamond shard rested in the domain of Valhu.

Something inside Atticus warned of danger behind them. He spun around.

A blue and grey, nearly hairless beast stood on top of a boulder. It had not been there a moment ago. The creature stood on its four muscular legs. Drool slid between its razor-sharp teeth and dripped out of its narrow mouth.

"Don't make any sudden moves," Zane whispered.

"A lonely Cygor," Atticus said to himself. Cygors were sneaky meat-eaters that attacked anything in their view.

The Cygor leaped onto the dusty ground and crept towards the three, its blurry grey eyes locked on them, backing them closer into the gates.

Zane kicked sand into the face of the approaching Cygor. With only the mesa and the gate beside them and nowhere else to go, the three of them drew their weapons and rushed at the beast. Maybe their display of courage would scare it off.

Apparently undaunted, the Cygor wiped its face and began to circle the three of them in the clearing.

Zane swung his sword at the nose of the Cygor. The creature snapped at them, then howled.

"Look!" Daria cried out as four more Cygors appeared.

"Over there," Atticus shouted and pointed to the ladder on the side of the gate.

She nodded, sprinted to the ladder, and climbed up.

Atticus and Zane fought side by side. The Cygors, with their hackles raised, stood on their hind legs and bared their claws and teeth

Atticus ran to a rock, but a Cygor leaped to block his way. These creatures were smart when it came to entrapping their prey.

An arrow swooshed past him from above, hitting a Cygor in its eye. One down! He focused on the Cygor's feet, he swung low, but the blade only managed to scrape one of the front paws. Atticus turned to see that Zane had swung low as well. The two injured Cygors limped off to the side. Atticus and Zane stood back-to-back.

The final two Cygors snapped and growled, the hairs on their backs rising higher. Atticus jabbed his sword towards one of them. The two animals growled and sprinted away.

"They might be back with more," Zane said. "We'd best hurry off."

Atticus pushed open the brass desert gate, giving the three enough room to enter The Badlands. Sand from the Valhu Desert breezed over the dry grounds. Weary but filled with zeal for their mission, Atticus stood between Zane and Daria and gazed at the horizon.

Atticus spotted a large cluster of trees surrounding a small cliff. He then pinpointed the Kingdom of Mizeria half a day away. The claystone and sandstone rock beyond Mizeria led into Valhu's Desert. The breeze brought air much warmer and dryer than at the pillars, where they'd met Zane several hours ago.

They trekked across the sandstone. The wind grew fiercer, blowing sand into their eyes. Daria covered her face with a scarf. Zane walked with his head down, and Atticus pulled his hood over his eyes. "Make way to those trees," Atticus shouted. They struggled towards the tree cluster, pushing against the sandy wind.

The wind calmed as they neared the trees, and Atticus took a deep breath of fresh air. He leaned his head back with relief.

They hiked through the trees, glad to be away from the sandstorm. Birds chirped and fluttered about the branches. Other small desert creatures scurried around. A rocky hill became visible between trees.

Drawing closer to the cave, they could see water trickling down. This would make a perfect place for them to camp for the night. He and Daria made a fire as Zane stood at the cave opening and sang.

Sofos stared upon the gems, and with one command, he created.

Opal created the Skyarl Realm, warriors, sky, and its lights.

No fragments left behind.

Topaz, topaz, hurry fast to create the shape of the land.

Sapphire of the mighty blue flood, make the seas and rivers too.

Ruby, ruby, shake the day with mountains both stone and clay.

Diamond, do your work so fast, create the badlands and desert vast.

Emerald, emerald, finish with our plants, such beautiful life.

For the last act, something living to roam the lands, Bonvidians, they will be named.

Elves and Isrus shall come first. And then Bonvidians, each unlike the rest,
Goblins, Dwarves, Brus, and Giants, oh mighty tall.
Warriors watch them from the gates, guide them in what they need.
When all is done, five simple shards remain, for these will rest within a blade.

The fire crackled, and sparks floated in the air and vanished. The smell of firewood overwhelmed the inside of the cave.

Daria opened her jar of berries and passed it to Atticus. "You seem scared."

He picked two berries and passed the jar to Zane. "I'm terrified, Daria, but I can not let fear get in my way."

Zane popped a few berries into his mouth. "She's right, Atticus. The enemy wants your fear. He thrives on it. Keep the seed of faith growing in you, and you will conquer fear."

Atticus focused on the fire. So many questions lingered in his mind.

***

Two Bonvidians crouched and watched Atticus and his friends. "That's them. That's who fought off those Cygors."

Prince Victor rubbed his eyes. "Let them rest. We will approach them in the morning. Now let's return to our camp and fetch extra horses. I have a good feeling about those three."

Chapter 17

The next morning arrived way too quickly for Atticus. He sat up and stretched.

Daria crouched by the water trickling into the cave and filled her flask.

Atticus stood up and walked to her. "You going hunting?"

Daria lifted her flask and capped it. "I am. Not sure what I'll be catching out here, though."

Atticus glanced at Zane, who lay curled up on one side, snoring away. "What do you think of our new friend?"

She strapped the flask to her side. "He's different, smart, makes you wonder what Sofos has planned. Zane is a gift to us. Anyhow, I should go get us some food."

Atticus watched her leave the cave. Then he grabbed his sheath, drew the sword out, and stared at the grooves. Wonder filled him. Did the shards that had created the land power the sword? Or did he? What was the purpose of gathering the shards anyway? Why couldn't he, as the chosen one, just use the sword without the shards to kill the darkness?

He glanced at Zane, who rubbed sleep from his eyes. Maybe Zane had the answers to the questions floating in his brain.

Zane splashed water on his face and sat next to him. "Amazing, isn't it? How did Sofos in an instant create all of this?"

Atticus touched the empty grooves designed to hold the shards. "I thought the gems created all of this."

Zane shook his head. "Fair point, but Sofos created those gems. He used them, their color, to form and bring life. Technically, the shards you are gathering are parts of the land, each part of his creation, coming together into one final weapon."

Still puzzled, Atticus slid the sword back into its sheath and attached the sheath to his side. "Daria went hunting for food."

Zane patted down his hair and stepped out of the cave. Atticus followed. They stared through the treetops. "The sky looks dried up." The Badlands brought warmth and dried everything.

At that moment, Daria wandered out from the bushes with slumped shoulders, wide eyes, and flushed cheeks, looking like she had lost an argument. But she did have a little smile on her face.

"Daria? You okay?" Atticus asked.

Her grin grew larger, and her eyes sparkled. "I didn't find food. I, um . . ." She paced forward and hurried to his side.

From the treeline, seven mounted horses trotted out. Riders led three more horses with empty saddles.

Atticus gripped his weapon but froze. He rubbed his eyes and glanced once more at the riders. Their armor . . . they wore the crest of El-Valr. "You're from El-Valr."

A rider with a thick greying beard and balding head cleared his throat. "I saw you three fight those Cygors, quite skillfully. We tracked you to this location."

Daria shuffled closer next to Atticus and nudged him.

He snapped back to reality. "Thank you. I am Atticus. This is Daria"—he pointed to his companions in turn—"and this is Zane. Are any of you the prince?

The center horseman pulled back his hood, revealing a young face and a head of silver hair. "That would be I. Prince Victor of El-Valr. I assume you three are here to join our fight against this darkness. We can use all the help we can get. There is one issue, though. We are awaiting someone special, someone important to lead us into victory."

Atticus, Daria, and Zane bowed before him. "My Prince."

As Atticus straightened, he considered what to say. The youngest prince of El- Valr was here. Should he tell him about their quest? Maybe not.

In awe, Atticus rubbed his head while hoping for inspiration. "We would love to join your fight, Prince. But we must make our way to Valhu's Domain."

Prince Victor combed a hand through his silver hair and glanced from Daria to Atticus. "Valhu's Domain? Why would you dare cross the desert to go there?"

A most unusual horsewoman behind the prince leaped off her horse and approached. "They seek the diamond shard, the shard that goes into the sword of the chosen one."

She circled around Atticus, Daria, and Zane. "I am Lena of the Brus. My father used to tell me tales of the chosen one."

Atticus had never seen anyone with ice-blue skin, but he had heard of the Brus, the only intelligent water beings. While they weren't a kingdom of the land, Brus had a connection with both the land and the kingdoms.

Prince Victor jumped off his horse, looking Atticus over. "Can it be? You . . . you're the chosen one?"

Atticus bowed his head. "I am, your majesty."

Prince Victor grinned, his eyes shifting to Daria once again. He turned his attention back to Atticus. "We must go to Mizeria to check in with the Master. He's been hosting us until we go and fight." Victor glanced over Atticus' shoulder at Zane and took off one of his brown leather gloves. "He's not the most enjoyable host, but you can enjoy a tasty meal there."

Prince Victor used two fingers to whistle. "Barlos, bring the three extra horses up front."

Atticus eyed the man with the thick greying beard. He recognized the name: Barlos, the commander of the El- Valr army.

The El-Valr commander hopped off his horse, made his way to three dark brown Friesian horses, and led them forward.

Their long mains and tails gave them a graceful look that contrasted with other odd features. One had a scar on its side, the second had five tails, and the third horse bore two heads.

With not a moment to lose, Atticus, Daria, and Zane packed up their belongings and mounted the horses.

Prince Victor climbed back onto his horse and gave it a tap with his boot. "Let's ride off."

The horses galloped through the woods and across the hot sands, the grit blowing behind their hooves with each stride as they headed to the city of Mizeria.

A vast wall surrounded the kingdom. In the center stood a square palace with cylindrical towers so tall they seemed to pierce the clouds. Outside the gates, guards armed with crossbows paced back and forth. They each wore a crest on their armor, a black "MZ" in a sand-colored square.

The gates opened, and the horse rushed into the kingdom. Mizeria was not a fully developed city because the Master did not care for his Bonvidians and their needs. As the final horse entered the kingdom, the gates screeched shut.

They rode up the main path, poor Bonvidians on either side of them reaching out for food, drink, and money. Atticus' heart ached at the sight of them. They continued up the path until they reached the palace gates. Once inside, an elderly man directed them to the horse stables, where a few stable workers tied their horses to a wooden pole.

They dismounted from their horses.

Prince Victor pointed out wooden doors centered in the palace wall under a large triangular window. "My brothers are elsewhere, so it's just us here, along with the ruler of Mizeria. I do give you fair warning. The ruler of Mizeria is harsh and not fond of us from El-Valr."

Barlos hurried alongside Atticus. "Don't mention your quest to the Master. If he finds out, I don't know what he'll do."

Atticus tapped his sheath and peered at Daria, whose cheeks were flushed. She had barely spoken a word since meeting the prince.

He and his companions paused at the doors of the palace.

The doors opened, and they stepped into a large hall. A large silver chandelier with candles dangled above their heads; a scarlet carpet lay under their feet. And a huge spiral staircase rose before them. The Master stood at the top of it, peering down at them. Beside him stood his wife and two children, who had to be at least twelve years old. They all wore rich robes decorated with jewels along the edges.

The Master placed one hand on the railing and held his other out as if to show off a glorious set of rings. "Prince Victor, what is this that you bring to us?"

The Master's family followed him down the staircase, using the same affected mannerisms. Too weird for Atticus' liking.

Prince Victor approached the Master as he reached the last step. "These are some friends."

The Master walked up to Atticus, Zane, and Daria, examining each of them. "I don't like the looks in their eyes. How do we know your friends aren't spies or even here to kill me?"

Prince Victor turned to Atticus and rolled his eyes, then he shifted back to the Master. "Because you're not worth the effort of being killed."

The Master straightened his shoulders. "Hmm, I'll keep

an extra close eye on you all. Follow me to my dining hall."

The group followed the Master and his family down the ornate halls. Two palace guards opened the dining hall doors. "Please, have a seat," the Master said, motioning towards a golden table and chairs. "Eat, drink, and enjoy. My family and I will return soon to join you. I have . . . unfinished business to attend to."

Servants pulled their chairs out, and they all sat at the table before an amazing spread of food of all kinds. Golden cutlery flanked fine China plates—gold-rimmed too. So much gold, fine jewels, and rich foods.

Not in a million years would Atticus have expected to find himself eating like this. It hurt to sit here and enjoy this meal when just outside the palace gates was so much hunger and suffering. However, he could not refuse to eat and risk being rude.

Atticus reached for a piece of meat and plopped it on his plate. He directed a low tone to Victor. "How will we explain to the Master that we must go to Valhu's Domain? He isn't the most charming man."

Prince Victor scooped a spoonful of vegetables onto his plate. "We don't. We'll come up with a plan to get us to the Domain."

Atticus' ears perked. He could not contain the excitement in his voice. "My Prince, you're coming?"

Prince Victor sipped from a goblet. "Aye, of course, I am, Atticus. How could I leave this mission to just the three of you? You will face many dangers out there. And the closer you get, the tougher it will be. Nine months ago, I vowed to save the land of Bonvida, and what better way to do such a thing if not by your side."

Atticus poured gravy over his meat and potatoes. He eyed Daria, his first companion. A beam of joy glowed on her face as she scooped mashed potatoes. He stared across from him at Zane, a scholar from the captured city

117

of Maljooi. Had it only been by chance that they had met this Bonvidian man who had knowledge of the shards' locations? And Prince Victor, his commander, Barlos, and the Bru, Lena, also intended to lend aid in this most dangerous quest. He cut up a juicy piece of ham, mixed it with his mashed potatoes and vegetables, and took a bite.

While savoring the mouth-watering flavors, the doors of the hall swung open. Atticus turned.

The Master had come to join them, a mischievous look in his eyes.

Atticus swallowed his mouthful. Something did not feel right . . . and it wasn't the food.

Chapter 18

Atticus glanced at Daria, who sat beside him loading her plate. Using his napkin, he wiped gravy from his mouth.

He scanned the dining hall, counting a dozen El-Valr soldiers and nearly twenty Mizeria guards standing around the perimeter. He shifted his attention across the table to the prince, remembering how he had once longed to become a knight and journey with the El-Valr princes. Now here he sat across from one. He cut another piece of ham and dipped it into mashed potatoes.

The Master, his wife, and two children stormed into the dining hall as if making a grand entrance in a play. The sense of comfort Atticus had found while eating dissolved into discomfort.

The Master waved his hands, showing off his many gold rings as he approached the table. "Ahh, my guests."

Atticus narrowed his eyes, a bit annoyed by the flamboyant way the Master carried himself.

Stopping at the head of the table, the Master looked at each guest in turn and then cleared his throat. "Well, stand for me. Am I not a royal ruler?"

Victor grumbled under his breath as he arose.

Atticus and the others followed suit.

The Master beamed. "Good. That's more like it." He snapped his fingers, and servants scurried over to four empty chairs. The Master and his family waited for the servants to pull their chairs out. Once seated, he signed for Atticus and the others to sit down too.

Victor cleared his throat. "You have provided quite the meal."

The Master pointed to the meat, and a servant grabbed the serving plate. "That I have." The servant brought the plate over and plopped meat onto his and his family members' plates. "That I have," he said again.

The Master waved the servant away and stood up from

his seat. He came up behind his two children and placed his arms around them. "Children, you are witnessing your father doing a great deed. I allowed these Bonvidians into Mizeria, and as much as I want to hang them, I can not." The Master bellowed a laugh. "Not yet, at least," he said under his breath.

Atticus straightened in his seat. How could this man call himself a ruler? He disrespected his people, was rude to his guests, and only seemed to care for riches. Should they even have come here? They should have stayed on high alert.

The Master swiped his wife's goblet and swaggered around the dining hall. He stopped at a side table that held jugs of beverages, and he hummed as he poured water into his wife's goblet. He glanced over his shoulder, then turned his focus on the goblet.

The Master's behavior rattled Atticus. What was he up to?

The Master rustled his robe, turned back around, and sauntered back to his wife. He handed her the goblet. "This is my kingdom, and once this battle has ended, no one from El-Valr will pass through my gates again." He pointed to his two children. "Children, why don't you scurry off to the study and work on lessons."

The two children exchanged confused glances, then slid their chairs back and shuffled from the room.

The Master's wife gazed at him uneasily, taking a sip from the goblet. After setting the goblet down, she grabbed her throat and coughed once ... twice. Panic filled her eyes as she struggled to draw a breath. In the next instant, she fell face-first onto the table.

The Master ran to her. "Guards! Guards!" he shouted, pointing at Atticus. "Your lot did this." At that moment, ten extra guards swarmed into the room.

"What?" Atticus exploded. They had not done anything.

The Master must have put something in her drink while fiddling with his robe at the beverage table.

Prince Victor slammed a fist to the table and stood up, his chair scraping back behind him. "You must be looking for a fight, but your blood is not worthy of my sword. We will go."

"Guards, we have been betrayed," the Master shouted. "Seize them. They poisoned my wife."

Atticus, Daria, Zane, Lena, and Barlos stood up and headed as a group towards the door.

The El-Valr knights and palace guards drew their weapons. The palace guards stepped in closer, and the room went silent.

Atticus counted the Mizeria guards as they circled around him, his friends, and the dozen El-Valr soldiers. They were outnumbered. This could not be good.

"We wish you no harm," Victor said as he raised his sword. "But you give us no choice. We are innocent and will not stand for this."

The Master spat at Victor's feet. "Guards, tear them apart." He waved his hand and walked out of the dining hall.

Atticus, Daria, and his newfound allies drew their weapons.

"Stay close," Prince Victor said.

The palace guards moved in.

Atticus scanned his surroundings and tried to make a plan. This would either be a quick end to his quest or a brutal escape.

Victor held a firm position as he peered around the room. "Barlos, stay back with the soldiers and have them retreat to one of our secret bases."

Barlos nodded. "And what about you? I must protect you."

Atticus turned. "We will wait for you at Valhu's

Domain."

Victor pointed his sword at the doors of the hall. "Stay close."

Atticus, followed by Daria, Zane, and Lena, charged, their weapons clanging against the swords of the guards. Fortunately, they overpowered them and soon shoved open the doors and sprinted down the halls towards the main entrance.

As they neared a corner, two guards jumped out at them. "Sorry, Prince of El-Valr, we have orders to stop you," the taller guard shouted.

Not waiting for Victor to reply, Lena pulled a knife from her gauntlets and lunged at the guards, slashing the two guards across their chests. She landed between them and stabbed them once more from the sides.

As the group neared the palace doors, an odor filled the room. From the spiral stairs, the Master's body rolled down, his robes torn, his face bruised, and a fresh cut on his lower jaw.

The group paused in shock.

The Master looked at them from where he lay on the floor. "I-I'm sorry."

Grunting and scuttling noises drew their attention to a group of Arcods at the top of the steps, standing just where the Maser and his family had stood earlier. One Arcod, perhaps the commander, wore dingy bronze armor, unlike the other Arcods who wore no armor.

With their eyes on the creatures, they edged to the palace door.

The Arcod commander pointed its dangly arm at Atticus. "That is the chosen one. Keep him alive. Kill the rest."

The Arcods charged down the stairs at Atticus and the group.

As Victor turned to bolt, his knights appeared on the scene, running towards the Arcods with their swords drawn.

"To the stables!" Atticus shouted. His flight response kicking in, he bolted with the others across the empty courtyard heading for their horses.

Once on the streets, they looked around at the ragged civilians crowding the side streets. "The Master is dead. The Master is dead," Prince Victor shouted.

Unaware of the danger, Bonvidians of Mizeria smiled, while others pointed at the city walls where an Arcod appeared and more followed. Several Arcods had breached the kingdom walls.

Zane turned to the people. "Go into hiding. Protect yourselves."

"We have to go," Lena called.

Without another word, they raced out of the kingdom.

Atticus and his companions rode through the rugged landscape that soon gave way to hot sand. In the distance stood red and orange clay mountains, each one unique. Some rose gradually at an angle. Deeper shades of red and orange colored the foot of mountains with smooth, column-like sides that rose to craggy peaks. As they approached the nearest mountain, caves along one side came into view.

Atticus tried to picture a city within the mountains. Maybe the thieves had developed a network of tunnels and rooms.

"Thief City is just through those caves," Prince Victor said. "They'll probably kill us if they know I'm of royalty."

As the temperatures climbed, Atticus wiped the sweat dripping down his neck. He glanced at his weapon dangling from his side. "They're really that ruthless?"

Prince Victor nodded. "They steal for the fun of it and will kill once they get the information they want."

Atticus scratched his head. "Why would they kill a

stranger?"

Victor smirked. "They have no morals. But they probably figure that if they don't, their victims will go after them."

Lena glanced in every direction. "Keep your eyes wide open. They could be watching us now."

Just then, spears flew through the air and hit the ground nearby. Daria's and Zane's horses reared up. Atticus and the others jumped off their horses.

Victor inspected the area but only found boulders and cactuses. "Don't make a move," he hollered, reaching for his weapon.

"Who are you? What brings you to these parts?" a distant voice demanded to know.

Unable to see the thieves anywhere, Atticus glanced at Victor, who shrugged. The others in the group looked from one to another too. The thieves must have been hiding in the shadows or behind a boulder shaped like two elephants stuck together. Maybe he could reason with them.

"My name is Atticus," he shouted. "My friends and I seek passage to Valhu's Domain."

"The domain is just a myth," a voice replied. "There is nothing beyond these clay rocks but more sand and creatures. If you did make it through the desert, you would never get as far as the sea."

Atticus stared at the shadows. "Maybe you can't, but we must try."

From the shadows stepped a heavyset man with three eyes, pink skin, and a ring of hair encircling his head.

Was this thief a Triloyd? One rarely came across that breed. "I assure you, the domain is real. Now please let us pass." Atticus tugged at the neckline of his tunic, suffocated by the heat.

The Triloyd blinked all three of its eyes. "I have lived here for twenty years. Believe me, if Valhu's Domain is real, I would have found it and would have obtained the legendary power that it holds within."

"Since nothing is out there, then you won't mind letting us pass," Prince Victor interjected, walking beside Atticus. Keeping their weapons low, the two of them approached the Triloyd, stopping only a few feet away.

The Triloyd glared at Prince Victor and stood to his full height, a few inches taller than Victor. Then he shoved Atticus aside and smirked. "Well, well, a Bonvidian prince."

Prince Victor took a deep breath.

"You're worth a lot, Prince. Why are you traveling this way?"

"Bonvida, as you may know, is in grave danger. I, one of the princes, am building an army, awaiting the right time to strike against the darkness."

"You'll need more than an army to defeat the darkness. I've seen it with my own eyes." He blinked his three eyes again. "I and a few others were on a job during the siege nine months ago. That's when we saw creatures unknown to this land. We watched El-Valr fall." He lowered his head.

"Come then, come to Bonvida and fight alongside us," Atticus said.

"You want a bunch of thieves?" He chuckled.

"You're part of this land. You have the right to fight with us," Atticus replied.

The Triloyd looked at him strangely. "Go on. You may pass, but I promise that you will find nothing other than your painful deaths. However, if you manage to pass through the sands safely, then you'll be in good luck because we have a ship at the shoreline."

"What is your name?" Atticus asked.

"Yil," he said.

"Thank you, Yil." Atticus offered his hand, but Yil rejected it. Atticus lowered his hand. He and Victor returned to their horses and mounted them.

Yil strode to Atticus' horse and stroked its mane. He stared up into Atticus' eyes. "Be safe out there in the sands, young traveler. You can never be too careful, especially in this day and age." Yil puckered his lips and paced back to the thieves.

Atticus loosened his tunic, hoping to cool down. "Don't you worry about us, Yil. We are always on our guard." He patted his horse and tapped its backside. His horse trotted off, and the others followed behind.

Before they got too far away, Atticus could not help but look back once more. His gut churned. Something did not feel right. But there was no turning back now.

Chapter 19

Atticus admired the dunes that surrounded them. Not too far ahead stood a reddish mountain, no more than a ten-minute ride. It was likely the domain. He leaned forward and tapped his horse, signaling for it to gallop faster. The wind rushed around him, whipping his hair in every direction.

The domain became clearer, and he pulled the reins back. The horse neighed and shook its head. He patted its neck as he gazed upon the clay mountain that stood beyond an open stretch of sand. His breath caught as he took in the beauty before him. A tall statue of a female Bonvidian warrior, her arms outstretched, flanked a high, narrow door in the center of the mountain.

Zane nudged Atticus. "Valhu was known as the most beautiful warrior, gifted with great wisdom. Everyone was in awe of her beauty. She is the desert protector because she fought and tamed the mythical desert beast, Narlow, saving the desert and Badlands from its wrath."

Atticus continued to gaze at the sight. Scattered stones poked up from the sand.

"Bonvidians built this domain as a place to worship her. But one day, Valhu came and told them that she was not to be worshipped, only honored. She ordered them to respect her wishes, or Sofos would send his wrath back to the Badlands."

Atticus turned to Zane. "How did the shard end up here?"

"Before Desmond died, he came here to see Valhu. He gave her the diamond shard to keep and protect. After Desmond left, he sealed the domain. Valhu explained that if the land was ever attacked by the darkness, she could summon the mythical beast to protect the shard."

Atticus gripped the hilt of his sword, anticipation filling

him. *Valhu, here I come.* He had the topaz shard, and the next shard was just a sprint away, across this field of sand.

As he stepped onto the sand, something under it moved, zipping straight towards him.

Someone grabbed him from behind and yanked him to saftey. Not a second later, a creature shot up from the earth. A pale orange monster pinched the air with its crab-like claws and swung its scorpion tail in circles.

Atticus' heart thumped. He glanced behind him and smiled at Daria, who had just saved his life.

Zane's face turned ghostly white. "Narlow, the mythical beast that Valhu once defeated."

Narlow opened its mouth wide and let out an ear-piercing shriek that sent more sand and spittle into the air. Particles rained down on Atticus and the others.

Atticus drew his sword, as did Victor, who stood beside him. Daria, on his other side, unlatched her bow and glanced at Lena, who also stood ready to fight. Zane paced behind everyone, looking a bit uncomfortable with a sword in his hands.

Narlow thrashed about.

As Atticus studied the creature, he realized something. "Zane, it has no eyes. Maybe we can pass by without it spotting us."

Zane chuckled from behind him. "It may not be able to see us, Atticus, but it can feel vibrations. That's how it gets you."

Victor said to Atticus, "I haven't led many battles without Barlos by my side."

Atticus smiled at Victor. "We will stick by each other's side." Then he turned to his sister and pointed to a nearby dune that cast a shadow on the ground. "Daria, take to high ground with your bow. Lena, go with her and protect her."

He turned to Zane. "Zane, stay on the perimeter but do

not engage in battle unless needed. Your full knowledge of Valhu's battle with Narlow will come in handy."

Lena and Daria ran through the sand and climbed the dune. Daria drew her bow and aimed an arrow at the beast.

Victor and Atticus walked in step towards Narlow.

Zane sheathed his sword. "Watch its tail! If you get the tail, you have a good chance of actually beating Narlow."

Narlow buried itself in the ground and slithered around them.

"Don't move!" Zane shouted. "Narlow is listening for the vibration of our movement. One step, and he will spring up and kill you."

Atticus and Victor stood still. Atticus shouted to his sister, "Daria! Shoot an arrow. Let's force it to the surface."

Daria got into position and released the arrow. The arrow sailed through the air and hit the sand below.

Narlow shot up from the sand.

At that moment, Atticus and Victor charged at Narlow and slashed at the tail.

Narlow swung around and whacked both of them across the sand. They struggled back to their feet. Atticus spat sand from his mouth. They landed not too far from the two statues on either side of the narrow domain entrance.

Atticus scanned the area. "You hold it off. I'll get the shard."

"We've got this. Run!" Victor said.

"Atticus, go! I have a feeling Valhu will call this fight off once she realizes you are here," Zane said.

Atticus sheathed his sword, took a deep breath, and bolted for the entrance, all the while praying that Narlow would not catch him. With each hurried step, his feet sank in the sand, and he had to throw his arms out for balance. The monster shrieked behind him and the ground trembled, but he did not dare look back. Relying on the others to protect him, he kept his eyes on the safety of the domain and pushed himself forward. Closer, closer . . .

Almost to the domain, he pushed himself and leaped to cover the final distance. Then he landed hard on compact clay at the foot of the domain.

Safe now, he glanced back. His friends ran in circles in the open field, and the creature lunged at one and then another. He huffed, amazed at their tactics.

Atticus turned around and looked for the entrance in the mountainside between the two statues. He saw nothing other than the smooth red clay and stones of the mountain. The two statues had thrown him off. He assumed that the entrance was here between them.

Confused, he took a step back and sized up the statues. They towered over him, standing at least five times taller than he stood. Their faces glimmered in the sunlight. They had to mark the door somehow. Could it be hidden?

He ran his hands up and down the red stone before him. Nothing. Maybe the thief Yil was right, that there was nothing here. No, that could not be it. The door had to be somewhere.

With a weary sigh, he gazed at the foot of one of the statues and noticed something on it. A thin crack ran along the strap of the stone warrior's sandal. He pushed the foot of the statue, and the crack shifted. Then the outline of a low door appeared in the mountainside, reddish dust issuing from it and cascading to the ground. The door opened halfway, just enough for him to squeeze through.

Once inside, he blinked a few times while his eyes adjusted to the darkness. Flickering light came from a doorway at the end of the corridor. He traipsed towards it and stepped inside a room. Two lit torches hung on the rough clay walls. How had they remained lit all this time? Or was someone here?

Between the torches hung an engraving of Valhu. Flowers and markings surrounded the female warrior, who stood with arms stretched out and something in her hands.

Atticus sucked in a breath. She held a replica of the diamond shard, so the shard was likely nearby.

Atticus approached the engraving, captivated by the beauty of this woman. He brushed the markings with his hand. "What do they mean?" he whispered.

Just then, the markings lit up, and the wall slid open from either side. As the opening widened, it revealed a narrow path, and a chilly wind blew out from it.

He stared down the narrow path, making out a door at the other end. Mustering his courage, Atticus stepped from the room and walked down the path towards the door. Heavy cobwebs hung from the corners, and long strands dangled before his face. Then he spotted *it*.

He took a breath and twitched, hoping that the twenty-four-inch Arachnid that had made the webs was sleeping and not going to drop on top of him.

Arriving at a frosted glass door, he reached out a hand, but the door opened on its own. He stepped through the doorway and into a circular room. Firelit torches hung on the wall. His eyes locked on a silver throne in the center of the room . . . and on the beautiful warrior dressed in silk sitting on the throne. Two doves rested on her shoulders.

Valhu smiled at him. "Atticus, it is you. I had to be sure. Come forward, young man. You don't need to worry. I have pulled Narlow back, and your companions are fine."

She waved him closer. "I have been waiting for this day, Atticus. I am the warrior Valhu, the protector of the desert. I am also the protector of the diamond shard that goes into your sword, the sword that will defeat Luvanasis."

He listened to her every word, mesmerized by her pure

beauty.

Valhu opened her right hand.

In awe, he gazed at the diamond shard glittering in the torchlight.

She stretched her arm out. "Take it, Atticus, and go save this place, for it cannot save itself."

He reached for the diamond shard and held it in his fingers, finding it warm to the touch. It brought peace and warmth to his body and soul.

Atticus pulled the sword from its sheath and placed it on the ground. Then he knelt and set the diamond shard in its groove. Atticus bowed to Valhu.

She bowed back to him. "You have much bravery and respect in you, Atticus. Now go."

Atticus bowed his head and turned back to the doorway. As he strode down the hall, something tickled his neck. He wished he could protect himself like a turtle in its shell.

A scurrying sound came from above and behind. Skin crawling, Atticus jumped and sprinted the rest of the way without looking back.

The instant he passed through the once-hidden door and out into the sunlight, the scurrying grew intense—as if the spider raced madly after him. But as Atticus drew his sword and turned to look, the door swung shut with a thud and sank back into the wall. A cascade of reddish dirt covered it up again, hiding it in the side of the clay mountain. Relieved, Atticus exhaled and turned to go.

While heading back to his companions, he noticed something in the distance. Someone—no, two people— rode towards them on a single horse.

Atticus ran forward. "Valhu, wait!" He didn't want Narlow to jump out at the horse or riders. He believed that she was able to hear his voice.

As the horse came closer, he recognized the first rider.

Barlos tugged at the reins. "My friends!" he shouted and waved.

"Barlos, glad you made it," Victor replied.

Barlos grinned. "You're lucky I did. I ran into a group of thieves tracking you. They didn't want to stand down, except this one here." He glanced over his shoulder at the person who sat behind him on the horse. "She's interesting."

A young girl, about fourteen years old, peeked out from behind him. Freckles dotted her round cheeks. "Hi, I'm Meg," she said with a wave.

"Meg, do you know the way to the ship that Yil spoke of?" Prince Victor asked.

She nodded, her black shoulder-length hair bouncing.

"Thank you, Meg. Would you show us the way?" Atticus said.

Atticus and the others mounted their horses and rode off together from Valhu's Domain. The desire to eat grew on him and his companions. They would not find much out here except for a few cacti fruit or palm tree melons. But even those were rare.

As evening drew on, they came to an oasis and decided it would be the best place to rest. Four palm trees dangled their branches over a pond. Zane helped Barlos set up tents to protect them from the blowing sand. Meg and Daria picked a few melons, and they all enjoyed the luxury of the sweet watery fruit. Not long after, they readied themselves for an uncomfortable night's rest on the sand.

All too soon, morning arrived, and they packed their belongings.

Barlos inspected the horses and turned to Meg. "Young one, how much further?"

Meg squinted at him as she filled a flask with pond water. "A few hours at most. We'll get there just after midday."

Barlos strode to Atticus. "Atticus, I suggest we journey by foot. The horses won't fit on the boat. If we send them off from here, they will find a way home."

Atticus stared at the horses drinking from the pond. "Okay, let's unsaddle them and set them free."

Atticus unstrapped his horse's saddle while the others took care of the remaining horses. "Bring what is necessary. Traveling by foot in the desert will not be a joyous time."

Atticus' horse bobbed its head and gave a friendly snort, as if wishing them a safe journey. Then it turned to go and led the other horses back towards Valhu's Domain. Hopefully, they would find safety.

Atticus turned back to the group. Everyone hung their belongings over their shoulders. "All right, Meg, lead the way."

The young girl gave a nod and then strode with confidence towards the sand dunes. Daria walked beside her, and the rest followed. Meg took no obvious path but seemed confident as she led the group through the shade of a towering sand dune, then over a gradually sloped dune, and next along the ridge at the top of another one. Dunes now surrounded them on all sides, but Meg continued undaunted, zigzagging through the maze.

"This dune maze reminds me of the tunnels I took to the Maljooi cove when I escaped," Zane said and then turned to Atticus. "Now that I think of it, once we get to this ship, the closest place to steer to will be the Maljooi cove."

Atticus spotted a raven perched nearby on a palm tree. The long, red-tipped tail feathers reminded him of the one he saw the night he and Daria had first set out from home. "Would that mean that we would have to use the tunnel you spoke about?"

Zane glanced up at the clear sky. "Aye, it would. If you feel that trek would be too risky, we can find another way."

Atticus shook his head. "No, Zane, we'll go through Maljooi . . . and when we get there, we will free your fellow citizens."

Zane's eyes opened wide. "Are you serious?"

Victor patted Zane's shoulder from behind. "Aye, of course, he is serious. Zane, your city is great and does not deserve to be held captive anymore. Together the seven of us will set them free."

***

As the mid-day approached, they finally made it out of the dune maze.

"Look, the sea!" Daria shouted, pointing to the horizon.

Atticus took a deep breath, relieved to see it, even though it would take them a few hours to reach it.

Daria glanced at Meg, who still walked beside her. The young girl hadn't spoken much on the journey. "How long have you been a thief, Meg?"

Meg glanced at her. "Um, not long, maybe a few weeks."

Daria nodded. "Only a few weeks, huh? Can I ask what happened? What led you to them?"

Meg's eyebrows lowered, and she moved her lips from side to side. "My father . . . he sent me to them. He wanted to protect me."

Daria could not see how placing one's daughter with thieves offered any protection.

Meg slowed her pace. "Before everything happened, we lived in a small home in Portacrista. Then the creatures came." Her look soured. "My father said we had to go. So we ran, stole a trade ship, and sailed off to sea."

Daria gasped. "Sailing off to sea seems extreme." Although... she didn't think Arcods could swim, so maybe it was smart.

Meg sniffled and wiped her nose. "Three months into our sailing trip, we rounded the bend by Valindin and kept sailing onward. We visited a few islands . . ." She wiped her watering eyes. "We found this small island and decided on it. That's when it happened."

Daria turned to Meg, sensing an important revelation.

"That's when my father's visions started. We sailed to Goblin Point, and he told me to go but not to speak to anyone. He sent me to live with the thieves in the desert."

Daria glanced over her shoulder at Atticus, hoping he had been listening to Meg's story.

Meg sighed.

Daria placed her hand on the young girl's shoulder. "What happened on that island, Meg?"

Meg stared at Daria, then glanced at Atticus and the others. "On the island, before my father left me with the thieves, we found a strange cave, and in it was a pedestal surrounded by water. The pedestal held a tiny, blueish gem fragment, quite beautiful. My father jumped into the water and touched it."

Daria wiped the sweat from her forehead, unsure if it was from the heat or the excitement of the story.

"My father said he should not have touched it. He said it wasn't for him. It was for some chosen one. Then he said that because he touched that blue shard, he was under the control of the Kilo, the sea beast."

Daria froze and leaned in closer. "I'm sorry? What did you find?"

Meg stared deep into Daria's eyes. "My father called it the sapphire shard."

Meg continued forward, but Daria could not move. She stood still as a rock. The sapphire shard? Zane did not even know its location. But this girl, this young girl, did. This innocent girl was the key to Atticus' quest.

Chapter 20

Luvanasis stood with a unit of Arcods on the front steps of the El-Valr castle. Strangely enough, he had grown accustomed to their smell. "I feel a battle brewing, the long-awaited battle." He strode forward, passing rubble from a fallen tower. "I need every prisoner accounted for and brought to me. Also, summon the rest of the Arcods to retreat here as soon as possible."

The Arcods growled as they formed three lines. The evening sky reflected off their tarnished armor.

He took a deep breath. Sundown would soon approach. "And if possible, bring me the chosen one. It should not be this difficult to catch him."

Without another sound, the Arcods turned their backs to the castle and marched towards the destroyed marketplace.

Luvanasis squinted at a black dot gliding in the wind and growing bigger as it drew near. The raven. He grumbled under his breath, "This bird better have some good news. If not, it'll be my dinner."

The raven landed on a nearby stone and cawed.

"I don't speak bird." He clenched his jaw and glanced around for Raia. "She better get here soon."

The raven flapped its wings and cawed a second time.

Irritated, Luvanasis glared at it.

"It's hungry," Raia said as she strode up the stairs. Her one-piece olive tunic brought color to her pale face. "Sorry, I had to let your ugly creatures pass by me."

Luvanasis turned his back on her and pushed open the doors of the castle. He strode through the halls, trusting that Raia would follow. "Where's my descendant?"

"On his way," she said from behind. "You seem distraught, Luvanasis."

He stopped in place and glared at her. *How dare she tell*

me how I feel. "My commander returned from Mizeria. Atticus escaped, meaning he is getting closer to collecting those shards." His Arcods had had one simple task and had failed him. If they kept this up, he would have to find Atticus himself. He picked up his pace.

Raia scurried to his side.

The raven squawked.

Raia smirked. "My raven comes with news. I now know where they are heading. They'll be there very soon."

Luvanasis stared at her. "Continue."

She tapped her shoulder, inviting the raven to perch on it. "They're going to Maljooi. Raven heard them speaking about going in and releasing those who are still captive there."

Luvanasis glanced at the floor. *Maljooi? Why would they dare go there? Doesn't Atticus have more important tasks at hand? What is he up to?* Grinning and pleased with his new plans, he stroked the bird's beak. "Well, my little spy, it looks like I won't be killing you, after all."

He continued past a staircase and doors. "Lucky for us, Raia, we will be gathering the prisoners. I suggest you tell the Arcod commanders—" A brilliant idea sprang into his mind. "On second thought, don't strike them in Maljooi. Let them free those held captive there. Instead, ambush them just outside the city. There should be a convoy of prisoners already on their way here. Have that set of troops aid your ambush."

She nodded in obedience.

What would he do once he had Atticus in his grasp? Would he kill him instantly? Or wait for the very end and have Hematite do the deed? But before that, he would take Atticus' precious sword.

They continued through the castle, striding down the hall of paintings and stained-glass windows that led to the throne room. He marched to his throne and sat.

Raia stood a fair distance.

It pleased him to think that his intimidation was working.

Just then, a man—a Bonvidian—entered the throne room and stood beside Raia. The Bonvidian wore black from head to toe, except for a menacing brass mask. His head swiveled from one side to the other, apparently sizing up the room. When his gaze turned towards Luvanasis on the throne, he lifted his chin.

"Come forward." Luvanasis motioned and leaned back in his seat. "You, Raia, are free to go. Now is not the time for a reunion."

While Raia bowed and strode from the room, the man in black marched forward.

Luvanasis arose, stepped down from his throne, and took slow strides to his descendant. "You. We have a lot to discuss . . . follow me."

Luvanasis went around the throne and stopped at a long, old wooden box.

The descendant stood at his side.

"You may be wondering many things, one being your destiny." Luvanasis placed his hands on either side of the box. "Our bloodline is a cursed one. The stories speak about the Sword of Darkness and how it aids our blood. It aids the She Serpent that Desmond and his followers put into a slumber long ago." He opened the box halfway, and a cloud of dust fell away from it. "I do not know where she is. Raia does not know where she is." Luvanasis took a long pause while the dust settled.

The descendant stared at Luvanasis as eagerly as a young child awaiting a gift from his father.

"I came to Bonvida intending to help Hematite. My destiny has always been to kill the heir. The heir of Desmond, of Dane. The new chosen one, Atticus. He is my destiny. Awakening the She Serpent is not. Awakening her is yours." Luvanasis opened the box the rest of the way, revealing a black sheath. He lifted it from the box. "Whenever the time calls, awaken her."

He grasped the snake-shaped hilt and tugged the sword from its rusted sheath. Then he waved the sword, allowing evening sunlight that streamed through windows to reflect off the serrated blade.

His descendant stared at the blade through the brass mask, desire in his eyes.

Luvanasis slid the sword back into the sheath. "Descendant, this sword belongs to you. For I do not need it to kill Atticus."

The descendant unlatched his own sword, tossed it aside, and spread his hands to receive the mighty gift.

Luvanasis placed the sheath into his waiting hands, relief filling him. No matter whatever else might happen, She Serpent would be awakened.

Chapter 21

As Atticus trekked through the desert, he could just spot where the desert met the sea. Another few hours, and they'd be there. He bumped into Daria. Why had she stopped in her tracks? Zane, Barlos, Victor, and Lena strode passed him towards Meg, who'd gotten further ahead.

Atticus rubbed his head. "Daria, everything okay?"

Her eyes were open wide, and her eyebrows rose alarmingly.

He waved his hand in front of her face. "Daria?"

She shook her head, finally making eye contact. "Sorry."

A stone's throw away, Meg turned around and waved. "Come on! What are you waiting for?"

"Atticus," Daria said, walking beside him now, "did you hear Meg's story?"

Atticus shook his head. "No, I was too busy talking with Victor and Zane."

Daria pushed a strand of hair behind her ear. "She knows where the sapphire shard is."

Atticus lost his breath. How could this fourteen-year-old girl know where the shard was? And what were the chances that they just stumbled upon her?

"You have to tell her who you are. She has to bring us to it."

Before long, they neared the sea. The sound of waves crashing onto shore filled the salty, fishy air. The sea stretched out before them. Meg had brought them to a deserted part of the shoreline—no port, no structures, and no people. A single ship sat moored to a lonely pier.

Meg pointed to it, a weathered mahogany ship with two masts and white sails. Swirls decorated both sides of the old ship, and a rope ladder dangled over the starboard side.

Barlos grinned. "A fine schooner, she is."

Three hefty ropes attached to metal moors kept the ship from drifting off.

Meg sighed. "Well, here you all go. I wish you the best in whatever you're doing."

Atticus spotted two grey seagulls fighting over a dead fish. "About that, Meg. Daria told me that you came across the sapphire shard."

Meg gulped and stepped back, glancing around nervously.

Atticus unsheathed his sword and held it up with both hands. "See those grooves? Those are for the shards. Meg, you must come with us. You'll bring me a step closer to defeating this darkness."

Meg stared at him. Her jaw dropped. "You? You're the chosen one? The one my father had visions of? That must be it, why he sent me to the thieves. Sofos must've shown him."

Atticus slid his sword back into its sheath. "What do you say, Meg?"

She bit her lip and glanced to the side. "Aye, I'll come."

Atticus exhaled as he turned to face the abandoned ship. He wondered for a moment who had owned the vessel before Meg's thieves had taken it. But he could not let the thought trouble him. They had a mission.

"Okay, let's set sail and hit the seas."

One by one, they climbed the rope ladder. Once all aboard, Barlos took charge of the helm. "Release the moorings! Raise the sails!" he shouted to the group. "And, Atticus, hand me your map."

Atticus paced to Barlos and pulled the map from his pocket.

Barlos pointed to a spot in the desert. "I believe we are roughly around here, and Maljooi is down this way. Hmm, okay, I'll stay on course with the Maljooi mountains as my focal point."

Atticus folded the map and slid it back into his pocket.

The ship swayed to one side and then to the other as its new crew untied the ropes.

Atticus glanced at the orange and pink evening sky. "Sir, what about when it gets dark? The mountain range will be hard to see."

Barlos scratched his grey beard, grains of sand falling to the deck. "Glow Fish will lead the way. Keep your eyes out for them."

Atticus nodded and strode to the others.

With the sails catching wind, the ship moved out into the open sea, and the port dwindled in size behind them. The orange-and-pink sky faded to dark blue. An hour later, the outline of mountains and rough edges of land appeared off the starboard side.

"There." Victor pointed to a distant island on their left. "That's Balast Isle. It's inhabited by a hostile tribe of Bonvidians." He flashed a scar on his leg. "This is what they did to me." He shrugged his shoulders and joined Daria, Lena, and Meg below deck.

The ship rocked back and forth like a mother cradling an infant to sleep. The motion soothed Atticus, but he still tried to avoid looking too long at the dark sea. Somehow, everything seemed more ominous at night.

After glimpsing something strange in his peripheral vision, Atticus found himself drawn to the taffrail, the rail on the ship's stern. Little balls of neon green light swam in patterns beneath the dark waves. Some rose close to the surface, their form becoming clearer. Glow Fish! Atticus counted thirty or so, maybe even fifty chubby Glow Fish, surrounding their ship.

"Barlos!" Atticus called over his shoulder. "We have Glow Fish!"

"Aye, I see their light. Tell them where we need to go," Barlos said.

Atticus leaned over the taffrail to . . . talk to the fish? Seriously? "Uh, hey there, Glow Fish, can you lead us to the

143

Maljooi cove?"

Some fish swam forward while others remained at a distance. Amazed that they now had the cooperation of fish on their journey, Atticus exhaled an relaxed his shoulders. Then he walked to Zane, who stood at the bow staring at the starry night. "Zane, how are you holding up?"

Zane turned and gave a faint smile. "I'm fine. Just nervous, I suppose."

Atticus sat down on a wooden barrel. "I don't blame you. It's going to be a big task. There are seven of us against who knows how many Arcods."

Zane slumped on the barrel next to him. "Maljooi does have some great fighters—we have too—but the majority of those in the city are like me."

Atticus dropped his head to his chest, trying to think of what to say. "Zane, don't put yourself down. And if you'd like, Victor and I can teach you a few tricks."

Zane smiled, his white teeth glowing in the faint light. "I would appreciate that, Atticus."

Atticus peeked over the railing to take another look at the Glow Fish. "Zane, the stories also tell about Desmond's followers. And how his followers' descendants aided in defeating the darkness of Hematite."

Zane's eyes glittered. "Gion, Alia, and Bige were Desmond's closest allies, and then Shiesta, the betrayer. Atticus, when this journey is finished, I suggest you read about them, read the stories of Desmond and his followers. Because there will come a time where you and the other descendants will have to rise."

Atticus' mind wandered. The idea of meeting others like him lifted his spirits. But fear of the future brought him down again. "I will do that, thank you."

Atticus and Zane got up from the barrels and made their way below deck to see the others.

The night passed as Atticus, and his companions enjoyed a small meal and curled up in a quiet corner for a rest. When the following morning arrived, Atticus leaned against one of the masts and wrote in his journal.

As Atticus finished his first sentence, Barlos shouted. *Was there trouble at sea? Was it a ship of Arcods? Could Arcods even steer a ship? Maybe pirates.* Atticus recalled hearing that pirates ornamented their wrists with gold. He shook the thoughts from his mind, closed his journal, and tucked it away. Then he sprang up from the deck, ready to fight.

As he approached Barlos at the ship's helm, he peered at the water off the port and starboard sides. Nothing. They floated alone in the sea, but ahead of them, mountains rose behind a sheltered inlet. Maljooi Cove! They had made it!

Barlos barked commands at the others as he brought the vessel in. Daria, Meg, and Lena furled the sails, while Victor prepared the anchor.

The cove did not live up to Atticus' expectations. Rather than beaches and boats of all sizes, it had a rocky shore and a dock. Nothing else. Maybe the cove was only used in cases of emergency.

Atticus grasped Zane's shoulder. "Here we are. It's time to free your home."

Zane stood silent, his jaw clenched and determination in his eyes.

Victor grabbed a plank and lowered it onto the rocky shore of the cove.

One by one, they proceeded down the plank, following Zane.

Zane hurried to a pile of rocks and hefted one rock and then another aside. As he cleared the rocks away, a tunnel appeared. "We can use the string as a guide. It'll lead us to a grate in one of the alleys in the city. We go single file."

Atticus and the others followed Zane through the dark

tunnels underneath the mountains. Atticus took small strides, hoping not to step on Zane's heels. Not too far ahead, a glimmer of light appeared. With each passing step, the light became clearer until they stood beneath the source. The seven squished together like canned sardines and stared up at a dark metal grate.

"Here we are. We stand beneath the city of Maljooi." Zane's glance shifted to the grate, sadness in his eyes. "My city. Which Arcods took over months ago, capturing or killing all her citizens."

Sympathizing with his friend's pain, Atticus squeezed his shoulder. "Aye, we made it. And it is up to us to rescue them. No matter the cost."

Chapter 22

No sounds other than a bird chirping and wind scraping rubbish along the ground came from above. Daria, Victor, Barlos, Lena, and Meg, standing nearby in the underground tunnel, even seemed to hold their breath as they watched Atticus and Zane.

Atticus grabbed the cold metal bars of the overhead grate and communicated with a glance to Zane his readiness to lift it. They needed to lift the grate as quietly as possible in case an Arcod happened to be near. Stifling a grunt, Atticus lifted the grate, working in tandem with Zane, and slid it aside. A shower of dust fell, but no new sounds came from above.

Grabbing onto the overhead frame and pressing a foot to the tunnel wall, Zane hefted himself up. After peering around, probably looking for signs of trouble, he climbed all the way out. Atticus and the others followed.

Atticus stepped over two corpses and came to the end of the alley. Row houses and shops lined the desolate streets. A square building with a circular roof—maybe a library—stood between two shops further down. With no sign of Arcods monitoring the streets, he sprinted across the street with the others following close. They scurried to a wider alley a stone's throw away.

"Zane," Barlos whispered loudly, "where do you think the civilians are being held?"

Zane peeked out of the alley and then returned to the group. "The Maljooi Senate. It's the largest building in the city."

"Lead the way," Atticus said.

Zane crept from the alley, the others following, and dashed down one street and then another. He slowed as they neared an oval clinker-brick building with statues circling the rim of its yellow rooftop. A metal fence with evenly spaced prongs circled the building.

"Over there." Atticus pointed to a damaged house across the street from the senate. While one side of it remained intact, the other side had splintered beams for walls. "Let's head that way."

They jogged across the street and around to the side of the house, glancing every which way but still seeing no sign of Arcods. Strange. Where could they be?

Barlos glanced at Atticus. "You all stay here. I want to scout the senate." He dashed off on his own.

Atticus' stomach churned. He hoped Barlos would not get spotted. He peered up at the cloudless sky.

Meg leaned against the brick wall and moaned.

Daria glanced at her. "You okay, Meg?"

Meg nodded. "Aye, just tired of waiting."

Lena and Daria glanced at one another.

Lena bent down. "Meg, we are most definitely going into battle territory. Do you have fighting skills?"

Atticus glanced over. That was true. Knowing their luck, they would have to fight through a million Arcods. He could not lose Meg. She was his only hope for finding the sapphire shard. He strode over and stood next to Lena. "She's right, Meg. What skills do you have?"

Meg stared at him and Lena. "Aye, my father taught me a few tricks with a sword."

Lena unclipped one of her swords from her belt. "Strap this around your shoulder. It's a smaller blade, but with your size, it'll be perfect."

Meg grinned and took the weapon.

Atticus strode to Daria, who peeked around the side of the building. "Any sign of Barlos?"

Daria stepped back. "Nothing. I hope he's okay."

Atticus stared at his sister. He hoped so, too; they could not afford to lose anyone.

A few minutes later, Barlos returned. "I found some

Arcods. Roughly ten are walking the perimeter of the senate, and another eight are at the front doors. I also spotted a caravan of wheeled cages on the other side. They may have plans to relocate the citizens."

Relocate? Relocate them to where?

Zane stepped into the conversation. "There's no place in this city to relocate them. Unless they are bringing the prisoners to Luvanasis."

Atticus shivered. Was it the thought of being a prisoner or the breeze which rushed through a hole in the building? "Barlos, do you have a plan of attack?"

Barlos rubbed his beard and stared at the senate. "Aye, I do. We need to climb to the top of the senate building. The glass above the front door is shattered, so we will go in through there."

Atticus inspected the senate building. It stood about twenty feet high, and bricks jutted out unevenly all the way to the top. "And we do this without being spotted?"

Barlos nodded.

Atticus and his companions sprinted to the pronged fence. Then they crouched low and crept around to the opened fence gate. Atticus peered between the bars.

Three Arcods patrolled the grounds inside the fence, dragging their arms as they shuffled along. Fortunately, the creatures moved away from them.

Atticus glanced behind at the others. "I suggest we split up. Some of us climb the roof and go inside, while the rest stay out here."

"Agreed," Barlos said.

Zane crawled to the front beside Atticus. "I'm going in."

Atticus poked his head around the corner a second time. As he checked out the situation, someone tapped him from behind. He turned to find Meg beside him.

"I think I can help," she said. "The thieves taught me how to swipe things. If these prisoners are locked up, the

149

keys are likely on a commander's belt."

Atticus nodded. "If you are willing to risk this, Zane and I will be right beside you."

Lena crawled forward. "As will I."

Meg took a breath as if gathering courage and crawled forward with Lena.

"Now!" Atticus commanded, his voice a whisper. He charged to the senate building, grabbed hold of a brick, and scaled the wall. Once he reached the top, he helped the others.

Now on the roof, they crawled to the front of the building, fighting against a strong wind. There on the roof, a towering statue of a warrior stood above the city streets.

Atticus approached the statue, appreciating the fine craftsmanship. Aside from the unusual height, it looked so real. Atticus inched past the statue and leaned over the rooftop.

Arcods stood on either side of the door. Just below him, no more than a five-foot drop, was an open window with a ledge. Perfect. It was just big enough for someone to stand on. He pushed himself back and leaned on the leg of the statue. "We can drop just over the edge. From there, we can climb up to the window. That's our way in."

Lena smirked. "You make it sound so easy, Atticus."

Atticus crawled forward first and looked down. He turned around and maneuvered himself over the edge. His heart pounded, and he wished the wind would settle down. He'd better make the drop. They all needed to make the drop. He released his hands. Then he landed, wobbled on the ledge, and thankfully caught his balance. Relieved, he looked up. Lena was next. At least now that he was down, he could assist her.

Lena dropped, landing perfectly on the ledge. Meg dropped second, followed by Zane. One at a time, they helped each other climb up to the window and into the senate building.

Now they stood on a wide windowsill inside, overlooking a huge foyer. Stone columns spaced apart held the roof firmly. Statues and benches sat between some of the columns, while others connected to walls with doors leading to meeting rooms. The dim lighting and their distance from the floor prevented them from seeing much more than a couple of Arcods below.

Zane twiddled his fingers and gazed around the building. He shook his head, probably remembering some old memory of being here. He pointed to tall wooden doors seven to nine pillars away. "That leads to the center room. It has enough seating for the representatives of twelve kingdoms to gather yearly and discuss politics."

Meg rolled her eyes at the word "politics."

Atticus looked at the door. A chain with a lock was weaved around the door handles. "They must be holding the prisoners there." They were too high to jump. How would they get down?

They had little to work with. Several items lined the walls at roughly the same height: flagpoles, carved faces, and a ledge with a banner that draped down to about ten feet above the floor. He could think of no other way down than to try to reach the banner.

Atticus motioned to the group. "Follow my lead. We'll use that banner, the red-and-yellow one by that flat statue. That's how we'll get down." He pointed.

Atticus took the lead. He crouched, held tight to the thin ledge, and scooted across the windowsill. Then he grabbed one of the flag poles and swung like an acrobat until he picked up momentum to leap for the nearest carved face hanging on the wall. Hands tingling and sweating like mad, he swung like a monkey to the next face, repeating the process until he arrived at the ledge with the banner. He pulled himself up and leaned against the wall to catch his breath. Lena, Meg, and Zane followed.

Atticus huffed and wiped sweat off his brow. "Good job,

everyone. We managed not to fall."

Placing one foot in front of the other, Atticus and the other three stepped to the opposite side of the ledge. A lantern hung on a stone beam above the door below them. On closer inspection, he noticed a tiny crack running across the beam. Praying it would not break, Atticus jumped down three feet to the beam.

As he landed, the beam shifted a bit, and his foot slipped. Adrenaline kicking in, he slapped a hand to the wall and regained his balance. He looked down at the floor, plotting his next move. Could he leap from here safely? He didn't want anyone to jump from this height and risk breaking an ankle. They needed one more base, something between the beam and the floor.

A shelf stood next to the door, filled with books and antiques. It looked fairly sturdy and wide enough for their purposes.

Just then, the door below the beam swung open. Directly under his feet, two Arcods in armor trudged out of the room. Atticus stood still and held his breath, hoping those horrid creatures would keep their eyes forward and not turn their focus on him. The sound of keys jingling caught his ear. The Arcods marched down the hall.

Once they rounded the corner, Atticus hopped to the shelf, bumping books, which slid to the edge but did not fall. *Phew!* Then he jumped down to the floor, looked back at the others, and waved them down.

Lena went first, the others following, jumping from beam to shelf to floor.

The second Zane's feet hit the floor, they sprinted to the other end of the hall and split up. Some went behind a pillar, and the others a nearby statue. Atticus peered around the pillar. The commanders had turned around and now stomped towards them.

"They're coming this way," Atticus whispered to Meg. "You know what to do."

Meg exhaled and glanced down, her black hair hiding her freckled face.

"Meg, don't be scared," Atticus said. "We're right here with you. Just imagine how proud your father will be when he hears how helpful you've been."

Meg raised her head, the look in her eyes changing from fear to confidence. She sneaked around Atticus and scurried to the next pillar.

The commanders came closer and closer. She plugged her nose from their stench. The moment they passed her pillar, she slipped around the other side and tiptoed up behind them. She inched closer to them, crouched lower, and with one swipe, snatched the keys. Then she darted back to the pillar.

Atticus and the others ducked low as the commanders passed them. The moment they were out of view, Atticus, Zane, and Lena dashed to Meg. Then the four ran to the next pillar and the next. They came to the final pillar, only inches from the locked door. Atticus turned to see no sign of the commanders. Perhaps they had gone into a room or turned down the hall.

They dashed for the locked door. Meg's hands trembled as she slid the key in and turned it. The lock clicked.

Atticus and Lena pulled at the chains, which then clanged on the floor. Atticus cringed at the noise and glanced over his shoulder to see if any Arcods noticed.

Zane pushed open the doors, his eyes filling with tears. "My fellow citizens of Maljooi, we have come to set you free."

Atticus came up beside him. Hundreds of men, women, and children filled the room, all squished together, some standing, others sitting.

Zane grasped Atticus by the shoulder. "This is him. This is the chosen one, the one we have been waiting for."

Atticus glanced at Zane, anxiety filling him. How would they safely get all these Bonvidians out?

Lena paced forward. "I hate to be the bearer of bad news, but we have to go. Two commanders are heading back this way."

"Everyone, follow us." Atticus motioned. "If you have anything to use as a weapon, use it." He unsheathed his sword, turned around, and charged forward. The citizens hurried along behind him.

As the commanders turned the corner and saw the crowd, their bulging eyes almost fell out of their heads in shock. One of the commanders blew a warning horn. Seconds later, Arcods burst out from every door.

Atticus raced to the front door and shoved it open. The sunlight streaming between clouds blinded him for a moment.

Ahead of him, Barlos, Daria, and Victor battled the Arcods that were patrolling the grounds. Weapons flashed in every direction, and arrows soared through the air, some sticking into Arcods.

Victor sprinted to Atticus and the others.

Leading the crowd, Lena pointed to the streets. "Go! You're free! Find shelter!"

The citizens of Maljooi dispersed through the courtyard and streets. Some grabbed weapons from fallen Arcods. Those that fled returned shortly with weapons that the Arcods must have tossed when they were rounding everyone up.

Victor jumped onto a ledge just outside the doors. "Bonvidians of Maljooi, I advise you to take to the tunnels. Make haste to Old El-Valr. There you will find some of my soldiers."

As the freed Bonvidians dispersed, the doors of the senate building flew open, and an Arcod commander bolted outside. A troop of Arcods followed him, ready to attack.

The commander lifted his sword and swung at Victor's

back, drawing closer to him. From the crowd, a Bonvidian—no, it was Lena! She raced up behind the commander and wrapped her blue arms around him, pinning his long arms to his sides. The commander struggled, hefting his weight from one side to the other. Just then, he freed himself and turned on her, swinging his sword high. The two of them grappled with the sword. It flailed high and then low, and then blood sprayed out from between them. Who was hit?

Another Arcod commander rushed up, swinging at Atticus, drawing his attention away from the bloody scene. Then the first commander emerged from the fighting crowd, also heading Atticus' way.

"There are too many of them!" Zane shouted, swinging his sword at the nearest Arcod.

The two commanders charged at Atticus with saw-like swords in their claws. One swung high while the other swung low.

His mind fought, trying to remember all the sword training from his time in the well. He pivoted to the side, swinging his sword and managing to knock one sword from an Arcod.

Daria stood in the distance and repeatedly fired arrows at one of the commanders until it collapsed.

The commander Atticus fought had retrieved the sword that Atticus had knocked out of its hand and advanced.

Atticus leaped back and blocked the strike. Then he lunged forward and impaled the Arcod on its lower side.

It growled in pain, one hand going to its side, the other clawing at Atticus' neck.

Atticus ducked and swung high, cutting off its hand.

The commander's sword clattered to the ground, and the creature let out an ear-piercing shriek. The shriek made the other Arcods, who were fighting the civilians, freeze. The battle stopped for a moment, everyone silent.

The bulging eyes of the Arcods all shifted to Atticus.

Atticus raised the Sword of Bonvida high into the air and exhaled, readying himself for a final strike against the commander.

From behind the commander, another sword claimed the kill. Zane stood over the body, his sword covered in Arcod blood. "That's for taking my city hostage."

After the death of their commanders, the Arcods scurried off like beetles and climbed the surrounding fence, escaping out of the city.

Atticus lowered his sword, pride filling him as he stared at Zane.

"Oh no!" Daria grabbed Atticus' shoulder from behind. Then she took off, sprinting across the battlefield to Victor. Victor crouched by a figure that Atticus could not make out from a distance.

Fearing the worst, he sheathed his sword and chased after Daria.

Victor sat on his knees, holding Lena's hand. Tears rolled down his face. He let go of her hand and stood up, but then he collapsed against Barlos, who steadied him.

Sadness replacing feelings of victory, Atticus crouched and stared at Lena's lifeless body. *Why did this have to happen?*

Chapter 23

Everything around him seemed to have stopped. Atticus paced to Lena and dropped to his knees, transfixed by her frozen stare, wishing to see movement—the rise and fall of her chest, a blink of her eye—but Lena's body lay as lifeless as a rock. Lena was dead. His mind tried to wrap around this loss. Though he knew this mission would challenge them all, he never seriously considered the possibility of any of them dying. What if he died before saving Bonvida? He shook the thoughts from his mind and stood.

Running a hand through his silver hair, Victor turned to face them. "She saved my life."

Barlos wiped his nose and kicked a dead Arcod. "What do you wish to do with her body?"

Daria stared at the sky, tears streaming down her face. Zane stood a few feet from her, glancing from one person to another as if unsure how to show emotion—or unable.

Victor bit his lip. "We have to leave it here with the others."

Atticus' heart ached at those words. Poor Victor. He could not even give her a burial.

Meg strode towards them, crossing the battlefield with her eyes leveled on the group, as if trying to avoid looking at the bodies on the ground. Once her gaze found Lena, her face dropped. She stepped back and turned away, her eyes closing.

Daria went to comfort her.

Victor bent down and closed Lena's eyes. "Rest in peace. I'll be sure to tell your family of your heroic end." He crouched near her body for a few moments, then cleared his throat and wiped the sorrow from his face. His eyes now held a look of grim desperation. "We must go."

Atticus nodded. Devastation threatened every corner of

Bonvida, and they alone could stop it.

Zane led the group out of the senate courtyard and through the crowded streets towards the arched gates of the city.

"Wait!" a voice cried from behind, rising above the panicked and sorrowful noises of the crowds bumbling around them.

Atticus and the group turned as a woman and man weaved past a mother and her children.

Zane stopped in his tracks and spun around, a smile stretching across his face. "Mother, Uncle." He pushed the group aside and ran into their arms.

Zane's mother grabbed his cheeks. "You've grown. I am so proud of you, Zane. Look at you, a historian turned swordsman. Oh my, Zane, you're making history. You're living all those stories you read."

"It's not quite the adventure I would've planned for myself," he said, his gaze shifting from them to a ragged group passing by. "So much loss."

"But you will help bring an end to it. Now go back out there and help the chosen one defeat this darkness." She kissed his cheek.

His uncle stepped forward. "Your father would be proud of you."

Zane dipped his head and drew a deep breath through his nose. "I'll be back when our mission is complete."

Atticus and the others waved to his mother and uncle. Then Zane, with his chin held high and chest thrust out, led Atticus and his companions through the streets. Some civilians patted their backs, and others bowed their heads in thanks, while children waved.

The busy streets became less crowded as Atticus and his companions neared the squared archway of the city gates. The chatter and excitement from the civilians faded as they stepped under the stone-crafted arch and onto the path they needed to take for the next stage of their mission. Pleased that they had saved the city of Maljooi,

Atticus was filled with a sense of pride, but sorrow over Lena's death lingered.

With each stride, the city appeared smaller and finally vanished in the distance. Atticus and his companions trekked down a smooth, level path, mountain ranges visible to either side of them. Before long, they rounded a turn and came upon a boulder cluster not far off the path—a perfect spot for a rest.

While Daria, Victor, and Meg rummaged through their bags, Atticus pulled out his map and compass. "The Greystone Mountains are at the far end of Bonvida. Zane, you said that's where the ruby shard is."

Zane handed him a jar of nuts. "Aye, the ruby is there."

Atticus tipped the jar and spilled nuts into his hand. "Excellent!"

Zane sighed and looked up at the blue sky. "Listen, there's something I never mentioned before."

Atticus turned his full attention to Zane, sensing bad news coming their way.

Zane sat up straight. "Luvanasis' escape from Calsriv wasn't done by him."

Daria lifted one eyebrow.

"What do you mean?" Barlos hopped onto one of the boulders.

Zane's ears turned red, and his cheeks flushed. "Someone had to release him. Someone from *Bonvida* had to release him." He glanced at Atticus. "On the boat, you asked about the other descendants. And I mentioned Shiesta, the one who betrayed your grandfather, the one whose bloodline connects to Luvanasis. He is her child." He took a long breath. "Well, Luvanasis has a descendant who has carried on the dark descendant bloodline."

Atticus shook his head, his mind scrambling to understand what Zane had just said. "So, Luvanasis has a descendant roaming around Bonvida. And whoever this

Bonvidian is, they're the one responsible for setting Luvanasis and the darkness free."

Zane sighed. "Correct."

Atticus leaned his head back. "How could this be?"

Zane opened his mouth once more, but no words came out.

Atticus glared at him. "What else, Zane?"

Zane rubbed the back of his head. "Well . . . if the stories prove true, then Luvanasis brought with him The Sword of Darkness."

Atticus lowered his eyebrows, wishing he had learned this vital information sooner. "The Sword of Darkness?"

Daria sat up straight at the mere name. She gazed at Meg, who sat silently listening.

Victor gripped his sword and stared at Barlos.

Zane huffed. "Aye, it's a dangerous weapon, so dangerous that it's told to be the only thing that can awaken She Serpent from her slumber . . . but only when it is right in front of her. Thankfully I have discovered no records of her anywhere, so I say we are safe for now."

Atticus sighed. One problem at a time. "Thank you, Zane. I wish you had told us sooner. I'm sure you have your reasons for waiting."

"Oh, lookie here," Victor said, waving a loaf in the air. "I still have some bread from our dinner on the ship."

Victor divided the remaining bread amongst the group and sat beside Atticus. "So, which route are we taking, Atticus?"

Atticus accepted a piece of the stale bread and bit into it. Fine cheese from Valindin would go well with the bread. Even just a blob of butter or berry jam would have pleased his pallet. He swallowed his food and pointed to the map. "Our safest route would be through the Woodlands. It's not the best terrain, but I would rather walk through the sheltered hills and the woods than be out in the open."

Daria popped her head between him and the prince. "The Woodlands it is, then. But we also need to fetch some arrows. I'm running low."

After their rest, they continued down the Maljooi path, taking in the cool breeze from the mountains around them.

Meg glanced in every direction. "Do you hear that?" She put a hand to her ear.

The wind carried a low rumble, barely audible over their footfalls.

"Those are the echoes of the Giants in Giant country walking and talking to one another," Zane said.

Victor and Barlos both bowed their heads looking grieved. "A few months after Luvanasis' attack," Victor finally said, "the Giants tried to fight back, but the Arcods overthrew them, leaving many to die." Victor shook his head and then told them more about other kingdoms and how they tried to defend their gates against the darkness.

The conversation lifted after a bit, turning to how much they all missed different festivals and occasions that they'd traditionally celebrated. That turned into a discussion about different cultures of the kingdoms and islands. They talked about which of the three seasons they liked best and how each celebrated Winter's Moon at the change of the year cycle.

Zane and Victor chuckled at the idea that both of them would have attended the Winter Moon senate meeting. The conversation moved to the weather, how only a day or two ago they struggled through the heat of the desert, but now they enjoyed the cool of the mountains.

As the sun neared midday, their conversations trailed off, and everyone walked in silence.

A gust of wind picked up, tousling Daria's dark hair. She moved a strand from her eye, turning her gaze towards an endless pasture of grass some distance ahead.

Atticus picked up his pace, the pasture expanding in his sight. A mesa off to the right would make a great place to camp. As Atticus scanned the lay of the land to his left, his heart skipped a beat.

A great onslaught of Arcods headed their way, their deformed bodies identifiable even at a distance.

"Make for cover!" Atticus motioned to the others and made ready to bolt in the direction of the mesa.

Before he could take a step, Arcods trudged out from behind the mesa and every nearby boulder. They were surrounded. The smell of so many Arcods made him woozy. As the Arcods closed in, dozens of wheeled cages rumbled into sight. Bonvidian prisoners clung to the bars, watching the attack unfold.

Daria pulled the young Meg closer, like an older sister would do.

Victor grunted and gripped the hilt of his sword.

Barlos limbered up.

A group of Arcods stepped aside, and a thin older woman in an olive tunic strode from the midst of them. On her shoulder perched a raven with four red-tipped strands.

Atticus recognized the bird. He had seen it at the beginning of their journey when he and Daria had left home. Had it been in the desert too? Had it been spying on them?

The woman pressed forward, striding as if she owned the plains. In one hand, she held a dagger. "This is the end of your quest."

Undaunted, Atticus stepped closer. "Who are you?"

The woman chuckled. "You might as well know. My name is Raia. This can go one of two ways. You surrender, and we nicely toss you into that cage over there." She pointed to the cage behind her as two heavy Arcods dragged it forward. Two figures huddled in the corner of the cage.

Raia strode closer to Atticus. "Or we can fight, and maybe more of you die."

Atticus gripped the hilt of his sword, readying himself for another fight. At least a hundred Arcods surrounded them. They did not stand a chance.

Barlos stepped to his side. "Don't engage, Atticus. There are far too many of them."

She stared at Atticus as he let go of his sword. "Wise choice, Atticus, our lovely chosen one."

Atticus' pulse elevated as he stared Raia down, hoping to frighten her. "Are you the dark descendant?"

"Maybe." Raia waved her dagger then turned to nearby Arcods. She pointed at the cage behind her. "Arcods, toss them all in there."

The heavy Arcods trudged forward. "Their weapons, madame?" one of them grunted.

Raia's gaze shifted to the group, as if she only just realized that they were armed. "I don't think they'd be dumb enough to use them. But this one"—she pointed to Atticus—"take his sword. It is much too valuable."

The Arcod strode up to Atticus, and its dangling claws opened.

Atticus turned his head from the smell and looked down at his weapon, clenching his jaw. "If you want this sword, you'll have to take it off my corpse."

Raia stormed closer, fire in her eyes. She glared at the group, marched to Daria, and lifted her dagger to Daria's neck. "Then she dies. I know she means something to you. My raven saw you by the river."

Atticus raised his hands. Defeat stirred within him.

Raia lowered her blade, paced back to Atticus, and unhooked his sheath. She strapped it around her shoulder. "You, commander! Take this sword and put it in the cage with the other weapons we've collected."

She passed the Sword of Bonvida to the Arcod commander, who then trudged to a smaller cage in the distance.

Two by two, the Arcods shoved Atticus and his friends into the cage. Atticus' head slammed against a steel bar. As he settled himself, he turned to the old Bonvidian man and woman huddling in the corner. The man had a hefty beard, twice the size of Barlos'. The woman lay covered in a bulky wool blanket with only her pale face and dark hair showing.

The army of Arcods gathered in sloppy formation and started off, marching to El-Valr. The cage wobbled and bumped up and down as the two massive Arcods pulled it along.

Daria peered through the bars, her hair bouncing from the movement of the cage. "Well, might as well catch up on sleep, then we can figure a way out of this rut."

Atticus slumped under the heavy weight of failure. How could he have been so stupid? He should have known. This could not be the end, could it? There had to be a way out. They had escaped and fought through so much already. If only he had realized that the bird had been spying on them, sent by the enemy army. His throat choked up. He closed his eyes and rested his head back against the bars.

"Atticus," the big-bearded man said, his voice raspy.

He turned to the man and woman in the corner of the cage.

"Atticus, we knew your father. We were good friends," the man said.

"You knew my father? How is that possible?"

"Your father was one of the warriors. When Bonvida was attacked, Sofos sent us"—he pointed to himself and the woman—"here to Bonvida. You can call me Hark."

The woman pushed the blanket aside and sat up. "I am

Hara." She glanced around. "You still have shards to find. And you can not do any finding if you're a prisoner to this darkness."

She moved the rest of the blanket to reveal a shield, which she then picked up and handed to Atticus. "This was your father's shield. He left it behind, but it is rightfully yours."

His limbs tingled, and the burden of being captured lifted. Atticus stared at the white shield. He reached for his sheath but then stopped. The Arcods had taken it from him and put it in the small, wheeled cage that trailed along behind them. His sword outshined all the other weapons, making it easy to spot from here. Wondering how he would get his sword back, he strapped the shield over his shoulder.

"Wake your companions, and we will open this cage," Hark said.

As the cart rolled through open green fields, it neared a cluster of trees by a river. Atticus shook his friends awake.

"Atticus, what is it?" Daria yawned.

Atticus pointed to Hark and Hara. "These two are warriors. They're here to set us free."

Hark nodded at Victor. "Prince Victor, we will send word and begin to gather our armies."

Victor squeezed Barlos' shoulder, smiling with relief.

Zane rubbed his thumb against his finger nervously. "How? I understand you are warriors, but cutting through these bars would be impossible."

Hark grinned. "You're logical, friend. But don't you worry." He pointed to a cleft mesa that they should reach in about ten minutes. "The Arcods will need to march in single file to pass through. When they do, they'll pull the cages to the side and let the army go first." He shrugged his shoulders. "A handful may stand back, but we will use this to our advantage." He glanced at Atticus.

Hara smiled and shoved the blanket aside. "We've been cutting an escape hole. One at a time, we will slip through. You all must run to the patch of trees by the river, the one we just passed. Understand?"

Atticus glanced at the others.

They all agreed with the plan.

"I just need to finish cutting the last edge. It will only take a minute," Hara said.

One minute passed, then five, then eight, and finally, they neared the mesa. The Arcods dragging the carts—including their cart—pulled off to the side. A group of about twenty Arcods and Raia with her raven stepped to the side too. She glared at their cage. The remaining Arcods grumbled at one another, then one shoved another. Raia marched forward as if to settle their dispute.

"Now! Crawl under the cages and run. Run and don't look back," Hark said in a low voice just as Hara pushed the bottom of the cage out.

"Daria and Meg first," Atticus said.

Daria dropped down, followed by Meg.

Before Atticus crawled into the hole, Hark grabbed his shoulder. "In the ruins of Altigoran, you'll find a misplaced knight statue. Under it is a passageway to Advo."

Atticus nodded. Having no time to thank them, he climbed through the hole in the bottom of the cage and onto hardpacked earth. Daria and Meg had already crawled under the next cage.

The echo of Raia shouting at Arcods brought relief. With her focus on the Arcods, she wouldn't notice them.

Atticus peered out, seeing only a few nearby Arcod feet, then hurried to the next cage. They crawled under the line of cages, moving from one to the other, waiting a moment between each to avoid being seen. With only three more cages to go, Atticus peered behind to make sure everyone was following him.

Raia's voice quieted in the wind. They had to go faster. Any second now, she would return to her post and see their empty cage.

They reached the last cage. Fields stretched out before them, the cluster of trees a good hike away. One at a time, they crept out and crouched low to the ground. When all six were together, Atticus pointed to the trees. "Keep going. I have to get my sword."

Daria shook her head and quivered. "I'm not leaving you, Atticus, not again."

Victor stepped in, grabbing hold of Daria's hand and turning her to face him. "I've got you, Daria. And he'll be right behind us."

She took a deep breath, nodded, and sprinted off with the others.

Atticus crawled back under the cages. The weapons cage was back two, so he had to go fast. He crawled and counted, "One . . . two." Then he rolled out, sprang up, and stared into the cage.

His sheathed sword lay on a heap of other swords in the middle of the cage. He slid his arm between bars, wrapped three fingers around the strap, and yanked. He dragged it halfway, but then it caught on the hilt of another sword, so he lifted and tugged and maneuvered it past the obstacle. And finally . . . out of the cage.

Just then, an Arcod came around one of the carts.

Having no time to dive under the cage, he took a deep breath and darted out past the cages. Then he sprinted across the field just as the others reached the trees by the river.

Seconds later, a signal horn blew.

Running like mad, Atticus shot a glimpse behind him.

Arcods scattered across the area, searching for them. The horn blew a second time.

This time, the raven flew towards him, and Raia and the Arcods were on his tail, though quite a way back.

Gasping for air, Atticus reached the river. Raia and the Arcods were far behind. His friends had crossed the river.

"Atticus, let's go!" Daria waved for him to cross over.

Meg pointed to scattered stones in the river.

Atticus nodded and then hopped along the slippery stones to the other side.

Daria rushed to him and squeezed him. Then she let him go and held him by the shoulders. "Don't ever do that again."

He clipped the sheath to his belt. "I won't. I hope."

"We best get a move on." Barlos threw a glance down the river, indicating Raia and her Arcods as they raced closer. "They haven't given up."

"Come on," Atticus said, leading the way. They pressed on to the Woodlands.

Chapter 24

Evening took over the eastern sky as the sun neared the horizon. Atticus and his companions rested acres away from a thicket of thin trees. None of them had seen Raia and her Arcods for a while now. The river must have slowed them down, but they'd catch up before long.

Atticus opened his flask and sipped water. He wiped his mouth and then pointed to the trees. "The Woodlands. We're almost there."

From what Atticus remembered about the Woodlands, it stretched across the land, some of it flat, but much of it hilly with steep inclines and even swamps. The Royal Path cut through the center of the Woodlands. And at the farthest end was the Twisted Trail.

Daria stretched to one side and then to the other. "How much further, would you say?"

Barlos hiccupped as he closed his flask. "I say we'll get there by the time the whole sky is dark."

Atticus scanned their surroundings. Off to the far left, a towering barrier surrounded a sloping landscape. "Is that the crater?"

Zane glanced, a grin on his face. "Aye, the crater, and within it stands the chamber that Desmond and his followers built."

Victor stepped closer. "Only descendants can enter, though, right?"

Zane patted Victor on the shoulder. "Aye, Prince."

Daria pushed her hair off one shoulder. "Must be amazing inside."

A desire to see it tugged at Atticus, but now was not the time. He had shards to collect. "Let's press on. We can rest again once we enter the Woodlands." He led the march across the grassy plains. They trekked through ravaged farmlands, picking up any remaining food they could find.

The air chilled, and the sky grew darker. Raia and the Arcods would have little chance of finding them in the dark.

Atticus and the others stepped between thin trees on the edge of the Woodlands. The chirping of crickets and the occasional hoot of an owl filled the woods.

Barlos leaned against one of the thin trees and peered back the way they had come. "Atticus, do you think our friends lost track of us?"

Exhausted from the long hike, Atticus sat on the grass. "I hope so." He had put his companions through so much danger already. He hoped the Woodlands would provide safe travels.

Daria searched in her bag. "Should we make camp for the night?"

Atticus got up and stared out into the darkness of the Woodlands but could make out only the nearest trees. He would not want to make the trek in the dark of night. Curious to know the time, he took a few paces to the edge of the woods and gazed at stars and a crescent moon. He guessed that it was just after eight o'clock. By the time they set up their tents and ate whatever food they had left, it would be close to ten. "Aye, we should."

Daria smirked and tapped Meg asking if she could help with the fire.

Ten o'clock rolled by quickly as he and the others sat around a campfire, eating the last of their nuts and dried fruit. "Do we have anything else?" Zane asked.

Daria set a glass jar down. "Afraid not. On the bright side, I'm sure these woods are filled with food we can gather. Maybe tomorrow we will hunt and cook some nice meat."

As the night deepened, Atticus used his tunic as a pillow, his eyes closing. Fear of being attacked by Raia and the Arcods slipped from his thoughts as he drifted to sleep. He did not stir again until sunbeams pierced through the canopy of leaves and found Atticus' face.

Birds chirped and flapped from one tree to another. Atticus stretched and sat up. He unrolled his tunic and pulled it over himself. Then he glanced out at the plains and saw movement. He rubbed his eyes and reached for his flask but turned once more to the plains.

Something marched their way. Raia, her raven, and a unit of Arcods had found them. They had twenty minutes at most. "Wake up! Wake up! They're here. We have to go!"

Everyone sprang up and packed their belongings within minutes.

Barlos grabbed his blue metallic monocular and peered into the distance. "That's her all right, and she has quite the parade behind her."

Atticus and the others finished packing their belongings.

"Bring only what is necessary," Barlos said.

They grabbed their bags and weapons and sprinted deeper into the woods, weaving between trees and bushes and leaping over fallen logs. They climbed a steep incline, using roots and stones for footholds and support. Once Atticus reached the top, he turned and helped Meg, yanking her up the final few feet.

Then he noticed something moving through the trees back the way they'd come. His heart beat faster, and his adrenaline kicked in.

Daria nudged him, encouraging him to get moving. They had no time to rest or even to check the proximity of the Arcods.

Atticus and the others dashed off, ducking under fallen branches and diving deeper into the woods. After a ten-minute jog, Atticus, who had gotten ahead of the others, slid to a stop. Pebbles and dirt skittered down a deep cleft in the hill. The gap, too wide to step over, stretched across their path and to either side.

Daria peered down and then jerked back as if afraid to lose her balance. "What now?"

Assessing the distance to be about three yards, Atticus backed up for a running start. "We jump."

Zane chuckled. "Jump! That's risky. What if we don't make it?"

"I'll go first," Barlos said, coming to Atticus' side. "Jump towards me, and I'll catch you if you slip."

Before either one made a move, the sound of growling Arcods traveled to them.

"We don't have much time." Atticus readied himself to sprint. "If we do jump, we go now."

Barlos made the first move, charging to the very edge, then leaping over the gap. He landed with a thud on the other side, turned to the others, and motioned for the next one to go.

"I don't think I can do that," Meg said, anxiety in her eyes.

Daria grasped her shoulder. "Meg, you swiped a key from an Arcod. You can do this. Let's get back a good distance, then run for it and jump. Barlos will catch you."

Without waiting another second, probably not wanting to think about possible consequences, Meg did just as Daria suggested. She backed up several yards, bolted towards the gap, and with a grunt, leaped through the air. She landed at Barlos' feet, flinging herself forward, and he pulled her to safety. Victor and Daria raced forward at the same time, making the leap seem effortless. Zane hesitated, turning back a few times, then he raced forward somewhat awkwardly and hurled himself into the air. He landed just barely on the edge, but Barlos was ready for him and pulled him to safety in one smooth move.

As Atticus crouched before taking off, a strong odor tickled his nose, and the growling came again. Louder.

Closer. Too close! He sucked in a breath, sprinted to the gap, and leaped. He landed on the edge and fell onto his knees, then rolled clear of the drop, getting dirt all over him.

Growls and guttural complaints filled the air. More than a dozen Arcods stood on the opposite side of the cleft. Some slammed the ground with their feet, while others slashed the air with their claws. In the next instant, one of the Arcods leaped across the gap and landed near Meg with a gust of fowl air.

Atticus rushed forward, unsheathing his sword, and stabbed the Arcod before it could make another move. It fell back into the gap.

The other Arcods growled and backed up, making ready for the jump.

"Run!" Atticus said, sheathing his sword. He led the way, sprinting to the sound of Arcod's pounding the ground right on their heels. Arcod breath tingled up his spine. They were too close to these dangling-arm beasts.

Atticus drew his sword, stopped short, and turned swinging.

His companions followed suit. Barlos cracked one Arcod into another. Meg, keeping close to Barlos for safety, wielded a sword. Daria, standing at a distance, loosed one arrow and then another.

The Arcod nearest Atticus fell at his feet, an arrow sticking from its neck. As another Arcod lunged for him, Atticus swung his shield forward and smacked it in the face, making it stagger back. When it lunged a second time, Atticus stabbed it with his sword.

A dozen Arcods now surrounded them.

Pushing forward to overcome the final threat, Atticus lunged at the nearest Arcod, then pivoted to the next, striking an Arcod with each movement until he and the others defeated the final one.

Relieved and trying to catch his breath, Atticus wiped his sword on a patch of grass and slid it into the sheath.

Barlos paced over to him. "Ah-ah, let me help you."

Barlos unlatched the sheath and strapped it around Atticus' shoulder. He then grabbed Atticus' shield and clipped it onto the sheath. He patted his back. "There you go."

Atticus glanced over his shoulder to see what Barlos had done. A thought shot through his mind. Where were Raia and the raven? Were they still tracking them? Had they taken another route or given up altogether?

"That must've been the last of 'em for now," Victor said, pulling Atticus out of his train of thought.

Daria glanced at her quiver, which held only about seven arrows now. "Let's hope." She stepped through the fallen Arcod bodies and tugged an arrow free from one.

Atticus stood for a moment and scanned the trees on every side. No obvious path ran through the woods. Nothing looked familiar. They were very much lost.

"Which way do we go?" Meg peered into the woods too.

Having no idea which direction to take, Atticus marched towards the trees with less undergrowth. "This way, for now."

They trekked through the Woodlands for hours, only stopping to rest for brief moments. When they passed a bush filled with berries, Daria half-filled a jar. The berries would not last long, but at least they had something.

After walking through dense trees and overgrown shrubs for so long, the trees finally thinned out ahead. Atticus picked up his pace, his eyes on a sunnier section a good five minutes away. The others trailed behind him. They trudged closer and then stumbled through the thin treeline onto a sunny path. They had made it to the Royal Path.

"I would say we are now about halfway through the

woods," Barlos said. He stared up and down the dirt path and then waved for them to proceed. After they crossed the path, they climbed up an incline.

Atticus' legs ached. His friends seemed drained of energy too.

The top of the incline overlooked an expanse of trees, everything bushy and green. Dark grey clouds moved over them. At that moment, a raindrop plopped onto his head. He and the group descended a treeless slope. With each passing step, the rain fell heavier. In the sudden downpour, Atticus figured this must be what it's like to stand under a waterfall.

A rumble of thunder sounded above them, and lightning flashed moments later. The slope leveled out just as another crash of thunder and spark of light filled the sky. With their cloaks over their heads, they ran from tree to tree.

As the storm continued, Meg shouted, "Look! There." She pointed to a rock formation between evergreens and a little cave opening in the middle of it.

They raced each other to the natural shelter. They had to duck to get in but could stand easily once inside. The cave went back only a little way but enough for them to avoid the spray of rain as the wind shifted.

"We can finally dry off," Zane said, trying to find a place to sit.

Daria stood by the entrance, wringing water from her hair. "At least we're cleaner."

The rain continued for the rest of the day and through the night. Meg and Victor grabbed dry leaves and branches that had gathered along the edges of the cave, and Daria used her flint and started a fire. Everyone huddled around, keeping warm and letting their clothes dry.

Atticus grabbed the map of Bonvida from his back

pocket. As he unfolded it, he accidentally tore it in half and found the ink smudged. He sighed out of frustration. They were somewhere in the Woodlands but had no idea which way to go, and now the map was damaged.

A flash of lightning lit up the area. Zane peered through the sheet of rain outside the cave. "Prince, isn't the El-Valr royal graveyard around these parts?"

Victor shook his head. "Not anymore. My father's first wife, Damien's mother, Queen—"

Barlos shoved Victor's shoulder. "You know better than to speak that woman's name out loud, as per your father's decree."

Victor glanced at Daria and bit his lip with embarrassment.

Zane tilted his head, his eyes opening wide in confusion.

Atticus glanced at the prince. Victor's father, King Arldin, married twice? And his oldest brother was only his half-brother, the son of the first queen? So he and Raldon were the sons of the second.

The rain ceased by morning, so they hunted for breakfast and headed back to their path. Despite the lack of wind, tree branches swayed and creaked now and then, especially further down the path. As time went on, the path led them through strange trees with long, twisting branches that stretched overhead, forming an archway.

"Ah-ha! This is the twisted path. I took it once, long ago. It's a full day's hike," Barlos said.

The trees grew denser over time and the overhead archway thicker, blocking out much of the sunlight, but the steady birdsong and an occasional appearance of birds kept the mood light. A squirrel hopped onto the trail ahead of them, glanced their way, and scurried back under a berry bush. They'd only passed a few berry bushes and fruit trees so far.

Daria reached into a bush and picked a few mint leaves.

She probably wanted to make mint tea, her favorite.

As the day carried on, the path split in different directions, one turning right, another left, and the third curved.

"Keep straight. The other two routes will lead us further away," Barlos said.

Once through the twisted path, they made camp for the night in a small clearing.

The next day came, and Atticus and the group awoke to the smell of Barlos cooking up a fry of Oilio eggs with crispy Apori skins topped with honey from a nearby Stinger hive. After enjoying their delicious breakfast, Atticus and his companions continued through the wooded hills. Both the trees and the thickets thinned out, and before long, they emerged from the Woodlands.

Their trail now led through open plains. Not more than an hour away stood the Greystone Mountains. The mountains stretched farther and wider than the eye could see, the tips reaching high into the clouds.

Atticus and his companions crossed the pastures, passing a mesa with fallen soldiers on the ground around it.

"Hey, Daria," Meg said, pointing out two soldiers in particular. "Aren't those archers?"

Daria sprinted to the bodies, covering her nose and mouth from the smell. She bent down and grabbed the quivers, then hurried back to the group. One quiver held approximately fifteen arrows, while the other held close to ten. It wasn't much, but it sure brought relief and excitement to Daria's face.

They soon passed a ravaged village at the foot of the mountains.

The air had grown colder here. Atticus rubbed his arms and tore his gaze from the ruins of the village to the mountains looming behind it. "How are we going to climb those?"

Barlos chuckled and pointed at a steep, narrow path situated between boulders. "See that there? That's a mountain path, but be on your guard. We'll find more than Arcods lurking in the mountains."

Atticus and his sister exchanged glances as they followed Barlos to the mountain path.

It would make this mountainous journey much easier if they could locate the destroyed kingdom of Altigoran.

He stared up the steep and narrow path. Worry filled him. What dangers awaited him and his friends in the mountains?

Chapter 25

Luvanasis sat in the throne room of El-Valr. Eagerness and impatience filled him. Atticus would soon arrive in a caravan of prisoners.

The throne room doors opened.

He straightened himself on the throne and watched as an Arcod commander trudged into the room. He grunted, disappointed that the visitor was not Raia.

The Arcod lumbered closer to the throne.

Luvanasis tapped the throne rail. "Well, where are they?"

The commander stood within arm's reach of the throne and opened his mouth but then hesitated. "They got away."

Luvanasis clenched his fists, his knuckles popping. He sprang from his throne and grabbed the Arcod commander by his throat. Anger shot through his veins. He did not have time for foolishness, for failure. How he wished this Arcod was Atticus so he could crush his throat.

"What do you mean they got away?" He threw the commander to the ground.

The commander pulled himself up. "Two warriors freed them, along with other prisoners."

Luvanasis grunted, then he shouted, "And where is she? Where is Raia?"

The Arcod leaped back. "She and a unit ran after Atticus and his companions a day or so ago."

Luvanasis held back from screaming. "Their armies are gathering. Our army will be too. And soon, Bonvida will witness my wrath."

The Arcod rubbed its neck. "What do you want me to do, Luvanasis?"

Luvanasis turned and smacked the creature. "Address

me properly."

The Arcod grumbled. "I do apologize, King Luvanasis."

Luvanasis rolled his shoulders, liking the sound of that. *King* Luvanasis had a good ring to it. He paced back and forth in front of the thrones and crossed his arms behind him. From the corner of his eye, he glimpsed the Dark Descendant standing nearby.

"Arcod, go and greet your fellow creatures. Let's have a perimeter set around this castle. I don't want anyone to think they can free the El-Valr King and the hundreds of prisoners below."

The Arcod grunted and strode to the doors, passing the Dark Descendant.

Luvanasis stood straight. "Raia and her pathetic raven have failed me. She knows not to return."

His descendant strode closer. "Do you want me to find her and bring her back?"

Luvanasis chuckled. "Find her, yes. Bring her back, no."

The descendant tilted his head. "Then what shall I do when I find her?"

Luvanasis wrapped his arm around his descendant's shoulders. "I want you and her to begin the hunt for the She Serpent."

The Dark Descendant lifted his head. "And where will I find She Serpent?"

Luvanasis dropped his arm. "If the stories of old are to be believed, then somewhere within Altigoran, underneath the mountains."

The Dark Descendant nodded. "Altigoran it is, then."

Luvanasis strode with his descendant to the doors. "And don't be spotted. You wouldn't want your identity to be revealed."

The Dark Descendant tugged on his cloak and touched the brass mask which concealed his face. He exhaled and marched through the castle.

Luvanasis strode down a hall to the back courtyard. Two Calsriv dragons lay curled up together in the courtyard, steam rising from their thin nostrils with each exhale. The long, pointed black tail of one dragon wrapped around a fountain statue of a fish.

Luvanasis approached the dragons. "Advo is going to be awoken. Unfortunately for me, your master, Kanado the dragon, is off hiding, awaiting its appointed time." He placed his hands on the scaly face of one of the beasts. "You two will do the trick just fine when the battle starts." He admired the thick scales of the two dragons. A ring of horns surrounded each of their heads, reminding him of Kanado, the dragon he met when he first arrived in Calsriv.

As he stroked one of the dragons, he wondered about the coming battle against Bonvida. More importantly, he wondered about his battle against Atticus.

Chapter 26

Atticus had heard stories of travelers passing through the Greystone Mountains. Few of those stories ended well. From high winds to creatures of all shapes and sizes. Not to mention the occasional rockslide sending a shower of boulders onto one's path. Maybe they would encounter trouble, but as long as he wielded the sword, nothing could stand in his way.

Atticus and his companions followed Barlos' lead up the steep basalt path through the mountains. As they climbed, his skin chilled, and his ears popped from the altitude. Soon the path leveled out, and stones tumbled from the mountainside. He turned and scanned the nooks and crannies above, thinking he would spot a creature but saw nothing. It could not have been a rockslide either.

Misty clouds above hid the sun, and boulders and cliffs surrounded them.

Barlos pointed up the trail. At least he had an idea of which route to take.

The wind picked up and whispered around them. They leaned into the rougher gusts. More stones tumbled down the face of the cliff. Something or someone must have been above them, maybe on a higher trail.

"Barlos," Atticus called, getting a rush of wind in his mouth.

Barlos turned his head. "Aye, Atticus, what seems to be the matter?"

Atticus waited a moment for the wind to break. "I think we are being followed. The cliffside stones keep falling."

Barlos froze. In the distance, the path bent. "Stones, you say? Nobody move. Nobody make a sound."

Atticus and the rest of the group paused in their tracks. The wind whirled around his whole body. He waited and waited. A few more stones tumbled down the mountainside.

Barlos paced along the mountainside, inspecting it closer. "Just as I thought. Those are Finexos, aggressive mountain creatures known to camouflage themselves by blending in with the mountains."

Atticus glanced at Daria. Their parents mentioned those creatures once when they were children and had trekked near the mountains. That was the only time he had ever come close to the mountains.

When more stones dropped, Daria jumped.

Victor held onto her shoulder. "Don't you worry. I have you."

In the next moment, a Finexo leaped from the mountainside. With its legs tucked under it, its grey, rocky body resembled a boulder. The ground rumbled as it crashed down nearby.

Everyone in the group spun to face it.

Atticus ran through his memory. What else had his parents told him about those creatures? That was it! They did not attack unless threatened.

The Finexo growled and smacked the mountainside with its thick back leg.

"It's getting angry." Zane backed away from it, bumping into Atticus, and then glanced over his shoulder. "Why is it getting angry?" His eyes shifted from left to right as if he were searching for someplace to hide.

A familiar horrid smell floated on the wind, followed by an echo of gurgles.

Atticus turned towards the smell. Not far away from Barlos, a troop of Arcods came around the curved path.

Atticus pointed. "Arcods. Maybe that's why it's smashing the cliff."

Barlos spun around and drew his sword, holding his position.

The Finexo smacked the mountainside once more. Two more strikes would likely cause an avalanche of boulders to rain down and crush them. They must have considered the Arcods quite a threat.

Barlos swung his sword at two Arcods. "We have to keep going."

The Arcods growled and swung their claws frantically.

Following Barlos' lead, Atticus raced ahead and swung at the Arcods as they turned the bend.

From above, something rumbled and crashed, getting louder and louder. "Rockslide!" Atticus shouted.

Wasting no time, they bolted down the path. Rocks and boulders fell behind and before them. The largest of them crashed directly in their path, blocking their route.

Barlos could not hide the panic in his eyes.

"Over there," Atticus shouted, pointing to a narrow path up the mountainside. Without another word, Atticus and the group charged to the path while more boulders fell behind them. They weaved their way along the narrow, twisting path between sharply rising cliffs. Rounding the next bend, a cave came into view. "Make for the cave!"

Barlos dove into the cave first, followed by Atticus and the rest of the group.

Catching his breath and thankful to be alive, Atticus leaned against the cave wall and peered into the darkness. The cave seemed very deep. He went to poke his head out of the cave, but a boulder came crashing down, blocking their only escape and cutting off all light. Debris surrounded Atticus, burning his eyes and itching his nose.

Someone coughed and then spoke, the voice identifying her in the darkness. "Now what?" Meg said.

Atticus rubbed his eyes. "Daria, do we have any more flint left and something to use as a torch?"

He waited, hearing Daria rifle through her bag. It must have been ten times more difficult for her to find what she wanted in the pitch black.

"Got it!" she said.

"It might not be the best solution," Meg said, "but we can burn a piece of clothing in one of our jars and use it as a lantern."

"Grand idea! Meg, your ingenuity reminds me of my son," Barlos said.

"I didn't know you had a boy," Atticus said.

"Aye, I do. He's about Meg's age," Barlos replied.

After some time, a spark turned into a flame, and Meg placed the burning fabric in one of the jars.

Barlos put gloves over his hands and held the lantern.

Using what little light they now had, they headed further into the cave, finding a tunnel in the back.

As they shuffled along deeper into the mountain, Atticus wondered how they would get out of this cave. It had to end somewhere or come out at another part of the mountains.

Two steps later, something wet dripped on his neck. He reached behind and wiped it. Saliva? His heart rate quickened. Something was above them.

"Yuk," Meg said from behind. She must have been drooled on too.

As they continued through the tunnel, something occasionally flapped over them, and saliva dripped now and again onto someone's neck or head.

At some distance ahead, light fell on the floor of the tunnel. Could it be a way out?

"Look," Barlos said. "I see light ahead." He strode faster and faster until he was at a full-on sprint.

Atticus and the group followed.

They entered a large cavern circled with stone pillars that extended high to a crack of light.

Victor pointed. "The light! I think we found our way outta here."

The stone pillars started small, and each one was larger than the last, creating a stairway to the light.

Atticus jumped onto the lowest pillar. "The pillars. Hop

onto the pillars to reach the top." He jumped from one to another, each jump more difficult than the last. Behind, the others followed his lead. He jumped to the last pillar and reached the hard-packed dirt ceiling. He pushed with all his might, dirt and pebbles crumbling on and around him. Light streamed through cracks overhead, the opening growing bigger and bigger. With one last push, he heaved the ground out of the way. Using his upper body, he pulled himself up and onto a path. Then he lay prone and helped his friends climb out.

Once everyone made it out, Atticus wiped dirt from his face and tunic and peered out at the lay of the land. The underground route hadn't taken them far off track. In fact, they seemed even closer to the ruins of Altigoran, but they still had quite a long journey.

Barlos and Zane rolled a boulder over the hole. Zane wiped his dirty hands on his clothes.

"What was following us in there?" Atticus asked Zane.

"Baractus, cave-dwelling beasts, much larger than your common nighttime bat."

Atticus shivered at the image forming in his mind; then he turned to the matter at hand.

Since they were on a hill, the only way to go was down. Stepping with care to avoid sliding all the way down, they soon returned to their trail. The kingdom of Altigoran stood in the distance, the setting sun painting a colorful backdrop in the sky. They should reach the kingdom within two days. But until the morning came, they would do no walking along the rugged mountain trails.

Chapter 27

In the mountains, a mist covered the rocky ground. Atticus and his companions had trudged for two straight days. Just beyond a cloud of fog stood a structure of some sort. He picked up speed, filling with determination. Each stride brought him closer to the third shard. The structure became clearer and clearer.

Wide cracked marble steps led up to an opening. Pillars flanked the opening. One towered as high as the mountains. The other stood half as tall, the top of it lying scattered across the ground. Whatever had happened here at Altigoran did not end well.

Zane cleared his throat and sang loud enough for his voice to echo.

"Altigoran towered high, overlooking the mountain land, but alas, without warning, a battle 'twas at hand.

The king was first beheaded. Escape did the queen?

The heir of Altigoran's voice faded away.

And oh, how the towers crumbled. All but one remains.

Walls fell inward, crumbling, and cries throughout the land.

Advo came with Desmond riding.

But they were too late, for Kanado, the dark dragon, his wrath hurt the land.

Altigoran deserted, and thus unto this day, Altigoran is gone forever.

Its ruins are sure to stay."

Zane's stunned expression manifested his excitement over being in such a historic place. "Altigoran. Stories spoke of it as an incredible place. Unfortunately, as the song says, the kingdom and all its inhabitants are not gone."

Atticus stared at a circle above the gate. Had a beautiful stained-glass portrait once hung there? Or maybe the kingdom's crest.

Stepping on the first of many cracked marble steps, his foot knocked over a rusted steel helmet. His nerves tightened with each step up the staircase. His stomach clenched.

Victor and Zane pushed on the gate. "After you," Zane said.

Atticus glanced behind at Daria, Meg, and Barlos.

They decided to stay back and keep guard.

Atticus, Zane, and Victor paced through the grim, empty ruins. Broken pieces and skeletons were scattered about the place. Huge Arachnids had found quite the home here too. Atticus unsheathed his sword, preparing to fight if one came close.

Zane pointed his chin at a hairy grey Arachnid spinning a web. "You know, Atticus, they're more afraid of us. There's no need to draw your weapon."

The creature swung between two beams.

Atticus ducked his head even though it was nowhere near him. "It's for precaution, Zane. I don't like them in my space."

Victor chuckled. "I don't blame you, Atticus. They are quite creepy."

The further they went into the kingdom, the sadder it became. Caved in walls here, toppled statues and smashed pottery there. So much destruction.

They finally arrived at the castle's golden door. It stood partly intact.

Atticus sheathed his sword, hastened to the steps, and pressed on the door. A creaking sound bounced off the walls as the door swung open.

Atticus, Zane, and Victor paced through a dimly lit entry room filled with rubble. They stepped over large stones and pieces of flooring and finally spotted the knight statue.

"Huh," Victor said. "How it's still standing, I can't imagine."

Atticus nodded. "But there it is, just like the warriors Hark and Hara said it would be."

"Now what?" Zane stood back, peering into the shadows around them.

Climbing over rubble, Atticus raced to the statue. He grabbed the cold metal statue and slid it across the floor, revealing an opening beneath it. He peered down the hole, but it was too dark to see anything.

"Kind of dark down there," Zane said, coming up beside Atticus.

"Aye." Atticus sprang up. "We need a torch or something we can use as light."

Zane and Victor went off, searching in opposite directions.

Atticus stepped around the hole and over more rubble. He pressed further down the hall, passing two fallen columns. There had to be a torch somewhere.

Something inside the castle made a fluttering sound.

His skin crawling, Atticus turned, scanning the area but not glimpsing anything dangerous. He did, however, spot a wooden club in a skeleton's hand.

"That'll do," he said as he climbed over more rubble. Almost at the skeleton with the club, he climbed onto a column. The club was just within arm's reach. He reached out, and his fingertips touched something sticky. Heart thumping like mad, he yanked his arm back. He had just touched an Arachnid web.

Where was the Arachnid? Atticus lifted his gaze, scanning the shadows on the wall.

There, dangling on the wall just above him, was an Arachnid.

The hairs on the back of his neck rose, making him twitch. Maybe Victor or Zane found something they could

189

use.

Atticus eased back, hoping it did not leap at him. A lump formed in his throat. Should he make a run for it? Without realizing it, his hand had moved towards the hilt of his sword. Yes, he had the Sword of Bonvida. He could do this. He took a breath, then unsheathed the sword.

The Arachnid dropped a ways and swung from side to side.

Atticus lifted the sword, his hand shaking.

The Arachnid lowered itself even more, coming closer.

Skin crawling, Atticus jumped back and dropped the sword. The Sword of Bonvida slid down the column and landed right next to the club.

The Arachnid dropped all the way down now, probably thinking the sword was a fly.

Survival instincts kicking in, Atticus leaped from the pillar. He backed away from the Arachnid, away from the torch, and away from the sword.

Before rational thought returned to Atticus, Victor slid down the column with a sword at the ready and swung at the Arachnid, slashing off one of its legs.

The Arachnid hissed and scurried back up the wall.

Victor jumped down and snatched up the club and Sword of Bonvida. "Here you go, my friend." Victor handed Atticus the sword and patted him on the back. "Let's get this torch lit."

Irritated at himself for his cowardly move and thankful that Victor drew no attention to it, Atticus sheathed the sword and followed his two friends.

Zane pulled flint from his belt, and Victor yanked a spare tunic from his pack. He wrapped it around the club, while Zane used one of his daggers to scrape the flint. After a few tries, a flame ignited the cloth. Now they were able to go into the catacombs.

One after another, they jumped down the hole. Atticus

moved the torch around a long hallway. Drawings, symbols, and torches hung on the walls. Atticus lit the torches as he passed each one, giving them more light. Rats squeaked and scurried along the ground and in and out of crevasses.

As Atticus proceeded forward, Victor and Zane each yanked a torch from the wall. Coffin-sized niches in the walls held dead bodies. Atticus tried not to look at the skeletons, while Zane seemed to have a historian's interest in them. Victor kept his eyes on what lay ahead.

They reached a painted archway with more hand-drawn paintings. It led to an open area and a high platform with several jewel-encrusted tombs.

Not watching his step, Atticus splashed down in a deep puddle. He shook off his boot and moved his torch around, driving shadows away. Advo had to be somewhere in these catacombs, but where?

They marched closer to the jeweled tombs, which likely belonged to the royal family of Altigoran.

Victor moved his torch around, throwing light in every corner. "Are you sure this is the right place?"

Atticus sighed. "It has to be. The warriors said so. Zane, what do you think?"

Zane rubbed his thumb over his fingers. "Advo is here. He has to be here."

The three trudged down the other side of the platform of the royal tombs, Atticus leading the way. A few steps later, his foot sunk into soft dirt. The ground under their feet gave way, and they fell.

Atticus landed hard on his lower backside, losing his grip on his torch. He reached for it. "Everyone okay?"

Zane groaned and nodded.

Victor wiped dirt off his sleeves and picked up his torch. "Aye, I suppose so."

Atticus and Victor swung their torches around to check

out their new surroundings. An unusual door with ancient inscriptions stood before them. They moved closer to it.

"What does it say, Zane?" Victor asked.

Zane scanned the writings. "Descendant, behind this place, you will find Advo. Make haste. Bonvida is counting on you."

Bursting with nervousness and excitement, Atticus pushed open the door.

Rays of sunlight streamed through cracks in the ceiling, illuminating the room. This room was not grim like the rest of the catacombs. Stone walls surrounded a translucent white dove, the size of an elephant. Tucked under its beak was a small box.

The box! Did it hold the shard? Atticus stepped closer to the dove. As he reached for the box, his fingers nearly touching it, the large bird's eyes snapped open.

Heart leaping to his throat, Atticus jerked his hand back and stumbled away from it. He tripped over something and fell onto his backside in a puddle.

The dove cooed and spread its enormous wings. "Your smell, I haven't smelt that in years . . . Descendant."

Atticus sat up. "I am Atticus, ancestor of Desmond, and the one chosen to save this land from the hands of Luvanasis. To do that, I need the ruby shard."

Advo cooed once more and lifted the box in its beak. The dove lowered and fluttered its tail.

Figuring the bird wanted them to hop onto its back, Atticus waved the other two over. They climbed onto the soft feathers of the dove.

Advo turned its head to speak with them. "Hold on tight." The great dove lifted into the air and shot out of the mountains like a flash of lightning.

Atticus grasped feathers, holding on for his life, as the wind rushed in his face. They were flying. He could see all of Bonvida from up here. Advo flew smoothly, swaying now and then to ride various air currents. It was probably happy to finally be awake and free to fly again after so many years.

After a few minutes, Advo headed for the ground and landed near Daria, Barlos, and Meg, who seemed to be tossing stones down the steps. As Daria threw a stone, she and the other two reared back in surprise at the sight of the dove.

Atticus, Victor and Zane hopped off the back of the bird.

Advo set the box in his beak down. "The shard is in here."

Atticus picked up the box and unlatched it. The ruby shard sat on a small silk pillow.

Advo looked at Atticus. "I will see you again." Then like a flash, Advo flew away.

Atticus lifted the shard from the box between two fingers. A ray of sunlight glimmered through the jagged piece.

In the next instant, a bird swooped down and snatched it from Atticus. The bird—the raven he had seen with Raia—flew higher into the blue sky, the ruby shard between its talons.

Atticus stood there in shock, his heart sinking to the ground.

Daria reached for her bow and arrow and aimed at the raven before it flew too far. The arrow whipped through the air and closed in on the raven. But it just missed.

Daria grunted, drew a second arrow, and shot. This time the arrow grazed the raven.

The raven cawed and dropped the shard. Then it dove into the ruins, through the hole above the entrance.

The shard fell through the air.

Atticus dashed towards it, hoping he could catch it. Almost to his mark, reaching to intercept the little red gem—

Smack! Something hard hit his face, shifting his jaw to one side and loosening a tooth. He shook off the pain and blinked his eyes.

There in front of him stood Raia, tall and thin in an olive tunic. She picked up the shard from the ground.

Daria snarled and, without hesitation, grabbed another arrow. "Her!"

Atticus unsheathed his sword and leveled it at Raia. "Hand over the shard."

Raia didn't flinch. She only chuckled.

Atticus held the sword. "I said, hand it over." He took a breath, trying to keep his cool, but frustration boiled through his veins. He lunged forward and pressed the blade under her chin. "Look, you have nowhere to run, and you don't stand a chance fighting us. I would rather not kill you if I don't have to."

Raia huffed, stuck her hand out, and opened it, revealing the ruby shard.

With his free hand, Atticus snatched the shard.

Her thin lips curled. "Are you going to kill me now, chosen Atticus?"

Keeping the blade to her throat, Atticus glanced over his shoulder to the others. Daria seemed ready to loose an arrow, while the others held their weapons at the ready.

Atticus drew his sword back. He faced Daria and shook his head.

Daria lowered her bow.

"You're going to turn around, and you will not follow us anymore," Atticus said. "Understand?"

Raia smirked. "Letting me live? Hmm, the chosen one doesn't have the like to kill. How will you ever defeat Luvanasis? Though I suppose you won't have to. Your precious sword will do all the work."

After giving him one last smirk, she turned away and slinked along the mountain wall. Then she dashed into the ruins.

Relieved that the exchange had ended so well, Atticus

returned to the others. He dropped to his knees and set the Sword of Bonvida on the ground.

The others circled around him. If not for these Bonvidians, he would not have made it this far: Daria, his encourager; Zane, filled with knowledge; Victor, a strong leader and a growing friend; Barlos, a calm presence and commander; and Meg, the young girl who knew the way to the final shard.

He gazed at the sword, his mind reviewing the mission. This sword was his only strength. It was what made him the chosen one, what made him who he was.

He dropped the ruby into the groove. Then he stood up and sheathed the sword. Two more to go. The emerald was somewhere in the forest, and the sapphire was on an island. He glanced at Barlos. "Which way now?"

Barlos scanned the area and whistled. "This way."

Atticus and the group marched down the steps, leaving the ruins of Altigoran behind them.

As they followed a new path, wind blew at their backs, carrying with it snow from the Frozen Wastelands. As the cloudy day carried on, the snow fell heavier. Thankfully, they headed down and away from the snow.

With the wind still at their backs and the sun peeking through the clouds, Atticus realized that nothing dangerous had happened in a few hours. At that moment, a growl bounced up the cliffside. Atticus peered around, scanning for an Arcod. Smoke from a campfire swirled up from a small ridge beneath the path. Arcods sat around the campfire. He pointed them out to the others, and they all crouched behind a boulder to avoid being seen.

Atticus peered around the boulder, spotting a knife on one Arcod and a sword on another. "They're packing weapons."

Victor peeked over the boulder. "Must be making their way back to El-Valr."

Atticus and his companions tiptoed away, making sure not to kick any stones over the edge of the path. They continued on their way, the sun sinking lower in the sky, until Atticus glimpsed firelit lanterns sitting on stones in the distance. Beyond the lanterns, just visible from the trail, stood a cozy little cabin.

They trekked off route, following a secondary path that would take them to the lanterns and the cabin. A sign hung from wires above the door: "Garron's Inn."

Atticus glanced at the darkening sky. "I don't know about you guys, but I could use a rest."

Barlos rubbed his stomach. "Garron's Inn. I hear they make quite delicious meals."

Daria rubbed her belly. "Count me in!"

Victor glanced at Daria. "I'm up for a good meal and a good rest."

Zane tightened his belt and glanced at the sky as if trying to decide what time it was. "I could eat."

Meg bounced on her toes. "Me too! Me too!"

Atticus grasped the oak door handle and entered with the others right behind.

Chapter 28

The Dark Descendant stood at the bottom steps of the ruins of Altigoran. He finally made it to this desolate place. With each stride up the marble steps, he pondered the day he had released Luvanasis and the darkness.

He sneaked through the Evergreen Forest, a hood over his head, and turned to see campfire smoke in the distance. Someone else was in the forest too. He pressed on until he stood before a strange stone platform. He withdrew from his pocket a letter he had received days prior, and he read it.

"You are the grandson of Luvanasis, heir to Shiesta. You were born to aid in the releasing of the darkness. In the Evergreen Forest, there is a platform that connects Calsriv to Bonvida. But it is locked. You must open it from Bonvida, and from there, follow the instructions of Luvanasis. I will see you there. —Raia"

At the final step, he shook off his memory. The long dark entrance of the ruins stood before him. The darkness of the tunnel fired off another memory.

He stepped onto the platform, not sure how this was supposed to work. Was he supposed to do something? Say something? He dropped onto his knees and banged his fist on the stone platform. "Luvanasis! Luvanasis! It is I, your descendant. I'm here to free you."

He waited a moment, the moonlight shimmering down around him. A second later, a smaller tremor rattled the night. He jumped back as the platform cracked open and steam shot up. He leaned over, peeking into the crack, staring into darkness.

The Dark Descendant strode through the entrance, pushing the memory away. A stone's throw from him, Raia sat on what used to be a food cart. She didn't appear to see him.

From the shadows of the forest, a thin woman with a strange raven approached. She said his name.

"Who are you?"

"I am Raia."

Out of the crack in the platform, a man in dark armor climbed up and onto the land. Behind him, a ten-horned dragon flew out into the night sky. Two more dragons followed, but they hovered above. Then a smell filled the air, a disgusting smell, as thousands of creatures with bulging eyes crawled out.

Raia's raven cawed and flapped its wings, returning the Dark Descendant to the present.

Raia jerked her head towards him. "It's you. Are you here to bring me in? I can only imagine how disappointed Luvanasis is."

The Dark Descendant strode closer to her. "No. That is not why I'm here."

Raia's eyebrows raised, and she straightened. "Oh, so you're going to kill me then?"

The Dark Descendant bellowed a laugh. "I'm not here to kill you, Raia."

She tilted her head and twisted her lips. "That's sweet."

He huffed at the sarcasm in her voice. "You're going to help me on a quest."

Raia stroked her raven. "A quest?"

The Dark Descendant reached to pet the raven, but it snapped at his finger. He pulled back and glared at the bird. "You're going to help me find She Serpent. And awaken her."

Raia jumped to her feet, horror in her eyes. "She Serpent? Luvanasis is already jumping to his contingency plan? He must be scared."

The Dark Descendant stared at her. "Scared? He brought fear to the land. He can't be scared." A wind whistled through the entrance. A rusted goblet rolled across the ground and clanged into the ruins of a rowhouse.

She strode closer to him, peering through the eye gaps in his brass mask. "Before I accept, I want you to understand that I don't answer to you." She leaned to his ear and whispered his name.

He stepped back and grunted. "Let's get a move on. We're wasting daylight."

Chapter 29

Atticus and his companions entered Garron's Inn. The savory aroma of home-cooked food and the warmth of a roaring fireplace greeted them. Two musicians stood in a sitting room, one playing a four-stringed guitar, while the other played a dark wooden harp. Atticus stepped up to a long oak desk, where an elderly woman watched them and an elderly man hunched over a crate.

The woman clapped her hands, her face beaming with excitement. "My dear, we have guests."

The older man turned to the group and grinned, his face filling with wrinkles. "How long will yah folks be staying?"

Victor nudged Atticus and answered for him. "One night."

The woman puffed up her grey curly hair and adjusted her round glasses. "How many rooms?"

Atticus counted their little group, figuring they could each have a room.

"Oh, we can share one," Meg said, and Daria nodded in agreement.

"Five rooms, then," Atticus said to the old man.

The man cleared his throat and grabbed five keys, which he then placed on the counter. "There you have it, folks. Now breakfast is served directly at dawn. It's hunted by our grandchildren," he said with pride.

Victor stepped closer to the counter. "And how much is a one-night stay?"

The man looked Victor and the others up and down. "Oh, times are rough. You all seem to have traveled a long distance." He scratched the few hairs on his head. "Pay or trade?"

Atticus glanced at Victor. Did they even have coins with them?

Victor twisted his lips and then reached into one of his

pouches. He pulled out a gold locket and placed it on the counter.

The old man leaned closer. "Hmm, a pure gold locket from El-Valr, I see. I can accept this as trade."

Atticus and the group stepped up the creaky stairs and into their designated rooms.

***

Daria entered the room and laughed as Meg ran and jumped onto one of the two feather beds. Their big room had two beds, a small desk with a lantern, a wooden tub with towels, and a strange vase-like object to use for necessities.

Meg continued to bounce on the bed. It had been so long since any of them had slept in comfort. Then Meg stopped jumping and sat on the edge of the bed. "I can't believe I'm here, that we're here, Daria, and that in a few days, give or take, I'm going to see my father again."

Daria unlatched her bow and quiver and swung off her pack. "You must be beyond excited, Meg."

Meg smiled from ear to ear and pulled off her bag, and unstrapped her sheath. "Do you still have family? Other than Atticus?"

Daria sighed and sat next to Meg. "No, not anymore."

Meg looked at the carpeted floor. "Oh, well, come to think of it, we're like a family."

Daria chuckled and wrapped her arm around Meg. "You're right." She got up off the bed.

Meg sighed. "Daria, I always wanted an older sister, and now I have one."

Daria's heart warmed. "I've always wanted a younger sister. Say, how about this, we take turns washing up, then I'll braid your hair and teach you basic archery?"

Meg chuckled. "I would love that."

***

Zane tore off his cape and weapons and removed his

201

boots. He observed the room. The only thing he cared about was the table with five books. Books! How long had it been? He grabbed all the books and placed them on the bed. Then he stretched out across the bed and reached for the closest book. It was a red leather book with faded writing on the front. As he opened it, dust puffed out. He could tell by the smell that it was pretty old. He glided his thumb across the pages, which calmed him. All his troubles and anxiety seemed to vanish from his mind.

***

As Barlos unloaded all his belongings by the door, his back felt so much lighter. He strode to a little table and pulled the chair out, and then sat down. He unbuttoned a pocket, pulled out a thin metallic box, and opened it. Barlos' eyes welled as he stared at a hand-drawn portrait of his wife and son. He touched their inked faces and pressed them to his heart. "I'll see you again. I will," he mumbled to himself.

***

Victor placed his belongings on the floor, kicked off his boots, unstrapped his belt, and slumped onto the feathered bed.

Out of the corner of his eye, he glimpsed the El-Valr crest dangling from his sheath. He sat up straight, picked it up, and kissed it. Still holding the crest, he rested his head on the pillow, wishing for another pillow. He sighed, closed his eyes, and a memory popped into his mind.

Victor slammed onto the ground in the courtyard. Lena held onto his side. He slid out of her grasp as swords clashed on either side of them.

Lena cried out in agony.

Victor turned, seeing a thick gash across her body. He crawled closer to her and sat by her side. "Lena, Lena, stay with me."

Her scaly hand held onto his. "It's too late. Don't mourn

202

me . . . We were never meant to be."

Victor wiped his teary eyes. "Lena, what are you saying?"

Her breathing slowed. "There's someone else for you."

Victor clenched his jaw and glanced over his shoulder at the raging battle. There amid the chaos, Daria shot arrow after arrow at an Arcod.

He turned his attention back to Lena. Her voice grew softer by the minute. "Stay with me until I pass."

He shook off the memory, catching the muffled sound of someone singing in the room next door. Curiosity taking over, he got up and pressed his ear to the wall. He still could not understand the lyrics, but he recognized the voice, and he smiled. Daria. He strode to the door and reached for the knob, wanting to talk with her. He remembered their first encounter.

Victor and his knights rode through the woods. Victor peered forward, spotting a young woman maybe a year or two younger than he.

"That's one of them," Barlos said as they trotted closer.

A beautiful young Bonvidian woman stared at the trees, probably searching for something to eat for breakfast.

"Hello, there," Victor said, hoping not to startle her.

She turned towards him, and her eyes opened wide and sparkled. "H-hello."

His cheeks warmed. "You're one of those travelers that fought the Cygors? Can you lead us to your comrades?"

The young woman stood speechless. She nodded but didn't move.

Victor stared into her glittering eyes. "Can you take us to them now?"

She grinned. "Aye, of course."

He pulled his hand back from the doorknob as the memory faded. He should let her be. He backed away from the door and slumped onto the bed.

***

After shutting the door to his room, Atticus took off his sword and shield. He placed his weapons on a table next to some books. Anxious to remove some of the grime he had accumulated over the days, he stepped over to the tub and dunked his head in the cool water. Sleepiness overcame him as he wiped his face and pushed the water from his hair. He exhaled and plopped onto the feather bed. Wow, it was comfortable.

He lay staring at the log ceiling. After some time, he went to the window, which overlooked the forest. Atticus paced to the table and took out his journal and feathered pen. Right now was the first time he or anyone in the group had had the chance to be alone with their thoughts. His mind and heart filled with mixed emotions. He opened his journal and touched the pen to the paper, but his hand trembled. His heart ached, and his eyes welled. He bit his lip and turned away from the journal. He could no longer hold back his emotions—the fear of failure, the worry, and the doubt that consumed his every bone.

He looked around the room for his sword. The sword was his only strength, and without it, he would be a nobody. He would fail. He had to lock these emotions, these reckless thoughts, back into a box in his mind. Atticus took another breath and wept.

The following morning, Atticus swiped runny egg yolk around the rim of his breakfast plate. He took a final bite of toast. Across the table, Victor sipped the last of his tea, while Barlos served himself the third plate of food. Daria nudged Meg and pointed at her half-eaten meal. Meg slid her leftovers to Daria, who beamed. Meanwhile, Zane seemed to have his own concerns as he struggled to keep his eggs from touching his bacon and toast.

Everyone seemed refreshed, but Daria and Meg had outdone themselves. A braid wrapped around the crown of Meg's head, with only a few dark strands falling free.

Daria wore a single braid that fell down her back.

Atticus patted his stomach. His tastebuds wanted to go up for another plate, but his gut told him differently.

After Barlos finished his third plate, everyone waited to see if he would get another, but he pushed back his chair and said, "I'm about as full as I can be."

Atticus and the group arose from the table, picked up their belongings by the door, and said goodbye to Garron's Inn. Refreshed and ready to push on, they returned to the path and continued their trek down the mountain.

The Evergreen Forest became clearer, and the end of the mountain path was only yards away. They raced down the remainder of the path and entered the forest.

The scents of the forest tickled their noses: the pine and birch trees, cedar bushes, and even wildflowers growing in sunspots. The woodland sounds created a soothing melody. They tried to identify the different birds that chirped and animals that squeaked. And even the occasional insects buzzing.

Barlos and Daria whistled songs, and some birds whistled back.

Zane tried guessing the names of the songs.

Victor pointed to a strange wall of adjoining trees. "Elf Kingdom is just within that wall."

Zane's face beamed. "Should we stop? The Elves are amazing creatures. Their eyes change color with their moods, and they can tell others' intentions with just a glance. They have a rich history."

Daria picked a daisy from the path. "And they make the greatest pastries."

Atticus licked his lips, remembering their berry jam pastries.

Barlos sighed. "Best not. They are probably preparing their soldiers."

Zane nudged Atticus. "We'll visit them after this adventure then."

They walked without speaking for a time, but then somewhere off the path, something rustled in the bushes. Ever on guard now, Atticus and the others prepared to grab their weapons.

From a dense section of the woods, a young Bonvidian man with short hair and a unit of armed soldiers marched out.

Victor's eyes lit up. "Raldon!"

Atticus recognized the name. Raldon was one of Victor's brothers.

The two brothers embraced.

Raldon kissed Victor's cheek. "I have so much to tell you, Vic."

Victor glanced at the others. "As do I." Victor waved Atticus and the others closer.

Raldon glared at them. "We are going to the meeting point. Who are they?"

Victor chuckled. "This is Atticus. He's the chosen one. Remember, we were told that he would come and save us. Well, here he is. He's going to destroy Luvanasis."

Raldon scuffed. "Victor, no sword can harm that vile Luvanasis. Soldiers tried but failed." Raldon stepped back and pointed at Atticus. "I don't know what these Bonvidians put into your head, but I don't believe it. If there is even such a being as Sofos, well, he doesn't care about us. No one is going to save us except us."

Atticus' heart sank. Why didn't he believe? How could he say such things?

Victor placed his hands on Raldon's shoulders. "Let me help you to believe, brother. Let's help stir up the faith in you."

Raldon shoved his brother's hands off him. "I'm not like you, Victor. I hope to see you in the battle. It would be good to show that at least two El-Valr princes care."

Victor's eyes widened with shock. "What do you mean? Where is Damien?"

Raldon sighed and turned away. "The word is that Damien and his unit are dead or captured somewhere. Do you even know that our parents and countless others are in the dungeons of El-Valr? Or have you been too busy playing pretend to care?"

Victor huffed. "Raldon . . . we will see you in the battle, I promise."

Raldon gave a faint smile, whistled for his troops to follow, and marched down the path.

Atticus and the group continued their journey through the forest. Zane hopped into the lead as they trekked off the path, pushing between bushes and trees and over mounds of grass.

"Zane, where exactly are you leading us?" Daria asked.

Zane glanced over his shoulder. "To the Stones of Artel. If I'm leading the way correctly, we should get there by evening."

Overhead a white-tailed owl flapped its wings and carried off a rodent in its talons. "What are the Stones of Artel, exactly?" Meg asked.

Zane halted and turned to Atticus and the rest of the group. "It's a landmark. Artel is known to live there or at least to visit that place. Artel was Sofos' protector before the creation of everything. And now Artel is here in Bonvida. He keeps watch." He peered through the treetops at the sun. "At the beginning of time, there was only a cliff. All around it was an abyss."

Meg strode closer to Zane to listen to his story.

Zane spun around and continued down the path. "Sofos used his ultimate power to create the gems, which he used to create the land. Sofos knew that an enemy was in the dark abyss." Zane stopped and scanned the area. "He used

Artel the Great Wolf to protect him and the dome, in case the enemy would make a surprise attack."

Atticus tried picturing the story in his head.

Zane strode on and grabbed an apple dangling from a tree.

Meg leaned in closer. "Well?"

Zane glanced at the young girl. "Hematite sneaked behind Sofos, and Artel charged him, tackling the creature. Sofos told Artel not to kill the creature. Instead, Sofos used his power and turned the creature into a gem and kicked him back into the abyss."

Meg tilted her head. "Where was Advo during all this?"

Zane bit into the apple and talked around his chews. "Advo was using its bird's-eye view, for She Serpent lurked in the abyss. It was the only thing that Hematite could tempt." Zane pointed to a clearing a short jog away now. "The rest is known to all of Bonvida. Hematite and She Serpent were cast to Calsriv. While Sofos created the land, he gave Artel, as I mentioned, the job to watch and protect." Zane took another bite of his apple.

Nearing the clearing, Atticus and the group picked up speed, dashing to it. Towering cone-shaped stones, twice as tall as any of them, stood in the clearing. They circled a square stone about head high. Atticus stepped closer to the stones and peered around one and then another, looking for any sign of Artel.

While the rest of the group set up camp, the setting sun painted orange streaks across the blue sky, and Atticus circled the stones again and again. *Where is this wolf? I need that shard.* Atticus rested against one of the stones. He was so close to getting the last shards, but he had no idea of how to find the emerald.

"Atticus, dinner's ready." Daria stomped towards him and then returned to the campfire.

What kind of meal would the Elves have tonight? He

heard rumors about their glorious feasts. Maybe one day, he would join them for one. He sighed and returned to the rest of the group.

After a light dinner, Atticus and the others admired the beauty of the moon and stars glittering above the stones. A cool night breeze swooshed through the trees. Even after the breeze settled, some of the trees continued moving. Wait . . . something approached from the other side of the clearing.

Daria sprang up and ran to her bow and arrow.

Barlos, Victor, and Meg grabbed their swords.

Whatever it was, it took slow strides as it drew closer to the stones. Any moment now, the figure would be visible in the moonlight.

A large dog shape stepped between two stones and onto the square one in the middle. Was that him? Was that Artel?

The grey-and-white wolf sat on the center stone, lifted its head to the moon, and howled. Its head swiveled to Atticus, its blue eyes glowing in the night. The wolf stood up on all fours, leaped off the stone, and strode towards Atticus and the group. It stopped yards away. "Atticus and companions, I welcome you to the forest. I come to these stones every night and guard the forest. Tonight, until Atticus and I return, I leave you five to protect it."

Artel turned around and strode to the stones. Atticus followed. Artel stopped and looked back at Atticus. "I suggest you bring your sword and shield."

Atticus returned to his gear and strapped on his sword and shield. Then he followed Artel between the stones and into the dark forest. Artel pointed its snout at a hill with a crooked cave, not too much further ahead through the thick forest. Clusters of trees hid the entrance to the cave. "This is my den."

A group of fireflies fluttered above them, providing

light for this section of the den. The den extended back into darkness, and a tree stump stood in the center, a secondary den branched off.

Transfixed by pale green points of light—from the fireflies circling through the cave—Atticus almost missed it. Then his heart skipped a beat, and his attention rivetted to the stump in the center of the cave. The emerald shard lay on the stump.

Artel strode to the stump and sat next to it.

Atticus stood on the other side and reached for the shard, but his hand went right through it. How was that possible? Was this a trick?

Atticus drew his hand back.

Artel got onto all fours and circled Atticus and the stump. "Fear, worry, doubt, anxiety. These things are not good. They are not from Sofos. They are the lies the enemy feeds you as he drags you further from your goal." Artel lowered his head. "I sense these in you, Atticus, even if you do not want to admit it."

Atticus turned away. Why was Artel saying these things?

Artel tilted its head. "You cannot have the shard until you undergo a trial."

Atticus faced the wolf. "A trial? I gained the other shards without trials. Why is this one different?"

"Go, Atticus." Artel pointed with his snout to the back wall of the den. "Go. Time is precious."

Atticus peered around Artel to the back wall. What test would he face there? He tightened the sheath's strap and strode past the wolf. Fireflies danced around him as he neared the wall. What was he supposed to do? He stopped and looked back.

"Continue, Atticus," Artel said.

Continue? Through the wall? Atticus pressed a hand against the wall and found it soft like jelly. He sucked in a breath, closed his eyes, and pushed himself through it. The cool, jellylike wall pressed softly against him for a moment until he passed to the other side. Once on the other side, he found himself standing in a small room. Stone walls surrounded him, and glowing rocks lit up the ground. A curiosity at the center of the room commanded his attention. Atticus strode closer, coming within inches of a single mirror stuck between two roots that grew up from the ground.

Chapter 30

Atticus paced closer to the mirror, curiosity directing his steps. The closer he got to the mirror, the more his reflection blurred. Maybe the mirror needed cleaning. Standing inches from the mirror, he wiped his hand over the glass.

His reflection remained blurry. Something wasn't right with his reflection, his messy hair, and especially his grey eyes. What was that look in his eyes?

He leaned closer.

At the same moment, his reflection smashed towards him from the glass, propelling him backwards. He landed on his bottom and scooted even further back, heart racing, mind reeling. What had just happened? Before him stood—another version of him! How was this possible?

His reflection grinned as it pulled out a sword.

Jumping into action, Atticus sprang to his feet, unsheathed the Sword of Bonvida, and strapped his father's shield on his wrist.

His reflection pointed to the sword. "You are weak."

Atticus' blood boiled. Weak? "I am not weak," he said, his voice echoing in his ears. "I am the holder of the Sword of Bonvida. I am the chosen one."

The reflection leaped at him.

Atticus raised his sword, and their weapons clashed. Atticus tried shoving his opponent back but made no headway. What was wrong with him . . . with his sword?

Calculating his next move, Atticus stumbled back, almost tripped, but caught himself.

With wide, half-crazed eyes, his reflection charged at him.

Their swords collided again.

"You are weak," the other Atticus growled. "You do not possess the strength to defeat me."

Atticus pivoted and swung, their blades clashing

against one another. What did this imposter mean by calling him weak? That he could not defeat him? "You are my reflection! What do you know about anything?" He twirled his sword and jabbed, just missing his reflection.

The reflection countered and swung at him.

Atticus blocked the strike with the shield, causing his reflection to tumble to the ground.

Taking advantage of the moment, Atticus charged at him, gripping his sword tighter. His mind spun like a wheel. Without the sword, he would be dead by now. If he did not have the sword, he would be a nobody. He could not do this. But he did have the sword. The Sword of Bonvida had the power to defeat anything. He and it were one.

He pointed his sword at his reflection.

The reflection chuckled. "See, you are still weak."

Atticus stabbed his reflection with the sword, and his reflection vanished, leaving him alone in the room with the mirror. He took a breath of relief and was about to relax his guard, but wait . . . where had his reflection gone?

The hairs on his neck raised as his reflection reappeared before him.

How was this possible?

The reflection swung his sword. Atticus blocked just in time, but his opponent kept striking, again and again, beating him back.

He glanced back. He was about to be pinned against the wall. He shoved his shield, knocking the reflection onto the ground.

Panic filled his mind. Maybe the thing was right. Maybe he was too weak. Maybe he was not worthy of this sword, of his title as the chosen one. His heart sank into his gut, but at the same time, something else rose inside him.

"No!" he shouted. "You are wrong." He glared at his reflection, where he had fallen to the ground, and a strange fire burned within. "I am not weak. I have been entrusted with this sword, the Sword of Bonvida. I am the chosen one."

The reflection stood up and regripped his sword, a grin on his face. "Oh, so close to the finish line but yet weak."

Atticus huffed. What was he supposed to do? Then it occurred to him. That was it! But was it too easy? Could it be true?

Atticus exhaled. Without another word, he dropped the Sword of Bonvida and unstrapped his father's shield.

Raising his arms, he pressed towards his reflection.

The reflection charged and rammed him against one of the dirt walls. Scowling, he pinned Atticus in place, his sword to Atticus' throat and his hand to his shoulder.

A great truth slammed Atticus hard as he stared into the glossy grey eyes of his reflection, as their breathing became in sync.

"I am weak, and it took me this long to realize it. I hid behind my title: Holder of the Sword of Bonvida. I believed that the sword and title were all I needed. I made the sword my strength. All the while, I let fear and doubt overtake me." His eyes welled with tears as he exposed his inner wound. "I don't need the sword to prove who I'm called to be. Sofos called me to be the chosen one because of who I am. I am to use his weapon to defeat the darkness. But sword or no sword, I am still the chosen one."

The reflection loosened his grip on Atticus, withdrew his sword, and stepped back, the scowl gone now. "Remember that. It is your blood that makes you the chosen one."

In an instant, his reflection vanished.

Atticus dropped to his knees. His hands shook. After a moment, he arose. He glanced at the sword, picked it up, and sheathed it. He reached for the shield, clipped it on, and strode back through the cool, jellylike wall.

Flashes of green light appeared first, fireflies fluttering in the dim cave, then Artel, pacing in circles around the stump. He stopped as Atticus stepped into the room and lifted his chin. "The emerald shard is yours."

Humbled, weary, and relieved, Atticus paced to the stump. He unsheathed his sword and placed it next to the shard on the stump. The sword was just his tool, gifted from Sofos, to destroy the darkness. Thankful for his new understanding, he grabbed the shard and squeezed it in his hands. As he squeezed it, strength moved through his veins. Now, he was ready to face the darkness and whatever came his way. He was the chosen one.

He placed it into the groove. It glowed green, providing a striking contrast to the other shards, the ruby and topaz and glittering diamond. One more to go.

Artel led Atticus from his den and back to the stone pillars, then the wolf climbed back onto the square stone.

Atticus crept to the campfire, where his companions slept soundly. He raised his brow, wondering why they couldn't keep watch for the hour or two he was away. He took off his gear and drifted off to sleep.

The following morning, after a quick breakfast, the companions packed their belongings and left the Stones of Artel behind them.

Daria turned to Meg. "You mentioned Goblin Point in your story. Your father brought you there?"

Meg nodded. "Goblin Point is the closest dock to the island."

Victor leaned in. "Sorry to say this, but the rumors I've heard about Goblin Point say the ships left port. They won't have a ship for us to use."

Atticus glanced at him. "Then how can we get to the island?"

"Do the Elves have ships?" Daria asked.

"They have one, but it's not docked on the mainland of

Bonvida. It's on a distant island," Zane said.

As they strode through the thick forest, thoughts bounced around in Atticus' mind. He had one more shard to find but no way to reach it. They needed to find a ship. Even a rowboat would do the trick if it could provide safe passage to the island.

Chapter 31

Atticus and his companions trekked through the forest. The cloudy sky and chilly breeze brought a sense of gloom to the forest. Few animals scurried about or made any sound at all. Even the flowers along the path had closed up. Though the success of obtaining the fourth shard brought joy, frustration bit Atticus. They still hadn't come up with a plan to reach the island. The sooner they figured out how to get there, the sooner he would be able to fight Luvanasis.

Atticus sighed. There had to be some way across the sea. Sofos would not have made this mission impossible.

His ears perked. A humming came from one of the bushes. He glanced at the others, but no one seemed to notice. "Do you hear that?"

Everyone stopped walking.

Daria glanced towards the bush and then at him. "Singing?"

Atticus and Daria crept to the bush and divided the branches. Atticus jerked back.

A little beige creature sat curled up behind the bush. It shrieked and covered its face, its little body shaking uncontrollably.

Atticus leaned in for a better look. It was a beige goblin. It could not have been more than two feet tall when standing.

"Don't eat me. Don't eat me." The goblin sobbed.

Victor and Barlos both rolled their eyes.

Meg covered her mouth and giggled.

"Eat you? Why would we eat you?" Daria asked.

The goblin uncovered its eyes. "Oh, you aren't those horrid creatures."

Atticus glanced at Daria.

"I sure hope not! Sorry about the fright," Daria said.

The goblin sat up, brushed its scaly body, and stepped

out of the bushes.

The goblin's beady eyes widened in fright at the sight of the others, who had gathered behind Atticus and Daria. "Oh boy, there are a lot of you." Its voice was raspy but joyful.

Victor knelt, getting down to the goblin's level. "Goblin, we are travelers on a vital mission. I know the ships at Goblin Point are gone, but do you know of others? A backup ship or something that can take us out to sea?"

The goblin tapped one of its three fingers on its chin and tapped its foot up and down. "Ah-ha! We do! It's a big one. Well, regular size for you folk, I suppose. And it should fit all of you comfortably."

Victor reached out his hand. "Thank you, little one. Can you lead us to it?"

The goblin grabbed Victor's index finger and shook it. "I—I suppose I can fit it into my schedule. And you can call me Orli."

Victor stood up and glanced at Atticus.

Atticus shrugged. Make time? What had this goblin been doing that was so important?

"This way." The goblin pointed and marched down the path.

Walking at the goblin's pace made the day drag slower. By evening, they'd reached the end of the forest path. The sound of waves crashed below them.

Filled with curiosity, Atticus paced to a small clearing. A cliff edge dropped sharply to where waves crashed on the rocks below. Deep blue seawater stretched out to the horizon. Jagged cliffs jutted out all along the shoreline. The goblin leaned over the edge and pointed to waves washing over enormous boulders. "It's hidden in a cave down there. We will have to wait for the morning when the tide falls back."

"Let's set up camp away from the cliff's edge," Barlos

said.

Daria turned to Meg. "Let's go hunt. You can test the archery skills I taught you."

Meg nodded and strode into the forest with Daria.

Barlos dropped his pack. "Zane, can you and our goblin friend gather firewood?"

Zane nodded.

Victor glanced at Atticus. "Say, how about we practice sword fighting?"

A half-hour later, Barlos, Zane, and the goblin prepared a campfire while Daria and Meg returned with two geese.

Atticus swung high at Victor. Victor blocked the hit and stumbled backward. "You're a good swordsman, Atticus."

Atticus chuckled and sheathed his sword, then he sat on a log, pleased by the compliment, especially since it came from a prince. "Well, the day Luvanasis attacked, I had come to apply to be a knight of El-Valr." Seagulls squawked overhead and swooped down to the sea. "Now, here I am, traveling Bonvida with one of the three princes of El-Valr as a companion."

Victor grinned and sat next to him. "Before you arrived, I had almost lost all hope. But here we are on a path to victory. You are going to unchain us from Luvanasis and his evil." He paused and placed his hand on Atticus' shoulder. "No need to apply. I've seen you in combat."

Atticus could not hold back a grin. *Did the prince just say that after this is over, I will actually be a knight?*

***

After eating a late dinner of goose and berries, one by one, they settled down to sleep, leaving Daria and Victor to keep guard. Daria shifted her position around the campfire as smoke floated her way.

Across the fire, Victor smirked. "Do you want to step away?"

Daria's heart leaped, and she smiled. "I'd like that."

Daria and Victor stepped away from the campsite and to the cliff's edge. The stars brightened and filled the night sky.

"Victor?"

He glanced at her. "Aye?"

Daria sighed. "Do you miss her? Lena, I mean."

A distant look came into his eyes. "Aye, she saved my life. We were supposed to be married one day."

"Oh?" Daria struggled to keep her gaze. For some reason, her heart sank a little at the thought of him losing her . . . or was it the thought that he had been engaged?

"It was arranged, my father wanting to form an alliance with the sea. My heart wasn't really in it." He turned towards the night sky and ran a hand through his hair. "Nothing against her, really. She was a good Bonvidian, just not the one for me. I'm waiting for someone who makes my heart skip a beat every time she smiles." His eyes shifted from the sky to her eyes.

Daria's heartbeat quickened. "I'm waiting for that too. I have never been in love. I desire it . . . one day, I suppose."

Waves crashed on the rocks below, sparkling in the moonlight.

He nudged her with his shoulder. "You'll find him. And he will treat you like the brave woman you are."

Daria bit her lower lip, her cheeks burning. Thank goodness it was dark out. She turned back to him, their eyes locking once more. "You will too, Victor, and she will be a perfect queen for you."

He scuffed his boot in the dirt back and forth and then lifted her chin with two fingers and peered deep into her eyes.

Oh, how she wished she could be here forever, with the stars and moon glimmering around them and the enchanting sounds of the sea.

They inched closer to one another, Daria's heart

beating faster. Her mind spun, and her stomach fluttered. Was this real or just a dream?

Out of nowhere, a loud pop broke the silence. They both jumped back and rushed to the sound, discovering a log had rolled out of the fire.

He took a deep breath. "We should. . .we should get some rest."

Daria stroked her long braid, gazing at the fire. "Aye, we should."

They stood for a moment, gazing into each other's eyes, then they broke away and found places to settle for the night by the fire.

Daria lay down near Meg, taking one last gaze at the starry sky. Finally, she closed her eyes.

***

At the crack of dawn, Atticus and the group stood peering down the cliff. The tide had just rolled back, revealing a sandy beach littered with boulders covered in seaweed and slime and pools of seawater. One at a time, they climbed down the cliff. A rough wind blew, and the sun peeked out from the clouds.

They finally made it to the beach. Atticus strolled along the shore, the sand hard and compact, not soft under his feet.

He followed Orli to a giant skull and gazed out at the fierce ocean waves. He shut his eyes at the mere thought of one of those waves coming their way.

Orli scurried to the skull. "Ah, here we go."

Amused by their guide, Atticus turned to Daria, who shrugged her shoulders. "Orli, that's a skull."

Orli chuckled. "It is indeed." He stood at the nose of the skull and scanned the beach, the huge egg-shaped rocks, and the cliffs. He jumped and pointed at what looked like a steel door at the foot of one of the cliffs. "Ah-ha! There we have it."

The goblin sprinted across the beach, kicking up sand as he headed to the door in the cliff. Atticus and the others took long strides to keep pace with him. After a few minutes, Barlos swooped the goblin into his arms to speed things along.

Once they reached the cliff, Barlos stuffed his fingers into a slot—the door had no knob—and tugged. The door opened to a small, weathered rowboat.

Daria stood with her hands on her hips and head tilted to one side. "I don't know." She exchanged a glance with Atticus. "You think we will fit in that?"

Atticus grabbed one of the paddles from the rowboat. "I'm not complaining."

They lifted the rowboat out of its hiding place and dragged it across the sand.

Orli pointed to where the cliff arched over the sea. "See that arch? Just around it is a calmer shore. That'll be your safest bet."

"Well, we thank you." Atticus turned to Orli, but Orli had already made tracks back to where they'd climbed down.

Meg came up to Atticus. "I remember seeing that arch. The island isn't too far from here."

Atticus and the others lugged the rowboat across the sand, passing caves and pockets of water. Once around the arch, they trudged a bit further until they arrived at a rocky beach. The waves were much calmer here.

They placed the boat into the water. Once letting go of the boat, Zane took a deep breath and rubbed his arm.

Barlos chuckled. "There'll be no rest for our arms yet, Zane." Barlos pushed the boat further out, wading through the water. One at a time, they hopped into the rowboat. Meg sat on the smallest seat in the front, while Barlos and Zane grabbed the oars and sat in the middle. Atticus, Daria, and Victor squished into the back.

While Barlos and Zane paddled, Meg pointed out to sea. "We passed the arch coming from that direction there. If we keep on going straight, we will get there."

They rotated rowers every half hour. Their burning muscles kept them warm from the chilly sea air. Night settled, making it harder to see which way to row.

Smoke rose to the dark night sky, a faint grey line reflecting the moonlight. Atticus looked again to be sure. Yes, that was it! They'd found the island. Excitement filled him. If only this weren't a rowboat, they'd get there before dawn.

As morning eased into the sky, they drew near a small island with palm trees overlooking a sandy beach. A campfire glowed just off the shoreline. They passed a merchant vessel anchored on a small dock, a regular oak cog with a single mast, rounder than most ships.

Meg sprang up, rocking the little boat. "My goodness. We're here." A tear rolled down her cheek.

Though weary, Victor and Atticus rowed harder until finally reaching shore.

The boat tipped to one side as Atticus got out and splashed into the cool water. He and Barlos dragged the boat to shore. As soon as the boat entered shallow water, Meg leaped out and raced up the beach towards a man sitting by a campfire.

"Meg!" Daria shouted, hurrying after her.

Atticus and the others followed.

Meg stretched her arms wide. "Papa!"

The man climbed to his feet. His hair hung down to his shoulders, and a scraggly beard grew on his chin, but joy showed in his eyes as he ran to her. They fell into each other's arms. He spun her around. "Oh, my little flower, my Meg." He paused, wiping tears from his eyes.

The joy of the two reuniting touched Atticus. He shut his eyes, remembering his mother. Was she still beneath the well? Was she even still alive? A desire to see her again stirred inside him. He had to rescue her from the well as soon as this adventure was over.

The man set his daughter down, and the two of them paced to Atticus. "I'm Alec. You . . ." He squinted at Atticus, an intense look in his eyes. "You're the one I saw in my visions. You're the only one who can release me from the prison I am in. And you brought my daughter back to me."

Atticus nodded. "She's a brave young woman."

Alec wrapped his arm around Meg. "I know she is." He smiled and kissed the top of her head; then he let go of his daughter. "I can only guess that you are here for the shard." He sounded anxious.

"Aye, sir," Atticus said.

"Follow me. The rest of you stay here."

Atticus followed Alec across the beach into the palm tree jungle. They trudged over large roots, passing coconut trees and long bamboo posts. The wind whistled through the palm trees, but they heard no sounds of animals.

A few minutes later, Alec stopped walking. He pulled back branches and revealed a cave entrance. "The shard is this way."

Atticus followed Alec through a tunnel lit by blue, glowing stones that stuck out of the wall. Once at the end of the tunnel, Atticus stopped. The tunnel ended at a pool of water. In the middle of the pool, on a stone pedestal, rested the sapphire shard. It was the smallest of all the other jagged shards.

Figuring the water wasn't deep, Atticus went to take a step.

Alec put his hand out to stop him. "Kilo, the sea beast, protects the shard. I wrongfully touched it and have been a prisoner here ever since. Then I received visions of you. I saw that you would meet my daughter in the desert, that somehow, she had a role to play. That is why I sent her away." He lowered his hand. "And now my vision has come true."

He rubbed his scraggly beard, his gaze shifting back to the shard. "Once you grab the shard, Kilo will awaken. The faster you put the shard into its place in the sword, the sooner the sea beast will return to rest at the bottom of the sea."

Atticus bent down and dipped his hand in the water, finding it warm and murky. "What am I freeing you from?" He straightened up, wiping his hand on his tunic. The task seemed simple enough, but what on this quest had been easy?

Atticus stepped into the pool of knee-deep warm water, waded to the shard, and swiped it off the top of the stone pedestal. As he trudged back to Alec, the entire island rumbled.

Meg's father reached for Atticus' arm and helped him out of the pool. "Run!"

The two dashed out of the cave, rocks and stones dropping behind them.

Outside, the island continued to rumble, and water burst from the ground all around them. Atticus and Alec dashed to the others, dodging powerful streams of water and earth exploding from the ground. Kilo lived under the island. At any moment, the island would be under the water.

A spout of water shot up between Daria and Meg, making them jerk back.

Alec pointed to the docked merchant vessel. "Get on quick."

Following his lead and dodging spurts of water and clumps of dirt, Atticus and the others climbed up a rope ladder.

Once everyone was on board, Barlos and Victor rolled up the anchor. The palm tree jungle crumbled into the sea.

Atticus still clung to the shard. He had to calm the sea beast. A shadow the size of two whales moved through the water, causing waves to splash onto the ship.

The ship rocked wildly. Atticus darted into the captain's cabin and slammed the door. He tossed off his pack and unsheathed his sword.

He tried to steady himself against the tilting and pitching ship. He placed the sword on the desk and opened his fist. A violent, blood-curdling screech filled the air, raising the hairs on Atticus' arms and hurting his ears.

Kilo was fully awake.

Atticus' heart pounded. The final shard rested in his fingers. This was it. The moment he placed it in the sword, he was ready. He had what he needed to fight Luvanasis. He pressed the shard into the final groove.

Atticus grasped the hilt of the sword. All five shards were now intact. He turned to go on deck, but something strange was happening. Everything around him glowed brighter and brighter.

"What's happening? What's going on?" he shouted.

***

Daria burst into the captain's cabin. "Atticus, Atticus, we need—"

No one was in the cabin. Atticus had come in here. She had seen him with her own eyes. She took another step, tripping over his pack. Daria picked it up, panic rising inside her.

He could not have just vanished. Could he? The ship rocked to one side, throwing her off balance. She picked up his pack, strapped it around her, and sprinted back to the deck.

In the next moment, the waves calmed. Daria wanted a glimpse of the ginormous shadow lurking and shrieking under the water, but now the shrieks of Kilo ceased.

Daria turned to Alec, who stood gripping the ship's wheel. "Is it over?"

He held his head with one hand as if the beast's horrid

shrieking had penetrated his brain. As she approached, he lowered his hand and took a deep breath. "Kilo is gone."

She sighed with relief. But then something swooped down at them. It was Advo!

Advo glided closer. "Hop onto my back. I will bring you to the battle. Atticus will be arriving there any moment with the warriors."

Without another word, Daria and the others jumped onto the downy back of the enormous dove.

Advo flew higher into the cloudy sky. "Alec, I will drop you and your daughter in a safe place on the way."

Once over the forest, Advo flew in low over the Elf Kingdom wall and landed by an oval door.

Alec and Meg jumped off.

Meg wiped tears from her eyes and waved at Daria, Victor, Zane, and Barlos.

With its remaining passengers, the bird flapped its great wings and flew higher into the air, the sun starting to break through the clouds.

Chapter 32

Atticus dropped to his knees on hard rocky ground. What had just happened? He wasn't on the ship. Were the others here? He looked around him. A lush forest rose up on one side, while stones and rough terrain stretched out on the other. Where was he?

He picked up his sword and glanced at the grooves, where all five shards glittered as the sun broke through the clouds. He had done it. Thankful and relieved, he slid the sword into the sheath.

He got up and turned around. A large crystal dome stood before him. He strode closer to the dome, his reflection bouncing off the crystal, mesmerizing him. Stairs carved in the crystal led to a door with no handle on the outside. How did anyone use it?

As the thought passed through his mind, the door opened and near blinding light issued forth. He lowered to his knees. The light formed into a large brown stag with antlers that intertwined. Sofos.

Sofos stepped down towards Atticus.

Still on his knees, Atticus bowed his head, though he wanted to stare at the great Sofos.

"You can arise, Atticus," Sofos said, his voice soothing.

"Sofos?" Atticus said, his voice a whisper as he got to his feet.

Sofos gave a gentle nod. "Atticus, son of Dane, you have gathered all the shards. Now you must defeat Luvanasis."

Atticus tightened the strap of the sheath. He swallowed back his nervousness.

"What about his descendant? What if he opens Calsriv again? Or awakes She Serpent?"

"Do not worry about the future, Atticus," Sofos said.

"Do you believe we will win?" Atticus asked.

Sofos stepped closer. "This is not about winning,

Atticus. Victory sometimes comes with great sacrifice. No matter what happens, in the end, the light will always defeat the darkness."

As two lines of warriors marched towards the door, Sofos turned.

Atticus and Sofos stepped aside as at least a hundred warriors marched past them, their golden spears reflecting the sunlight. Sofos addressed the warriors as they stopped before him. "Are you ready to give our Bonvidians back their home?"

The warriors raised their golden, double-sided spears and cheered.

Still appearing as a stag, Sofos reared up on his hind legs and then dropped down hard onto the ground.

A soft breeze blew behind Atticus. As he turned around, a white funnel with glimmers of yellow appeared. Atticus paced to the portal with the warriors trailing behind him, his mind reeling with the realization that once through the portal, the battle would begin.

Chapter 33

Atticus led the warriors through the shimmering white portal. The open plains of Bonvida stretched out before them. The mid-afternoon sun shone overhead. On the plains stood row after row of soldiers and knights from every kingdom. The portal spiraled away, and the warriors who'd come with Atticus formed into lines, joining the kingdoms' armies. Across the open land stood El-Valr.

Rhythmic stomping sounded from the other side of the open pasture. Rows of Arcods of various sizes marched forward. Small ones, oversized ones, and ones the size Atticus had faced previously. Behind, soldiers grunted and yelled at the ever-expanding army of Arcods.

With no time to let anxiety take over, Atticus took a breath and turned to the warriors. He had to lead hundreds of strangers into battle. If only his friends were here. As he scanned the warriors, he spotted two familiar faces nearby: Hark and Hara, the two warriors that had helped him escape.

Hark gave him a wink. "We move on your signal."

The Arcods stopped marching. They growled and stomped and waved their claws and weapons in the air.

The soldiers shouted back, some beating their breastplates. The tension between the two armies mounted with each passing second.

Atticus exhaled and reached for the hilt of his sword.

From above, Advo landed at Atticus' side. Off jumped Daria, Victor, Barlos, and Zane.

"You're safe," he said, relieved to see them all.

Advo lowered his tail for Atticus to climb on. "I will fly you to Luvanasis while the others defend the land."

Atticus climbed onto the dove, his heart thumping like a drum and his palms sweaty. He drew out the Sword of

Bonvida and lifted it to the sun. The shards in the groove shot out beams of light purple, red, blue, green, and white. The colors fell on the soldiers on the ground. The Battle Song of Bonvida that he had learned as a child came to Atticus' lips, and soon, everyone joined in.

"We fight for Bonvida, saving her from our enemy.
We fight for Bonvida, standing strong to gain serenity.
We fight for Bonvida, the enemy no longer a threat to me.
Together we fell, now together, we rise.

We stand for Bonvida; prepare to meet your demise.
We fight for Bonvida, sending in all our Calvary.
We fight for Bonvida, standing strong to gain serenity.
We fight for Bonvida, the enemy no longer a threat to me.

This land is ours, and that'll always be true. Stand down, you cowards.
Bonvida, we'll die for you. This is our song, and we sing it out loud.
Oh-oh, Bonvida, we know we'll make you proud.

We fight for Bonvida, to keep the land forever in peace.
We fight for Bonvida, to honor all our deceased.
We fight for Bonvida; this battle will be bittersweet.
We fight for Bonvida; each step we take is destiny.
We fight for Bonvida and make the enemy flee.
We fight for Bonvida, set her loose, and make her free.
This is Bonvida, and we no longer carry fear.

We won't forget those who'll pass on. As the twelve kingdoms, we all fight as one.
This is our homeland; you'll never take her from me.
By the power of Sofos, this is Bonvida's decree.
We're going to march on her sacred ground.
You no longer have us, for we are unbound.

231

This is Bonvida, and we'll always stand for you.
This is Bonvida, across the land, sky, sea we honor you.
This is Bonvida; we'll always take care of you.
This is Bonvida; together strong, we live for you.

Their voices trailed off, and Advo lifted Atticus high. "Viva Bonvida!"

The armies, the voices echoed, "Viva Bonvida!"

Atticus lifted the Sword of Bonvida high, then swung his arm down, pointing the tip of the sword at the Arcods. The armies charged at their enemy, arrows and spears sailing through the air in both directions. The battle to save Bonvida from Luvanasis had begun. Feet stomped and armor clanged. The two armies collided, cries and shouts coming from every direction.

Advo flew overhead, swerving between arrows and spears. As Advo drew closer to El-Valr, a black, scaly Calsriv dragon flew from the castle courtyard.

A dragon! Atticus shuddered at the sight of it. Advo cooed and flew higher, picking up speed. Atticus' hair blew in the wind. He glanced over his shoulder at the dragon right on their tail.

Advo flew lower in the sky, pushing his wings back and head straight.

The dragon drew closer, its piercing red eyes locked onto Atticus.

Atticus flung face-first into feathers as Advo slammed his beak into the dragon, taking a part of its scales off.

The dragon roared and blasted flame after flame, but Advo swooped from side to side to avoid each blast. Then he shot up and smashed into the dragon a second time. Atticus held on with all his might.

The dragon roared and thrashed its razor-sharp claws.

Advo swerved around the beast, his wings whistling as he flew. Wanting to see the effect the Sword of Bonvida had on the dragon, Atticus waited until Advo swooped

232

closer. With the sword gripped in both his hands, Atticus swung, the blade dragging across the beast's neck.

The dragon shrieked.

Advo grabbed the dragon from behind with his talons.

The dragon lashed its tail around, the sharp point swooshing close to Atticus.

Advo dove straight down with the dragon still in his talons.

Clinging to the dove for dear life, Atticus leaned into the free fall.

Advo slammed the beast into the plains.

Atticus gasped from the sudden impact, the smacking sound of the dragon on the ground ringing in his ears.

Then Advo hovered over the dragon, flapping its great wings and peering down at the beast. The dragon's eyes closed and a last puff of smoke escaped its still nostrils. Advo swooped closer and cooed. Then Advo flew back to El-Valr.

In the distance, a second dragon flew into the sky, but this one had a rider on its back. Luvanasis.

Expecting to fight Luvanasis in the air, Atticus readied his shield. But then the dragon and Luvanasis flew off in the opposite direction. Where was he going? What was he scheming?

As Advo picked up speed, pursuing Luvanasis, Atticus' heart raced. They flew over his old home, over torn villages and fields, over ruins, and the Greystone Mountains and the Evergreen Forest.

Advo turned its head. "He's going to the Calsriv platform that his descendant split open. You should be able to squeeze through."

The dragon glided over a clearing. Luvanasis jumped off the back of the dragon and dove through the crack that led to Calsriv. The dragon flapped its wings and flew away.

Advo hovered over the cracked platform in the clearing below. The opening was just big enough for a dragon to squeeze through.

Atticus sheathed his sword and tucked his shield close to his body.

Advo glided closer.

Atticus tried to peer through the crack, but it was too dark. He tightened the strap of his sword, then stood on Advo's back and jumped into Calsriv after Luvanasis.

Chapter 34

The smell of the Arcods and sweat mixed in the air. The clank of weapons hitting each other, of shouts and grunts, filled the ear. Arcods swung their weapons and claws at every angle, and soldiers fought them off. This long-awaited battle expanded far beyond the eye.

Daria's heart ached for everyone who would die today. But she had to keep herself alive too. She gripped her bow in one hand and her hunting knife in the other. She glanced to her left, spotting Victor, Barlos, and Zane fighting side by side.

An Arcod shoved soldiers aside and charged at her.

She swung her knife, but it was too late. The Arcod dropped to the ground. Two arrows stuck out of its gruesome form, one from its back, the other from its head.

"Ah lookie, Spit, always saving the lass Daria," Tidy said.

Filled with relief and surprised to see the two Dwarves, Daria sprinted to them, ducking under an incoming spear. Spit and Tidy were dressed in their hefty armor.

"Aye, you'd think she does it on purpose," Spit said.

Victor glanced over and chuckled at the comments from the Dwarves.

Daria tucked her knife away and switched to her bow. She reached for an arrow. Then she and the Dwarves fired off arrows at Arcods that surrounded Victor and a few El-Valr soldiers.

The soldiers dove in front of Victor as they and the Arcods fell to their deaths.

Coming from off to their right, Raldon swung his sword at every Arcod in his path.

"Victor!" Raldon shouted.

Victor picked up a second sword from a dead soldier. "Brother."

Raldon pointed at El-Valr. It stood no more than a

twenty-minute sprint from where they were, beyond a field of Arcods and Bonvidians. "Will you join me?"

Victor waved Daria and the Dwarves over, but then an Arcod charged at Victor.

"You coming?" Victor said as he stabbed the Arcod.

"There ought to be hundreds in there, including our own," Raldon said.

One Bonvidian soldier fell, then another, too many, succumbing to the wrath of the Arcods. There was no time to think or speak. They had to get moving. Daria clipped her bow around her shoulder, and grimly, she tugged a halberd from the hands of a dead soldier.

They sprinted towards the Great Steps of El-Valr, Arcods and soldiers battling all around them. They ducked under spears flying through the air and struck any Arcod in their path. Daria glimpsed behind her. The Dwarves, Barlos, and Zane followed on their heels.

They drew closer to the Great Steps. Raldon and Victor stopped at the bottom of the hill.

Daria and the others arrived. The sounds of battle echoed in her ears. "What are we waiting for?" She sucked in air, trying to catch her breath.

With a deadly grin, Victor turned with his brother and charged up the stairs and down a path leading to the El-Valr market. They passed damaged rowhouses and neared the castle of El-Valr, which looked as if the Giants had stomped on it.

Victor froze in his tracks. His face paled as he gazed at his surroundings, and his face became grief-stricken. Daria wanted to comfort him, but now wasn't the time. Despite feeling his pain, they had to move on.

Victor clenched his jaw and gripped both his swords. He pressed towards the castle, determination evident in his unwavering stride.

Overwhelmed with grief for Victor and eager to bring

an end to this darkness, Daria jogged a few paces to catch up and then walked beside him, his brother on his other side. The Dwarves, Barlos, and Zane strode in a row behind them. Together they made a mighty pack of warriors. They would end this.

Arcods patrolled the castle grounds. Strange, no one guarded the front castle gates.

Zane touched a scrape under his eye. "Your idea of fun isn't what I had imagined, Daria."

Victor glanced at the Dwarves. "You two, ready your arrows. We are running nonstop to the front doors. Once through the doors, we'll make our way down a hallway until we reach the doors to the dungeon. From there, we'll take spiral stairs to reach the lower level of the castle."

"Aye, sounds like simple work," Tidy said with a crack in his voice.

Spit gave his brother a strange face. "Simple, ha. It's gonna be simpler than simple. It's going to be easy."

Daria and Victor made eye contact. She rolled her eyes.

Victor smirked. "As for the rest of us, fight with every last bone in your body."

The seven charged to the front gates of the castle. Daria's adrenaline pumped faster as she kept pace with Victor. The Dwarves shot arrow after arrow at any Arcod that ran at them.

They neared the gate, drawing closer. Raldon and Victor shoved the doors open, and they stormed inside.

Once entering, Daria and the others froze. The fattest Arcod Daria had ever seen stood before them. It grunted and stomped its heavy feet.

Raldon elbowed Victor. "You all go on. I will take this one myself."

Daria stared at Victor. There was no time for debate.

"Viva Bonvida," Victor said.

"Viva Bonvida," Raldon repeated.

Daria and the others fled from the foyer, Raldon, and the fat Arcod. They sprinted down a few dimly lit halls and stopped at a locked door. Barlos handed Zane his sword and nervously felt around his belt. He grunted and tossed Victor a ring of keys. "It's the black one."

After finding the key, Victor slid it into the lock. The lock clicked, and the door opened. They sprinted down the spiral steps, the air cooler now and the light dimmer. Victor unlocked the second door they came to. He swung open the door to a dungeon. Brick walls divided the room into cells. A heap of weapons overflowed from a wooden crate against one wall.

"Victor!" a woman cried.

Victor hurtled and rapidly searched through the cells until he found his parents. "We're here to set you free," Victor said. His hands shook as he unlocked their cage. He tossed Barlos the keys to unlock the other prisoners.

King Arldin and his wife, Queen Sioan, stepped out and hugged Victor. His mother kissed him on the cheek. "You've made us proud, son."

Grief at the loss of her parents struck Daria for a moment, but a faint sound—growing louder—shook her back to the present moment. Heavy footfalls echoed in the stairwell. "Arcods!"

King Arldin and other prisoners rushed to the open crate of weapons.

Victor's mother stared at him. "Where are your brothers?"

Victor glanced at Daria as if needing support to bear the news. "Raldon is upstairs fighting." His face turned to stone. "We believe Damien is dead or captured."

Queen Sioan placed her hands over her heart and sighed. "And Luvanasis?"

"He must be fighting the chosen one, Atticus, as we speak," Victor replied.

The smell of the Arcods grew thicker. Their shadows bounced off the walls of the stairwell. Daria, Zane, and the Dwarves got into fighting positions. The Arcods were almost down the stairs.

Victor squeezed to Daria's side.

In the next instant, an Arcod appeared at the open door. Daria shoved her halberd through its gut and yanked it out.

"Move! Let's go," Victor said.

Daria, her friends, and the prisoners fought their way up the stairs and spread across the hall of the castle. Thirty more Arcods barreled in.

Daria ducked from the swing of a sword. She stabbed the halberd through the attacking Arcod. As she turned to find the next threat, she glimpsed a figure stumbling into the room.

It was Raldon! Blood covered the chest of his tunic. After taking another weak step, he collapsed to the floor.

Daria threw her halberd, impaling an Arcod. She unlatched her bow and drew an arrow, covering Victor as he dashed to his brother. Daria moved up beside them, grabbing and shooting arrow after arrow.

Victor bent down, grasping his brother's hand. "Raldon."

Daria reached for another arrow but found few in her quiver. Panic filled her.

Raldon gasped for air. "Don't be sad for me, brother. I have regained my faith. I had to see the chosen one coming through the portal with my own eyes. Now I believe. I wanted to give you that peace before I die."

Daria glanced over. She swallowed a lump in her throat, watching Raldon take his final breath.

Victor got to his feet and wiped a tear.

Daria reached into her quiver, finding a single arrow left and fired it. "I'm out of arrows."

Victor handed her one of his two swords just as the fat Arcod entered the hall. Victor's eyes went fiery.

Daria and Victor nodded at one another and sprinted past nearby battles, their eyes on the Arcod that had killed Raldon. More Arcods crashed through windows and lumbered down halls. Daria's heart beat rapidly as Arcods overran the castle.

"Come on, Atticus," she said under her breath, knowing full well that if he didn't defeat Luvanasis soon, then she and everyone would die.

Chapter 35

Atticus landed hard on his feet; a pain fired up his legs. He stretched his legs, thankful he hadn't broken anything. A surge of adrenaline pumped through his veins as he scanned this desolate place—the land of his birth. A forest of dead trees and massive boulders surrounded him. And above him, rather than sun or moon and stars, thick fog drifted in odd patterns as if alive. Chills tingled up his spine.

There in the distance—Atticus had to look twice—Luvanasis stood with his back to the platform. Atticus had expected to have to search for him. But Luvanasis stood waiting.

Atticus stepped off the platform and strode to the forest. Mother had told him that his father had died saving them. A few steps later, he stopped.

There amid the mud and dirt lay a skeleton in weathered clothing. He trudged to the body and leaned closer. Could these bones be . . . his father's? Atticus made a fist and glanced over his shoulder to where Luvanasis gazed at the realm. This enemy had caused so much pain and suffering, and now Atticus needed to end it. He trudged across the ground, dirt clouds forming with each step, dusting his boots and trousers. Luvanasis turned and faced Atticus.

Atticus' heart pounded faster, confidence in himself and in Sofos' plan grew within him. Sword or no sword, this was his destiny.

Luvanasis grinned. "I was banished here by Sofos. But I'm sure you know the story." He pointed beyond the dead trees. "You were born there, beyond the woods, in the ruins of the banished Bonvidian city of Nandra."

He never realized his mother had lived in such a dreadful place.

Luvanasis lowered his arm. "I assume you saw where I killed your father."

Atticus flushed with anger. He wrapped his fingers around the hilt of the sword, hoping to steady himself. He shook his head and loosened his grip. No, the sword was not his strength.

Luvanasis sighed, his hand moving to the hilt of his sword. "Eighteen years later, and here we are, you and I. Not face to face in Bonvida. But standing here in Calsriv, the place where I failed to kill you. Here in this prison." Luvanasis' eyes filled with hatred.

Atticus maintained eye contact. They stood at least five yards apart. He had to be ready to strike Luvanasis any second.

Luvanasis unsheathed a long sword and pointed it at Atticus. "I am going to destroy you, Atticus. I hope you understand that. And after I do, I am going back to Bonvida to finish what I started." The grin on his face turned more menacing, and his eyes blazed with hate and anger.

Atticus unsheathed the Sword of Bonvida and latched his father's shield onto his other wrist. He strode closer to his enemy. "You're wrong, Luvanasis, so wrong." He paused halfway, his chest expanding with confidence. "You will not be returning to Bonvida."

Luvanasis leaned his head back and laughed.

Anger flooded Atticus at the sound of Luvanasis' laughter.

Luvanasis charged towards Atticus, swinging his sword before him, and went for a strike.

Ready to confront this darkness, Atticus swung his shield and blocked the attack. Then he thrust the Sword of Bonvida high, threatening a counterattack.

The two blades pressed against one another. Luvanasis' much larger blade did not intimidate Atticus.

Luvanasis pressed harder and shoved Atticus.

Atticus grunted as he stumbled and had to catch himself from falling. Unwilling to give Luvanasis another chance to strike, he advanced and took a low sweep at Luvanasis' ankles.

Luvanasis jumped over the blade.

Atticus and Luvanasis circled one another. Atticus' mind ran through a strategy for taking down his foe.

Luvanasis lunged at Atticus.

Ready for it, Atticus thrust his shield up and slammed it against Luvanasis' blade. But as the blade hissed against the shield, Luvanasis made another move—a knife clutched in his other hand.

Atticus twisted his shield to block the second weapon, but it skimmed his upper arm, drawing blood. Coldly furious now, he spun away to throw Luvanasis off. As he turned back, he landed a kick to Luvanasis' head.

A growl filled with rage escaped Luvanasis, and his next moves came quick and fierce. He swung with the sword, then with the knife, then with the sword again.

Atticus blocked each strike, one with his shield, the next two with his sword. Switching from defensive to offensive, he swung for Luvanasis' head.

Luvanasis grunted and blocked the strike, his counterstrike so powerful it did the unthinkable. He knocked the Sword of Bonvida from Atticus' grasp. It clanked to the rocky ground, too far for Atticus to reach easily.

Atticus backed away, eyes flitting to his sword, panic and anxiety gripping his mind. Luvanasis' taunting chuckles filled his head as his enemy strode closer for the kill.

Without a second to spare, Atticus dove for the Sword of Bonvida, scraping his arm on a rock. As he gripped the hilt, a surge of power surged through his veins. And he rolled onto his back.

Luvanasis hesitated, as if not expecting the speedy recovery, but then drew back for a strike.

Using his courage and determination, Atticus thrust the Sword of Bonvida at Luvanasis, skimming past his sword and piercing his lower abdomen. Drawing the sword back, Atticus jumped to his feet.

Still clinging to his own sword, his enemy held his bleeding side and growled, his veins popping from his neck.

Atticus tapped his sword and shield together. He got one hit, but it wasn't a deadly blow. He circled the injured Luvanasis. This was it, the moment that he would finally save Bonvida. He pushed the prideful thought to the back of his mind and stepped up onto a nearby boulder.

Then he turned and leaped from it, ready to swing at Luvanasis.

Luvanasis no longer held his side in pain. He put away the knife, gripped his sword with two hands, and swung.

Atticus just barely blocked the attack with his shield. With the sword in his other hand, he jabbed at Luvanasis' ankles.

His enemy stumbled back. In the next instant, the two charged at one another and locked swords.

Atticus' muscles burned. He could not lose his position. He stared into the pain-filled eyes of Luvanasis.

Using the Sword of Bonvida, Atticus pushed Luvanasis back, and their swords lost contact for a few seconds. Then their blades made contact, scraping against one another. Neither one would give up until the other was dead.

His enemy stepped backward, lowering his sword to one side. He was up to something.

Atticus stood ready, his eyes locked on his foe.

An eerie silence filled the air, making Calsriv even more uncomfortable than it already was. Was Luvanasis waiting for him to strike? Was he thinking of what to do, or had he given up?

Not wasting another second, Atticus lifted his sword and attacked.

Luvanasis remained in place and blocked Atticus' strike. Then he feigned a strike from the left, and as Atticus moved to block, he swung from the right.

Avoiding the blade, Atticus leaped aside and rolled onto the dirt.

Luvanasis came at him again.

Atticus rolled over, just missing the hard slam of the strike. He pulled himself up.

A screech echoed in the fog above, making both men look up. Luvanasis glared at the fog and chuckled, but Atticus swallowed back worry. What was up there?

Before Atticus turned back to the fight, his enemy dashed at him.

Atticus leaped to the side and swung his sword, not intending to block the attack but to strike. His blade met its mark, piercing Luvanasis' chest. Just then, the hilt of his sword shot warmth through his entire body. He tugged the Sword of Bonvida from the chest of Luvanasis.

Luvanasis fell to his knees and struggled to hold himself up.

Atticus stood shaking, covered in sweat, dirt, and blood. He peered into the distance, behind his foe. Something flew towards them.

A large bird—had to be at least thirty feet across— glided closer and screeched.

Atticus picked up a jagged stone by his foot and whipped it with all his might. The stone flew past Luvanasis' head and smacked the bird in the eye.

The bird squawked, its eyes fiery. Then it flew higher and circled over the two of them.

Atticus grabbed the sword of his enemy and tossed it out of reach.

His enemy labored to breathe. He mumbled to himself, his eyes locking with Atticus'.

The screeches of the bird continued in the fog above.

Relief filled Atticus. He had saved Bonvida and defeated Luvanasis.

Luvanasis' arm shot up. He grabbed Atticus' tunic and yanked him closer.

Panic threatened Atticus, but pity soon replaced it.

"You may have defeated me, Atticus." He coughed. "But you haven't saved Bonvida yet. No, you're not even close." He chuckled as blood dripped from his mouth.

Shivers tingled up Atticus' spine. *What does he mean? What is Luvanasis saying?*

Luvanasis tugged Atticus closer. "I was only the beginning of Hematite's dark reign. Hear and remember my words. You didn't save the land." His grip loosened from Atticus' tunic.

The screeches of the bird ceased.

Atticus stumbled back, Luvanasis' words haunting him.

In the next instant, the bird swooped down and stuck out a claw-shaped tongue. It wrapped its tongue around Luvanasis' dying body, drew him up, and swallowed him whole. The bird squawked and flew in the direction of the volcano.

Moments later, growls and grumbles came from above the platform. The remaining Arcods were being pulled back into Calsriv. They climbed off the platform and scurried across the realm.

Atticus wiped blood from his sword and sheathed it. A rush overtook his body and his mind as he tried to process all that had happened. Luvanasis was gone . . . but his final words, his final taunting words . . .

Shaking the words off, Atticus strode to the platform. How could he get out of this place?

"Atticus," a soothing voice said.

He spun around. Sofos stood behind him in stag form. "Hold onto me. I will bring you out."

Overwhelmed with all that had just taken place, Atticus strode closer and grasped Sofos' side. He exhaled and gazed around the shadowy realm of Calsriv. The dead forest and jagged ground where his father's remains lay began to fade. Then the foggy sky and distant volcano faded too. In the next instant, a blue sky domed overhead, and a forest surrounded him. At his feet and Sofos' hooves was the cracked platform he had entered to defeat Luvanasis. He was back. Eight warriors rushed from the treeline and positioned themselves around the open platform.

"What's going on? Can't close this?" Atticus asked, stepping off the platform.

"No. Not until the rest of the darkness is vanquished. These warriors will remain here and keep guard." Sofos sighed. "Luvanasis was one layer of the darkness of Hematite. Each layer protects Hematite. With each defeat of Hematite's darkness, Bonvida moves closer to facing Hematite in its fullness."

Atticus clenched his fists. That must have been the purpose of the other descendants. He needed their help to defeat the rest of the darkness.

Sofos nudged Atticus' side. "Hold onto me again, Atticus. There is one last place I want to bring you."

Atticus grasped Sofos. The forest faded and then vanished.

In the next moment, he stood with Sofos by the well. "Remember, Atticus. I am always with you."

Questions formed in Atticus' mind, but Sofos vanished before he could speak.

A sense of urgency overtook him, and he rushed to the rubble of the well. He moved large stones away until he finally unburied the well. He peered for a moment into the darkness, trying to formulate a plan, then he found a long vine hanging from a tree and tied it around a boulder. He wasn't going to fall in this time.

Using the cracked walls inside the well to maneuver, he climbed down to the bottom and found an opening and a flickering light in the distance. He moved towards it and soon arrived in the cave.

Memories flooded his mind as he entered. Lavender lay on a bed by the fire. Love welling in his heart, he rushed to her side. "Mother!"

Lavender turned, her face much paler than the last time he was with her. Her eyes were barely open. "A-A-Atticus," she whispered, as if struggling to speak.

Atticus quivered, his heart wrenching at the sight of her poor health. This could not be happening. "Mother, Luvanasis is defeated. I can bring you out of here. To a doctor." He squeezed her ice-cold hands.

"Oh, my Atticus, you are going to do great things. You have so much ahead of you. Adventures, friendships, love, losses, trials. Hold your faith close like you would a shield." She tried pushing herself up, but a rough cough overtook her, so she lowered her head back down. "I knew that I would see you one last time."

Tears streaming down his face, Atticus leaned over and kissed her cheek.

Lavender took a last gasp of air. Then her head dropped to the side.

Atticus gave into his grief and sobbed. After a few minutes, he looked around and considered the situation.

He cradled her still body in his arms and trudged back the way he had come. He tied the vine around his mother. Then he used the vine to climb back out and lift her body from the well.

He carried her lifeless body through the mist, to where two trees formed a natural arch over flowering vines and bushes with purple blossoms. Using a thick branch with a pointed end, he dug a hole deep enough to bury her. Then he eased her body into the earth and gazed at her until he knew it was time to move on. He wiped more tears away then filled the grave and made a cross out of branches.

After a few minutes, he straightened the strap of his sheath, ready for the next stage of this mission. He needed to meet up with his friends. He dashed through the mist and into the plains, his eyes focused on El-Valr.

Chapter 36

As El-Valr came into view, bustling with activity, Atticus forced his weary, aching body to move faster, almost to a jog. He scanned the scene, hoping to find his friends.

A horrible stench wafted in the air, not from Arcods this time but from the remains of fallen soldiers. Soldiers set about collecting and organizing weapons and gear. Others worked on setting up tents for the wounded and those searching for family members. The enemy was gone, but the devastation would be around for a while.

The sights and sounds, while tragic, motivated Atticus to hurry, scanning faces as he passed through the gates. Civilians milled about, some even crowding the wide pearl steps leading up to the kingdom of El-Valr. Everyone looked weary and drained.

A group stood at the bottom of the steps. Atticus' spirit lifted as he recognized them. His sister and his friends—Barlos, Victor, and Zane—all disheveled, huddled together with two short folks, probably Dwarves, maybe even the Dwarves Daria had told him about: Spit and Tidy. Daria sat on the step, talking to the Dwarves, her bow and empty quiver by her legs.

Zane stood talking to Victor, swaying from side to side, his pack over his shoulder. He probably could not wait to go back to Maljooi—and his books.

Barlos stood as strong and proud as ever, a bit off to the side, his eyes on a burning pile of corpses. So many good soldiers had died to keep the land safe from Luvanasis.

Once he was a stone's throw away, Atticus waved his arms and dashed to his friends.

Barlos noticed him first, then the others turned to see. When Daria lifted her head, her face beamed with joy, and she sprang from her sitting position. "Atticus!" She ran to him and flung herself into his arms, embracing him the way she had when they had reunited in the barn.

Atticus held her tightly. His sister had grown from a girl who loved adventure to a strong young woman—with amazing skills. He still could not get over how well she had picked up archery.

"You did it," she whispered, stepping back and smiling.

"*We* did it," Atticus corrected, pushing a strand of hair from her face. Then he took her arm, and they walked back to the others.

"Good to see you," Barlos said, greeting Atticus with a firm handshake.

Victor shook his hand too, then he lowered his head, his countenance depressed and exhausted.

"Bonvida is saved!" Daria said, her voice full of enthusiasm.

Atticus averted his gaze, wishing her words were true.

"What is it, Atticus?" Daria must have read his mood.

Atticus watched Bonvidians pass by. The smells and smoke from the many piles of burning corpses drifted their way with the wind. "We're not saved yet."

Daria gasped and wrinkled her brow. Zane's eyes opened wide. Barlos gripped his weapon. Victor clenched his jaw and straightened the strap of his sheath. The redheaded Dwarves shrugged.

Daria shook her head. "Wh-what do you mean?"

Atticus' hand went up protectively to the stinging wound on his arm. "I'll explain later. For now, let's enjoy this victory."

Zane cleared his throat, drawing everyone's attention.

Atticus turned to the once nervous scholar who now stood like a brave fighter of Bonvida.

Zane rubbed his fingers together, and his gaze shifted to the steps of El-Valr. "I will be going now, back to Maljooi."

Atticus reached out to shake Zane's hand. "Thank you, Zane, for everything. This isn't goodbye. I'm sure our paths will cross again someday."

Zane grabbed Atticus' hand. "No, Atticus, thank you. You gave me an experience I will never forget."

Atticus swallowed back his emotion. "Be safe on your journey home."

Zane let go of Atticus' hand and nodded. He shifted his attention to Daria, Barlos, and Victor and shook each of their hands. Still looking them over, he gave a confident little smirk and tightened the strap to the scabbard on his side. He waved his hand and strode off on his own, following a group of travelers.

Victor chuckled. "Well, there goes the bravest scholar one would ever hope to meet."

"Agreed," Atticus said and then turned his attention to the Dwarves. "You must be Spit and Tidy?"

"Aye, we are. I'm Spit. This one's Tidy," Spit said.

Victor nodded at Barlos, who then placed his hands on the Dwarves' shoulders.

Victor bent to their level. "I heard that you saved Daria not only once but a second time in the battle. You both deserve a spot in the El-Valr army."

The two Dwarves puffed out their chests. "Really? What'll the Dwarves say, though?" Tidy asked.

Barlos chuckled. "Don't you worry. Now come with me. I need to find my family, and we can discuss it on the way."

Barlos and the Dwarves strode off towards one of the many white tents.

Atticus glanced around. "What became of Meg and her father? Are they okay?"

Daria rubbed her drained-looking eyes. "They were dropped off at the Elves on our way to the battle."

Atticus lowered his head. "Never got to thank them."

Victor rubbed his shoulder. "I'm sure we will see them again."

Daria unlatched Atticus' pack and passed it to him. "Oh!

You left this on the ship. Your journal and everything else are in it."

Thankful to have his journal back, Atticus swung the pack over his shoulder. "I guess this is our turn to say goodbye?"

Daria bowed her head.

Victor pressed his lips together, a thoughtful look in his eyes, then he blurted, "Where exactly are you two from?"

Atticus pointed in the direction of a distant field, where their home appeared as a mere speck. "Our farmhouse is that way. And we have a lot of work to do to make it liveable again. The sooner we get started, the better."

Victor shook his head. "That's where you used to live. Now you can live in the castle in El-Valr."

Atticus' heart jumped.

Daria raised her head, joy replacing the sadness. "Really?" Without waiting for an answer, she ran to her weapons and pack and flung them over her shoulders.

Atticus and Victor strode to her.

Victor reached for her hand.

She hesitated, giving him a shy glance, but then took his hand into her own. As their fingers interlocked, she blushed, a smile wavering her lips.

The three of them strode up the wide steps, their shoulders tapping others who were making their way up or down.

Once at the top step of the Great Stairs, Atticus stopped in his tracks.

Daria turned to him. "Atticus, you coming?"

Atticus nodded. "You two go on ahead. I need a moment."

Daria smiled, then she and Victor strode on ahead.

Atticus turned and considered the view from the top step. As the sun set along the horizon, the sky filled with colors, and sunbeams stretched out across the land.

Atticus set his pack down and pulled out his journal. The desire to write his thoughts overwhelmed him as memories formed into words and were scrawled across the pages.

Perilous was this journey, perilous 'twas indeed.
For a moment once divided, months later reunited.
Kissing farewell to loved ones, saying sweet goodbyes,
This journey was a long one, and it drained our bones dry.
In the early mornings, with the sky so fiery bright,
We continued onward towards our destiny.
No matter what came at us, we fought side by side.
Even though death befell us, still we carried on,
Through the basalt mountains, across the sinking bogs,
Through the thick pine forests, through caves, and over ocean.

Crawling through the desert, parched and in need of drink.
Through stormy weather where lightning brightens skies.
Meeting new companions and foes along the way,
Growing ever closer than we were at dawn of our first day.
Taking down the first darkness with a few uneasy swings.
Perilous was this journey, but the song inside me sings,
We will all be changed forever, and that is for our best.
It was Sofos who had called us on this perilous quest.
Though this adventure ended, I can hear the next one call.
Other descendants, I am coming to lead you in this fight.
And together, we will vanquish the remaining darkness and, in the end, Hematite.

ACKNOWLEDGEMENTS

I want to thank my family, who have supported me in their special ways, whether reading drafts or listening to me ramble on about ideas and characters. I want to thank Author Ellen Gable Hrkach and Artist James Hrkach at Full Quiver Publishing for their guidance and advice in getting the book up and running. I want to thank Author Theresa Linden for the countless hours of editing and teaching, the copyeditors and beta readers who gave me wise advice, and the time they took from their extremely busy lives to help!

About the Author

Chris Smith found his gift of writing in the second grade when he was asked to create his own fairy tale story. Since then, when he wasn't with his friends, Chris would escape, creating stories and playing in this world that he named Bonvida. He is the fourth of five children, works at a private Catholic school, helps run a youth group at a local parish, and is a member of the Catholic Writers Guild. Today Chris lives with his family and black lab in the small rural town of Embrun, Ontario.

A Look at Book 2:
Bonvida
The Quest of Light

The Dark Descendant sat atop a black stallion as it galloped across the Bonvidian plains. With each horse stride, he and Raia sat at the back, her arms wrapped around his waist, and came closer to their destination. Sweat drizzled from behind his mask from the heat of the beaming sun.

He tugged the horse's reins. The plains had come to a crater that expanded wide. Leaping off the horse, he focused on what stood in the crater's center. – The Chamber of the Descendants. He grabbed a bag from the horse's saddle and glanced at Raia.

Raia scooted into the center saddle. Her raven glided over their heads. "Luvanasis would be proud of you."

He stared at her and the raven through the eye holes in the mask. "I will meet you later."

Raia whistled for the raven to land on her shoulder. She then tapped the stallion with her heel and rode off.

The Dark Descendant proceeded to the chamber in the center of the crater. He skipped down the rocky slope and marched over the rough grounds. He soon came close to a barrier. To his knowledge, only those descendants of Desmond and his followers could enter through the barrier. Without hesitation, he entered through the barrier.

Now through each stride, he came closer to the chamber, cravings of Sofos, Advo, and Artel engraved on the exterior walls.

Drawing closer to the door, he shoved it open and
proceeded down the hall, trying to ignore the stained
glass and statues that decorated the building. He had to
remain focused and not pay attention to the decorating.
He paused at large scarlet red doors and pushed them
open. Four tombs scattered the room with a few stained-
glass windows. The center tomb caught his eye. He
paced closer and read: *'Desmond.'*

Walking to one side of the tomb, he pressed his hands
on the edge and pushed, his muscles and veins popping
out of him with each inch the tomb moved until it
revealed a hole big enough for someone to squeeze into.
He couldn't hold back the grin on his face. Without
another thought, he climbed down into the hole.

As he stood in the dim cavern, the only light was from
the sun beaming into the hole and bouncing off puddles
and shiny stones. No more than thirty paces, he spotted
a strange door. He strode onward, stepping into a puddle,
glared at the reflection of the brass mask, and picked up
his pace. Finally reaching the door, he inspected ancient
Bonvidian writing. *"For yee who finds this place, be
warned, for chaos is behind it. Turn back and avoid, for
she is in a slumber, and as long as she slumbers, chaos
and darkness will not reign."*

He chuckled and pushed at the door harder and harder
until it opened. – The opening of the doors shook around
him. Hopefully, that didn't rumble the whole land.

He fell face-first on his mask as dust filled around him.
He coughed and gagged as he pulled himself to his feet.
Fear struck him every bone so much he couldn't move.
It had taken him and Raia a year and a half to figure out
that Desmond hid the She Serpent beneath the chamber.

Realizing he hadn't moved a muscle in at least five, maybe ten minutes, he turned his attention to what rested before him. – The She Serpent. He paced around the forty-foot serpent, the thick body of the ancient creature covered in a layer of yellow honey-like amber. Coming back to the front of the ancient creature, he touched the face and shivered.

How does he awaken her? He tapped the serpent-shaped hilt that dangled on his side. He wrapped his hand around the hilt, his fingers fitting perfectly, and unsheathed The Sword of Darkness. The scissor-tipped blade resembled the tongue of a snake. He swung the sword over his head at the amber. – But nothing, he grunted, frustration kicking in. He had been here now much too long.

He tore off the brass mask with his free hand and tossed it to the side. The echo of the mask hitting the floor filled the room.

The Dark Descendant exhaled and hit the amber, again and again, each hit stronger than the next. Finally, part of the amber cracked between the eyes of the serpent. Luvanasis' secondary plan is finally falling into motion.

He stepped back as the crack in the amber moved in different directions. One piece after another crumbled off the serpent.

The She Serpent opened its yellow circular eyes, shook the remaining amber off her head, and scanned the area.

He paced closer to the massive creature, but her focus wasn't on him. He spun around, spotting two others in the cavern. - No two others strode towards him. He then pulled a long hood over his head as it draped to the tip of his nose. There wasn't time to pick up his brass mask.

The glimmer of the leader's sword glittered in his eye. It was the Sword of Bonvida. Atticus had arrived, but who was that second Bonvidian?

He glanced back at the She Serpent.

"Descendant," her voice hissed.

The Dark Descendant turned his attention to Atticus and the other Bonvidian and charged at them. Not a moment later, three weapons clanged.

Manufactured by Amazon.ca
Bolton, ON